I0523038

Unawqi, Hunter of the Sun

*The story of a boy who overcame the Sun
and raised the world a little closer to the stars.*

Second Edition

Kali Kucera

ISBN: 978-1-0878-7206-3

for Thomas Merton Brightman
and
Julio Cesár García Lenís

CONTENTS

THANKSGIVING 1

2 THE UNAWQI AWAKENING 6

3 UNAWQI, HUNTER OF THE SUN 12

4 MOCHE 16

5 FLIGHT FROM THE FOREST 20

6 UNAWQI AND THE THIEF 26

7 JAQUNQAY 30

8 STORM WITH A VIPER'S TONGUE 37

9 INSTRUMENTAL DESIRE 45

10 TOMÁS 51

11 THE MOON'S WHISPER 59

12 THE GREAT MANGROVE GATHERING 62

13 ATAMA'S JOURNEY 69

14 THE MEETING WITH THE MOUNTAIN 74

15 THE BUTTERFLY INTERVENTION 81

16 BACHUÉ: MOTHER OF THE SUN 87

17 THE DAY THE SUN RETURNED HOME 94

18 WEDDING FOR A NEW EARTH 100

19 ON THE ROAD TO ANTISANA 107

20 THE DEMON ON THE WALL 110

21 TUNGURAHUA AND THE BALAO PROPOSITION 114

22 TAPAIPI 119

23 THE PURSUING SHADOW 123

24 KUKANIBO 127

25 HEARTLESS 133

26 DEFIANCE..137

27 CONDOR ROAD..141

28 TUNGURAHUA'S TOWER 144

29 THE WESTERN DEEP 147

30 THE MUD RUT 150

31 SAVING REVENTADOR 155

32 SANGAY..159

33 IN THE RING OF FIRE 164

34 CONVENING THE CONGRESS 170

35 TOUCHING MIBA 173

36 Reunion 180

37 LIGHT COMBAT..184

38 QINA'S ARMY 190

39 THE CONGRESS DECIDES............................193

40 CROSSING OVER...196

41 OLD MAN...199

42 THE EMPEROR'S ROBE 203

43 THE END...209

GLOSSARY 210

ABOUT THE AUTHOR 212

OTHER BOOKS BY KALI KUCERA............................213

May all arrive.
May none be left behind.
May all be one.

K'iche' traditional proverb

THANKSGIVING

Beware the empty chair.

It was the only one unclaimed in the room of hungry diners in the basement of St. Rita's church in Tacoma. The legs were slightly turned out, as if an invisible waiter had pulled it back to let me slide in.

Guilt had gotten the best of me to be there in the first place. It was Thanksgiving morning, and a day earlier, my neighbors, who were never ones to shirk a promise, came to me with panic on their faces. Their son's house had burned down, they said, and they needed to leave immediately.

I gave them my sympathies, but something else was still bothering them. They had obligated themselves to help prepare free breakfast at St. Rita's in the morning, an annual tradition for the city's homeless. I tried not to wince at the pious sound of it all, but I could sense what they were leading up to and I remembered the many times they'd watered my garden when I was out of town. I knew my morning would be free before needing to drive to my aunt's house for our family dinner, so, of course, I told my neighbors I would be glad to fill in for them and they should think no more of it.

Never having even been to St. Rita's, I was loathe to socialize and threw myself into the work, but after a couple hours of scrambling eggs, I was impressed by my neighbor's commitment to do this year after year. My feet felt like two ends of a barbell, and I was ready to grab a plate myself and take a break.

Thanksgiving

If I had not been so tired, my finicky nature would have guided me to pass up the solitary chair and look for a less conspicuous corner of the room where perhaps there were fewer people. The less forgiving angel on my shoulder bit me with the words: "You hypocritical, insincere, lazy ass." It was right. The people were streaming in through the door. Most had no home, no job, and no money. Their bodies told their stories of broken dreams, crippling work, and damaged minds. And here I was, fancying an emperor's throne somewhere, so I could separate myself off to swallow my grits and baked apples?

The lonely chair in front of me could have been reserved for someone else, so I asked the person sitting on the opposite side of the table if it was taken. He said no, gestured for me to claim it, and I sat down with my plate and coffee without giving it another thought.

It wasn't until I looked back up that I noticed something about him seemed out of place. I glanced at him across the table as he salted his eggs, observing how his right hand moved gracefully to the shaker. He had none of the typical displays of mental edginess. He was not disheveled, or weary on the brow. His hair was combed, and he wore a leather jacket that didn't bear a single tear. His eyes were calm, like having emerged from a prayer, and he was happily occupied with his own thoughts.

But his left hand remained fixed in place on the table, appearing to be hiding something underneath his palm.

I must admit, it was also plain to me how strikingly handsome he was. His jet-black hair, and his face with the sheen of a brown eggshell, suggested he was Latino. So I wondered what had brought him here, far from where he might have been born.

Normally, it's prudent in these settings not to ask. People are scarred enough by their circumstances and they don't want to be interviewed as the price for their meal. I wanted to protect his privacy and let him eat in peace, and in my own defense, didn't want to unleash an emotional outbreak. But still, his appearance challenged me, and his seeming self-confidence broke through my etiquette, and I asked him that inadvisable question anyway: "So, what's your story?"

His face sprung up like a soldier's salute and he gave me a smile, wide with contentment.

"I am Unawqi. I am hunting the Sun."

It was such an absurd thing to say, and yet he was perfectly composed in saying it. I smiled and nodded back, disguising my disappointment, and now sure he was just as crazy as the rest, albeit happily crazy.

I thought some more about the strangeness of his name, sounding out the phonemes in my mind, "Oo-naow-kee". Was it Finnish or Japanese? Apache, perhaps? A second later I thought again that maybe he was making a clever joke in order to break the ice. After all, Tacoma has plenty of days of being overcast with gloomy clouds refusing to budge, and talking about the weather is indeed how we all usually start a conversation. So, I returned to him again and said,

"Yes, the Sun has a lot of good hiding places in November!"

Unawqi dropped his fork on his plate and his eyes bore into me as if I had just given him the key to paradise.

"So you have seen him?" Unawqi beamed.

Regretting, now, that I had not taken the warning sign of the empty chair, I searched my mind for an excuse to get up and return to the kitchen.

But before I could finish my breakfast, Unawqi had lined out enough of his story that I found myself not only glued to my seat, but devoid of any fatigue or hunger but for the feast of his very next word.

I fell in love with Unawqi instantly, as I imagined everyone did. In the first thirty minutes he made me laugh more than I had over the course of a year. It puzzled me how such an energetically positive young man could end up in a basement of broken heartedness, but this only compelled me to listen all the more.

I wouldn't be telling you this story if Unawqi was, in fact, merely making a joke about the weather! His opening line was literally and plainly what he had meant: he was a hunter, the Sun was his prey, and his extraordinary pursuit, which had begun ages ago, had finally brought him here, to Tacoma, of all places. And it was here, in Tacoma, that he was just as zealous as he had always been to see his hunt come to an end.

Naturally, I had to ask why would one hunt the Sun, and this was when his story grew more complicated, his face showing pain, at many points, as he labored to justify the emotional struggle of his journey.

Thanksgiving

He set his plate aside, for the heaviness in his heart overtook any appetite he had left, and he reached out and took my hand, asking me to listen.

"Think back, if you will, to the first time your father took you for a walk in the night. The darkness, how it horrified you. It swallowed you whole, and the only link you had to the light was the touch of your father's fingers in your palm. So small and tenuous a wall were his fingers, you remembered, separating your life from your death.

"For a brief second he let go of your hand, to instead put his hand on your shoulder, and in that moment of absence you felt in your body the meaning to be…forsaken. You gasped a small cry of terror, and even when his hand returned, you realized his hand could leave again, throwing you into the vastness of space to be on your own.

"Still, he urged you to continue, to go further, deeper into space, farther away from home. So you trusted him again, and you walked together until you shivered from the cold.

"But for some reason still a mystery, imagine that he truly chose to let his hand go, and his voice to go silent. You would pray it wasn't true, that he must soon return, and yet he would not. No matter how many times you called, he would not answer. He just left.

"This time you would be all alone, a boy, abandoned to face the boundless night, led to the loveless abyss, rejected by your own genesis, without a compass or line to find your way back.

"No greater a cruelty can be imagined than this. But this is just between one father and his son. How much greater is the cruelty when the father casts a million sons, indeed, the whole world, to the abyss?

"That is the crime. That is why I'm here.

"But there is more, for now the father is no less the boy, and the boy no less his father.

"We are all in danger of casting each other out."

Unawqi told me he was not hunting for sport or pleasure. He was a bounty hunter of sorts, and the Sun had committed a crime against humanity, a preconceived crime that had not yet fully been accomplished, but still could, if the right conditions were met. It was a crime that Unawqi said he himself needed to overcome. Indeed, that we all must overcome the crime at some point or another.

My mind came around again to his left hand, which still had not moved.

"And what is this you're keeping?" I asked.

"Oh, this," he answered with a little chagrin and lifting his palm. "This is a gift. A little silk worm I hope will bring me good fortune and make things right."

The tiny insect underneath his hand was crawling around in a nest of straw, making spindles of silk that played with the overhead light. This smallest of living things, manufacturing the miraculous in the middle of such a somber place, enchanted me to no end.

Unawqi, of course, wanted to protect it, which is why he kept it covered so securely. His hand was its shelter, its mighty fortress, and he would be certain to never abandon this creation for as long as he lived.

His story would not have come from Finland or Japan or the mesas of Arizona. His beginning belonged to a patch of green, high in the Andes, where farmers herded goats and unearthed potatoes when they were not dancing to the sounds of their magical flutes.

It was a peaceful place, and he longed to return home as soon as he was able, but only if he could bring the whole world home with him.

2 THE UNAWQI AWAKENING

Titu Ilumán walked swiftly, his steps close together to keep the altitude from decaying his pace. He was in a hurry, but he knew the Quijos canyon well enough to calculate that it would defeat him if he broke into a run.

Beneath his punchu, he clutched onto his treasure, Aakti Amurugana. Those were words from an ancient language no longer spoken, but everyone knew what the words meant.

He was carrying the seeds of the Sun.

At that moment, Titu knew what he had in his hands, but he did not comprehend the devastation the seeds would bring.

He only knew of the seeds from legends he had heard as a child, legends he'd come to mock. He was unlike most everyone else. He was not a believer in legends, and so he had forgotten their crucial details, including the one about the seeds of the Sun.

The legend says Aakti, who is the Sun in the sky, is not an unfeeling object hovering above us. It is not an it, but a he, a being, no different than are we. He has a relationship with us, albeit a contentious one. He is none other than the emperor of Earth and sky, who is to be both worshipped and feared.

And here, Titu, a rather common man, had stolen the emperor's seeds from the hands of Titu's newborn son whose first cries of life were still piercing Titu's ears from the valley floor below. Titu knew what he had done, but he bristled at the notion of his deed as a theft. The way he thought of it was that if he were the father of the child, then the seeds delivered through this birth were his rightful property.

Besides, Titu had a further motive.

Titu was born in a place where his ancestors had lived for thousands of years, but it was also on the edge of what his parent's generation called "the next world."

Just over the next few hills from his own village, a people with pale skin had built their own village, made up of strange buildings, with everything laid out in squares. They were driven and ambitious. They behaved as if nature was theirs to command, and they used tools he had never seen before, but that worked more efficiently than the kinds of tools used in his own village.

Titu craved to be a part of "the next world" and was a malcontent at home, uncomfortable with leaving the supernatural to gods and magicians. Mysteries were gifts meant to be unwrapped, he believed. They should be studied, tamed, and put to use for the purpose of advancing the lot of people like him, and not just the people of the pale town a few hills away.

His parents did not encourage him as much. They wanted to maintain the family tradition and see Titu growing cassava and plantain as had they and their parents.

But from the first time Titu lay ill in the house of the local shaman, he wanted to know what was in the bowls and baskets lining the healer's walls, and how healing worked according to nature and not according to magic. His parents chided him for asking, for they believed such matters were not his business to know, which made Titu even more determined to know!

Hence, these seeds were a continuation of his rebellion, his determination to demystify nature and control it.

In the second and larger drama, Titu was the next in line to be in possession of the Aakti Amurugana, but this was the first transfer of hands in almost a millennium, as the seeds had gone missing for 888 years. During all that time, the emperor and the world did not know where they were hidden, but in truth, they had been held captive by the sorcerer of Antisana, the one they called Moche.

Moche lived in the great mountain, Antisana, but he was a completely foreign entity to the people of the Quijos that lived beneath the mountain. He was not of the family of the mountains, but a demon who had usurped the mountain in his control, burying its rightful goddess somewhere inside. Where Moche came from, no one in the Quijos valley knew, but his ways, though different from theirs, were oddly obsessed with the Sun.

The local people feared him terribly, for he would hunt them and bring them back to the mountain to be sacrificed, drinking their blood, saying it pleased the Sun, even though this was not according to anything they believed or practiced.

As far as Titu was concerned, he didn't care to think about all of that. For his interests, the seeds were the most powerful medicine he could ever hope to find, and there were no parents this time to deny him from taking and deciphering this magic. This was an extraordinary opportunity for him to become a legend himself, if he could but harness the power of the seeds.

Still, the fact that he was running arrested his conscience. He was a fugitive, and he knew it. He left Tamaya behind, a woman whom, at one time, he could not keep himself from. She was weak and without aid, the blood of her womb flowing cold onto the floor of her grass-roofed hut.

Titu loved her, and many times had thought of bringing her home to marry her, but he had convinced himself that by running away, he was protecting Tamaya from danger. A great many powerful people –sorcerers, kings, witches– would kill to possess Aakti Amurugana. He needed to get the seeds far away from Tamaya to keep her safe; so far that indeed his footprints would be lost, even if it meant Tamaya would never be able to see him again.

Tamaya never laid her eyes on the seeds because her eyes were closed tight with labor's pain when they were snatched from the child's hand. So for her, Titu's sudden flight was as mysterious as it was cruel.

Lost in his thoughts, Titu stumbled over a stone in his path. He rolled down the side of the canyon and would have encountered his death if another death had not encountered him first.

The still warm belly of a dead, black goat was braced to the edge of a cliff. The goat was still bleeding out, having succumbed to a thicket of barbed tarapacana shrubs. Its bulging eyes stared directly into Titu's as if pleading with him a little too late.

Another legend Titu rejected said to beware if one ever saw a dead, black goat in the wild, for it was an omen of a bad future. This legend was not so easy for him to shrug off now that he was encountering it in the face. So, Titu delicately raised himself to his knees, and blessed the goat with a nod of awe, fearing it might awaken from the dead if he should be disrespectful.

The black goat's eyes would not leave him as Titu pulled himself back up the hillside. Those eyes would never leave him.

Through the indigo night Titu ran west over the Papallacta plateau. The Aakti Amurugana under his punchu harassed him by imposing upon him a strange gravitational clash. Some seeds were craving the fleeting sun in front of him, while others were pulling him toward the cries of the child he had left behind. He wondered if the seeds were his captives or his captors. Who had the greater power, him or them? What if the seeds were to forever maintain two opinions and paralyze him from going any direction at all? Titu managed to keep moving forward, but he hobbled sideways and backwards as he went.

When the Sun, the emperor Aakti, passed over the Quijos valley the next day, he sensed his amurugana had reemerged, and that they were pulling at him from the west. This meant that once more they had been stolen, after 888 years of captivity, and Aakti heated up with anger, ready to burn the grass roofs of the huts underneath him into ashes.

But Tamaya, who had no familiarity with the seeds or that her child had been holding on to them at birth, and only knew her abandoned child was suffering as much as her in Aakti's merciless heat, did something only the Quijos people would do in desperation. She cried out for Moche, the sorcerer of Antisana, to save her, to send wind or rain to contest the Sun.

Little did she know that Moche knew why Aakti had been angered. It was Moche himself who had kept Aakti Amurugana successfully concealed from the emperor for almost nine centuries, and now Moche had been robbed of them, the same as Aakti. Aakti's heat provided the clue as to their whereabouts, and Moche wanted the seeds back, just as much as the emperor. So, he was pleased this call from a common woman would give him a head start on Aakti to recover what they both were looking for.

Having heard Tamaya calling, Moche put some coca leaves in his mouth, chewed them, and spit out a plume high into the air. In turn, it made the sky sneeze, expelling a squall of hail into the valley and throwing a blanket under the Sun.

By the time the squall settled, Aakti had grown tired of waiting and fled west to hunt for his seeds.

But life would not go back to something more bearable for Tamaya.

She had barely a moment to be grateful when Moche showed up at her door to collect his debt.

Moche was a scrawny demon, and no taller than Tamaya's waist. He looked like any of the other people of the valley, but seven times older than old. His clothes were scavenged from whatever travelers had lost in the mountains: a white Cañari hat, loosely enveloping his tiny head; an Otavaleño scarf he had fashioned into a vest; and pants made from of a woven sack that probably had carried spices from the Amazon.

He held out his shriveled hand.

"I saved you from Aakti, but he wants what is mine. Give me the child before the emperor returns."

The startled mother looked at the little sorcerer, no bigger than her dog, but with enough strength to squash her like an ant between his fingers. She knew well Moche's traditions, and of his sacrifices.

"But this is my son! I cannot let him go!" Tamaya contested.

"Listen to me," Moche warned, "for I will only tell you this once. You will not survive tomorrow if you stay, and you will surely die in the caves of Antisana where the child and I will live. Run away, east into the cloud forest, where the emperor does not know your name and will pass over you. The child will only be safe with me. Everything else here in this valley will die."

Helpless and terrified, Tamaya ran from Moche, but though he was smaller, he was the faster and stronger. He caught up with her and pulled the child into his arms, pushing Tamaya down and onto the ground. She screamed at him for mercy, and tried to pursue him, but the sorcerer stamped his foot on the ground, creating a wide hole between them that she could not cross.

Despite his size, Moche had no problem bearing the weight. He carried the child away without hurry and disappeared over a hill, and Tamaya wept until she had no voice left with which to scream. Now both Titu and her child were gone. All that she had were the words of Moche promising the child would live, and it was upon that promise that she determined she would get him back.

Unlike Titu, Tamaya believed the legends of her ancestors were true. She had just looked into the eyes of one of them. And so, fearing for the emperor's return and destroying the rest of her life around her, Tamaya quickly packed her things, gathered her goats, and fled down into the cloud forest, as Moche had told her to do.

But once there, Moche chewed some more coca leaves and blew his plume at the forest so that it closed so densely around Tamaya's path that she lost the trail she had made. She could not find her way back to the valley, as much as she tried.

Moche brought the child into the cool underworld of Antisana, a spectacle of a thousand tunnels and crystal streams, with glowing pools of azure-colored lava emitting light and warmth. It was a land the emperor had never seen, the land where his seeds had once been held prisoner.

The sorcerer entered a chamber so grand it seemed to have a sky of its own, its clerestory heights filled with flying bats, ventilating the air. There, he laid the sleeping child down on a bed of eucalyptus leaves, and one of the bats flew down and hung over the child's head to protect him.

"The day will come," Moche whispered to the sleeping child, "when Aakti will forget you, but I, on the other hand, have found you, and you are now mine. I will train you to be a hunter, but not of mere beasts. You will hunt for the *atama* who stole my seeds in the night, and you will return them here to my keeping. The seeds are crying for you already; I know you hear them. They need you to keep them planted here in the world. Until then, I know who you are. You are the most gifted creature to ever touch the earth. You are…Unawqi!"

The child awoke upon hearing his name, and cried like a shrill flute from another world, and all the million bats in the chamber fell stunned to the floor.

3 UNAWQI, HUNTER OF THE SUN

Deep in the caves of Antisana, below the steamy lakes where cold falls and gushing geysers mingle, there in his cathedral, Moche the sorcerer leaned over the slumbering boy he'd named Unawqi.

With his reptilian fingernails, Moche scraped the fossils embedded in the cavern wall, releasing flecks of emerald dust into his palm. He blew them into the boy's nostrils, making him convulse in mounting fits of anger, for Moche was trying to induce Unawqi into the world that surrounds the world, the land of the Sun.

"Unawqi! Unawqi!!" Moche yowled, increasingly louder and higher. He blew more emerald dust into the boy's face. With each curl of dust Unawqi inhaled, the muscles in his thighs swelled, and the veins in his arms and neck bulged with a greenish glow.

Moche raised his voice to a climax, "Unawqi! Unawqi! The hunt awaits you, Unawqi!!"

The boy finally sprang to his feet, but with an unforgiving look in his eyes. His arms rose above his shoulders, and he looked down on Moche like a bear about to pounce on his prey.

"I am Unawqi!" the boy roared with such a thunder the cavern walls shook and the bats in the vault scattered.

Moche cowered, quite afraid, but also relishing the success this promised child would bring. He got back onto his feet and placed around the boy's shoulders a punchu made from eucalyptus leaves, so that during the day when the Sun would pass over the boy, Aakti would not be able to distinguish him from a sapling tree.

The leaves bristled around his Unawqi's shoulders when they sensed the immense energy inside his skin.

Moche led Unawqi back up the ribs of the cavern to the mountain's entrance where they had entered when the boy was but an infant, and which Unawqi had not seen since that time. There, Moche put a stick in the boy's hand and let him go. The stick had no magic in it except to cast a shadow for Unawqi to detect whether the Sun was behind him, in front of him, to his left, or to his right.

In letting him go, Moche gave Unawqi a solemn order: to hunt Atama down. Moche believed Atama was in the Pasochoa Forest to the west, and in Atama's hands would the boy find the stolen seeds, which Unawqi was to capture back and return them to Moche's vault.

But who was Atama? Moche could not give Unawqi an answer to this question, because Atama was able to change appearance. So, Unawqi was instructed to do what he had been trained, to ask the forest, and wait for the forest to eventually gossip.

Unawqi went on his way, climbing down and through the Quijos Canyon, until he came to the plateau over the Tamboyaco River. He could smell and hear all of nature around him. The eucalyptus and the pine whispered loudly, so Unawqi eavesdropped to see if they would gossip about Atama. He noticed little birds like the purple tapaculo and the red cotinga, arguing with each other whose coat was more attractive. He thought maybe they would change the subject to something more of interest to him. But alas, he heard nothing of Atama.

So, he climbed on a boulder to get his head higher into the dancing breeze, and there he could hear the faint voices coming from the communities dotted alongside the river below.

But it was one voice he heard, very far away, that particularly drew his attention. He did not know it was she, but it was Tamaya, his mother, talking to her animals in the cloud forest to the east. There was something about her voice that resonated inside of him, so he turned in that direction to search for her, though he knew not how he would find her or why. In addition, it was in the opposite way the Sun traveled, and Unawqi was tasked to follow the Sun, not walk away from it.

This became his first act of disobedience to the sorcerer. It was the first of many to come.

For many days, Unawqi traced the Tamboyaco river into the cloud forest, using his eucalyptus punchu to disguise him whenever the Sun was close. Once in the forest, the giant Huasquila trees created their own shield over him, and so he did not notice it when the punchu slipped off his shoulders and fell into the bush.

Eventually, he came to a clearing where some goats were chewing the bush, and behind them was his mother, using her machete to clear a new path for her animals to follow.

When Tamaya lifted her head and saw the boy, she jumped back in fright, for she thought he must be another demon. She lifted her machete to him and shouted at him to leave her alone, but Unawqi remained in his place, looking intensely at her to record all he could of her face.

Tamaya screamed and ran at him with her machete, threatening to cut off his head. Her shouting scared the goats more than Unawqi, and they ran in every direction, knocking both Unawqi and Tamaya off their feet. When Tamaya fell, the machete left her hand and flew up into the air, and when it came down, it sliced into the neck of one of the goats, severing its head from its body. The goat's decapitated head rolled across the ground until it settled directly between the mother and her son.

Tamaya looked upon the frightful sight, believing it to be an omen that harm would befall her if she disturbed the boy any further, so she backed away from the goat's head, and would not go past it. She also shook her finger at the boy to tell him that the sign applied to him as well, and that he should back away, never to cross her path again.

Unawqi did not know where the word had come from, as he had never learned it, but his lips formed the word, all the same: "Mama?"

It really was a question. An intuition, yes, but a puzzled intuition. For his mother, however, the single word was like the machete had fallen into her heart instead of the goat's neck, and she gasped, and stumbled backward.

Yes, it was him. She looked closer at his face and saw her own. The creases around his nose, and the lashes over his eyes were the same shape as hers.

She wanted now to run toward him, but the head of the goat stopped her, its ghostly brown eyes looking directly at her as if warning her to stay away. She believed they were the eyes of Moche, using the goat to find and hunt down both mother and son, and as much as she wanted to claim her son and take him in her arms, she wanted even more to protect him.

She looked at the trees around her, hoping one of them might give her an answer, and Unawqi was impressed that she could also talk to the forest. Indeed, one Huasquila, the biggest one at the edge of the clearing, showed her a sign. At its base of its trunk was a path that led to the dwelling of her neighbor, someone she could trust.

"There!" Tamaya pointed for the boy to see. "Run that way, and you will find the house of a woman with hair like red clay. Go to her, for she will hide you, and put clothes around you."

Unawqi, not knowing what else to do but to obey, took one last look at his mother's eyes and followed where she had pointed under the Huasquila tree. He went downhill, deeper into the cloud forest, where the ground became wet and muddy, and the blood-red sap of the Yawar Wiki trees drained to the edge of his feet.

Next to a waterfall, he spotted a house. It had a roof, but only three walls. In front of it sat the woman with red clay in her hair. She was old, blind, and had a bent back.

Unawqi approached her. She heard him, but was not frightened, and did not move. When he came close enough, she reached out her hand to him, and he gave it to her. She felt it was the hand of a rather young child, so she had nothing to fear.

She ran her hand up his arm and felt that he had nothing covering his naked back in the cold forest. So she raised herself up and felt around for an earthen pot that was sitting near the fire. Inside, the pot held a liquid form of warm red clay. She dipped her hand into it and gently bathed the boy with the clay, covering first his upper body, and then his legs and feet. When she was finished, she rested her hands on his head for a long time as they radiated warmth throughout his body.

Tamaya had quietly followed him down the path, bringing with her one of her goats. When she was near enough to the old woman's house, she hid behind a stand of guadua, and released the goat to wander toward the woman's dwelling. When it bleated, the woman heard it, and called it close to her.

That night, the old woman and Unawqi feasted on the rich goat with boiled yucca, while Tamaya kept watch from her place in the dark some distance away.

It continued this way for many weeks. The woman with the red clay hair kept the boy fed and protected him from all harm, while the mother sent miracles to appear in front of them, but never revealed herself.

4 MOCHE

It had been uncomfortably long since Unawqi left Antisana. Moche thought that, certainly by now, Unawqi would have returned, but he had neither heard nor seen any sign of the boy.

From his perch atop Antisana, he scanned the treetops of the Pasochoa Forest, while tracking the Sun to sense any disturbances.

It was much too quiet, so Moche called upon one of his bats, and instructed her to fly to the Pasochoa at dusk to investigate. When the bat left, Moche returned to his chamber to sit alone.

It was the first time his aloneness felt lonely. He was the master, but he was unable to master his own feelings, and the boy's absence had brought back memories Moche preferred to forget.

He recalled his much younger days in his own land, and his rapid ascent to the priesthood. His masters had marveled at the sharpness of his wisdom, and his ability to captivate the people's attention when he spoke.

Performing ceremonies in the temple of the Sun was his lifelong ambition--training warriors not to kill, but to hunt, and bring him the conquered as candidates for sacrifice to Aakti.

The temple there was magnificent, grander than any royal palace he had ever seen. The outer wall, as wide as half of the city, rose straight up from the sand to a height so imposing, it challenged the surrounding mountains. Upon the wall, in red and gold, were carved the faces of the gods, and the tales of great battles. Moche imagined how, one day, he too would be a legend, and his life would therefore also be depicted on the wall, covering enough stones to make even the gods jealous.

Inside the temple there were hundreds of rooms, and Moche knew them all. He would pace through each one, overseeing rituals, administering tributes, and receiving audiences. It was there, at the very top of the temple, where he would perform his most solemn duty, in front of the thousands of spectators stretching out below him: the sacrifice to the Sun.

When a candidate, usually an enemy soldier captured in battle, was prepared, he would be presented to Moche, kneeling at the priest's feet. Moche would pace around the candidate on a highly decorated and canopied platform, which was the holiest of holy places at the top of the temple. He would recite incantations and help the candidate drift off into the dream world by imbibing him with a mixture of potent plants and corn alcohol. The dream world was the world of the Sun, the same world that surrounds the world that Moche induced Unawqi into upon his being brought to Antisana.

Eventually the candidate would drop his neck back from exhaustion, and Moche would slit his throat, drawing the candidate's blood into an earthen vessel. The crowds watching from the base of the temple would cry out in awe as Moche drank the blood and poured the rest into a pedestaled fire, the smoke of which rose to the heavens and toward the Sun. The people feared they would never see a day they would be so presented to Moche, for his manner was so commanding and serene, it scared them. It was as if he himself were not of this world.

But as time passed, Moche knew he could still be more than a priest. He wanted to be closer to Aakti--an advisor, perhaps, maybe chief viceroy. Knowing the other priests would not willingly allow him to pursue this and become their overlord, he concealed his ambition from them and descended underneath the temple to meet with Amaru, the great serpent who could travel between the underworld and the heavens.

Moche offered to build Amaru a temple of his own, equal to that of the Sun's, if the serpent would transport Moche to the Land of the Sun. The serpent accepted the offer willingly, and asked for Moche to guarantee his promise by making occasional sacrifices in the Sun's temple, not to Aakti, but to Amaru instead, so the people could better justify building a new temple.

Though Moche knew this would be a challenge, he agreed, and one day made a sacrifice, using both names of Aakti and Amaru, thus confusing the priests. The second occasion he made the sacrifice to Aakti, but asked for Amaru's blessing to seal it, making Amaru a more final authority. This caused the priests to admonish Moche for straying from the true religion, and they ordered him to return to their orthodoxy. On the third occasion, Moche made the sacrifice fully to Amaru, and pleaded with the people to build a separate temple for the great serpent.

The priests were horrified at Moche's appeal, but waited until after the ceremony to decide his fate. But while the other priests deliberated, Moche wasted no time and hurried underneath the temple to inform Amaru he had completed his side of the agreement. Amaru, in turn, took Moche upon his back and slid through a labyrinth of tunnels, until they came to a place where they could see the whole of Earth beneath them, and in front of them, the gates to the court of the emperor of Earth and sky, Aakti.

Moche went inside the palace. The emperor was impressed at the priest's ability to have convinced Amaru to bring him there. The priest told the emperor his effort only represented the degree of his fealty to the Sun, and that he would like to be Aakti's highest representative on Earth.

The emperor liked Moche's boldness and determination, and consented to the request, making Moche his high consul, an honor never bestowed upon any earthly being. Filled with pride, he rode back to Earth on the back of Amaru to announce the emperor's decision.

However, when he returned to announce his new and superior role, he still had one more promise to complete; the one made to Amaru. Moche embarked upon building Amaru's temple so that it would be separate but equal to the splendor of the Temple of the Sun nearby. The emperor eventually noticed the serpent's temple challenging the size of his own temple, and was furious, sending fire down on Amaru's temple until it burned to the ground.

Amaru was now terribly afraid of traveling between the worlds, embarrassed at his affront to the Sun, and refused Moche any further assistance. The other priests saw the burning of Amaru's temple as divine judgment, and therefore resolved to strip Moche of the title and privileges Aakti ordained. Moche's sacrifices and rituals grew rambling and flat, devoid of their usual energy, and the people stopped listening.

The priests met again to ratify their belief that Moche was no longer worthy of being high counsel, and furthermore, no longer fit to be a priest. They called the city before them, accusing Moche of misusing the religion for his own gain, and that he should be banished to the farthest frontier.

The people agreed in a loud voice, and Moche was immediately escorted by warriors across the desert to the north to the very edge of their known territories, where they knocked him unconscious, and then carried him a day further into an unknown wilderness where they left him.

When he woke up, Moche knew it would be to his own demise if he tried to return, and he had nothing with which to survive a long journey back. The wilderness around him, though, had plenty, and he decided to make his new start there.

It was a sore memory, and he was still bitter at the emperor's rejection and the humiliating removal from his people.

Moche desperately wanted revenge, and Unawqi was to be his weapon. The day was coming soon on which he would prove to the whole world—including his former people—that not only would he reclaim his position as their high priest, but that even the Sun would come to fall at his feet. If only he could reclaim the seeds!

Nonetheless, after all the years he had invested in Unawqi's training, Moche was afraid to admit the one thing his magic could not control, and that was the boy's free will. How could he not have foreseen it? If he desired, Unawqi could simply reject him and walk away. The thought upset Moche, for he would not suffer being spurned a second time.

5 FLIGHT FROM THE FOREST

It was the first night of the clouds festival, when the monkeys drink palm wine and laugh high up in the trees. Unawqi had been staying with the woman with red clay hair for several weeks by then.

The monkeys were carrying on loudly when they were stopped by an even more vocal exchange higher in the heavens.

Mama Killa, the Moon, confided to the cloud spirit Puyo Supai, that the sorcerer Moche, who was also Puyo Supai's lover, had raised a boy in secret.

This made Puyo Supai very angry, for she thought Moche had taken another lover and fathered the child. Puyo Supai paced rapidly up and down the slopes of the forest, wailing tears from her clouds and making her head boil so that even the monkeys could not enjoy their drunkenness and they scattered for cover.

She became so enraged with her lover who had betrayed her, she stirred up lightning which fell from her belly, lighting up the forest with fire.

One of the bolts hurled downward and struck the forest canopy directly over the dwelling of the woman with the red clay hair, creating a hole to the sky through which torrents of Puyo Supai's tears poured down, enough to equal the waterfall next to the woman's house.

Even without the eyes to see, the old woman moved quickly to pull Unawqi and her belongings inside, trying to spare them from the deluge. But the rain was so great, the pool at the foot of the waterfall grew into a lagoon in no time at all, surrounding the house.

Eventually, Puyo Supai cried herself to sleep, and the next morning, Unawqi and the woman found themselves trapped up against the embankment of the ravine, surrounded by water on all sides.

When Aakti, the Sun, passed over, he saw through the gaping hole in the canopy. He felt a great disturbance in his heart coming from the hole that was Unawqi, and then poured an intense ray of energy down into the cavity in an attempt to make the pain go away.

The heat of the Sun began to wither the skin of the old woman, but not Unawqi's. His clay kept him moist and cool. But he sensed the danger they were in, and felt it urgent they should escape.

He grabbed the frail woman's hand and led her into the lagoon, swimming under the falls to the other side where they emerged in the shade the Sun could not reach. It was there Unawqi remembered he once had a eucalyptus punchu to protect him from the Sun, and that he had lost it. He also remembered he had left his stick behind at the woman's dwelling.

The Sun continued to sear its way through the hole in the canopy, and in time, incinerated the woman's house and all her belongings.

Unawqi and the woman retreated into the forest until they found a place where they could rest to nourish themselves on lemon ants. It was there that Unawqi's mother, Tamaya, spotted them, but because she could not reveal herself, she waited until Unawqi fell asleep on the ground. Tamaya then approached her friend, the woman with the red clay hair, put a blanket over Unawqi's body, and left next to his head some cassava cakes and goat's cheese wrapped in a large yarumo leaf.

Tamaya took the hand of the blind woman and led her away, assuring the woman that Unawqi was at Tamaya's other hand, even though this was not true. Tamaya was sure that Puyo Supai's flood and the blaze of the Sun were further proof that the omen was still upon her, and that destruction would continue to target them unless they separated themselves from Unawqi. This would throw all the demons and gods off their track, and Tamaya could keep continue keeping an eye on Unawqi from a distance.

In the humid forest the old woman's skin revived, and her flesh grew plump again. In fact, as she walked next to Tamaya, her voice grew so strong that Tamaya could hear it on both sides, as if the one old woman had become two, and then three, and four. From all sides of the forest the woman's voice could be heard talking, even though she appeared to be standing right next to Tamaya. She knew from that point on, the old woman with the red clay was much more than an old woman and was instead someone able to use her way with the forest to bend it to her will.

When Unawqi awoke, he didn't understand why he had been left alone, but he saw the food left for him, and thought the old woman was simply out exploring for more. He feasted on the cassava and cheese. When he was done, he noticed a path in front of him that perhaps the old woman had taken. In truth, the woman had gone the opposite way with Tamaya. Unawqi searched all day for her until he found himself so deep in the forest he could not remember the way to return.

Unawqi had nothing—no punchu, no stick, no food, only the red clay that covered his body. Nevertheless, it proved to be enough for one of the old woman's friends to recognize that Unawqi must have belonged to the old woman; and he was in need of help.

This friend of the old woman was a rather shy chinchay, a medium-sized yellow cat with black spots. Even though she was bashful, the chinchay made herself visible to Unawqi, coming just close enough for Unawqi to see her so that could follow her up the ravines to the edge of the forest.

This edge of the forest was a ridge from which Unawqi could see the villages and farms below. Drifts of smoke from cooking meat and the sounds of goats being milked made his mouth water, and he was filled with hope that he would reunite with the old woman there.

He turned to thank the chinchay for showing him the way, but when he turned around, he saw no sign of the spotted cat.

Unawqi descended the grassy slope dotted with pampas and yarumo and approached the nearest farm.

Upon seeing the muddy red boy emerge from the dusk on the edge of their farm, a farmer and his son went to greet him. Unawqi had no language to match theirs, and thinking he must be an animal, they put him in a stable with the goats and pigs, where he would be raised like those animals to do some work.

The farmer and his son studied Unawqi, giving him grass and corn to eat before putting him out in the field to see what he could do. But Unawqi was not an animal, so he simply turned his eyes skyward, making the farmers think that perhaps he might be waiting for a bird to fall, or that he might be a type of hunting animal, perhaps one of the legendary hunters of condors they had heard of but never witnessed.

Unawqi, however, was simply concerned for when the Sun might reappear from behind the clouds that were so thickly covering the valley, for he was without his eucalyptus punchu to hide.

All this made the farmers annoyed, so they thought about how else thy might find some use for the strange creature before them.

They put a white smock over his body and brought him over to a big clay tub behind their house, filled it with water and soap, and plunged his hands into it, moving them up and down to produce a rhythm. Then they put bowls into his hands, and he continued the rhythm until the bowls were clean.

All they wanted was to keep him in the same motion, whether or not he had anything to wash. They brought Unawqi all their plates and then all their soiled farming tools to wash. They kept him going all day and all night, for this was especially useful to them and they always had many things to wash.

Unawqi find some rest only when the farmers themselves could no longer keep their eyes open, and he fell asleep hanging over the edge of the tub. As soon as the farmers awoke, they picked him up off the ground, and set him back to his washing motion.

Unawqi knew not how to get himself out of this predicament. Every day his back stooped a little more, his knuckles scraped and bled, and his feet were very sore. He continued to think of the woman with the red clay hair and how he might find her. He longed to return to the forest where he could be cool and free, but something else inside of him equally pulled him to wonder about the absent Sun.

He remembered Moche's charge, to find Atama. Perhaps if he could ride on top of the Sun and make it carry him around the world, he would find a great many things.

Before the farmers awoke the next morning, Unawqi felt something pinching him on his forehead. He opened his eyes to see a piercing ray of sun breaking through the clouds to the east. It rallied him up, and he jumped to his feet with a vitality he had not had for a long time, to stare up through the ray like a hunter, fixing on its prey.

He ran across the field, pursuing the Sun's ray before it could disappear. All the former fear he had of the Sun had transformed into desire, and Unawqi could not distinguish between fear and desire. It occurred to him they were much the same thing; that a hunter cannot hide from his prey because he is afraid of it; rather a hunter chases what he is hunting because he thirstily desires to confront his fear.

Maybe, he thought, by arresting the Sun, they would find Atama together.

The clouds opened more, and the Sun sent new streams to pour through. Unawqi ran faster and faster, almost jumping into the air as he tried to catch the Sun, all the way to the edge of the valley, and up into the canyon.

He was far from the farm now, completely out of the farmers' sight, when they came out of their house to find him gone.

Instead, the sorcerer, Moche, who had raised the boy to send him on this undertaking, was sitting on top of Antisana. He looked out across the world and spotted Unawqi running east, which was not the direction in which Moche had told Unawqi to go. Unawqi was on the wrong mission. He was supposed to be searching for Atama, not Aakti.

Moche screamed into the air for help from his mistress, Puyo Supai, to cover up the Sun in order to make Unawqi return to the west.

But Puyo Supai was still angry with Moche, and she did not respond to his call.

Eventually, the great condor from Reventador also saw Unawqi running, and was impressed by the youth's passion and velocity. The condor swooped down from the ledge of the mountain to entertain a race with Unawqi.

The boy called out to the condor and said, "Take me! Take me to the Sun! Let's wrestle the yellow beast to the ground, you and me together!"

The condor grinned at the fearlessness of the young boy, and couldn't help but attach himself to Unawqi's fire. He swung over to the boy and let him jump aboard his wing, and then the great, brave bird shot upward into the currents like an arrow, soaring with Unawqi on his wing, climbing toward the Sun in a spiral motion.

Aakti noticed as Unawqi approached closer, becoming alarmed by this precocious boy and the bird on which he flew.

Aakti turned his heat upon the boy to try and ward him away, but Unawqi was anything but harmed. On the contrary, it only served to make him feel stronger. The more Aakti turned his heat on

Unawqi, the more Unawqi trapped the energy into himself and the condor, making the condor turn silken gold and red, like the emperor himself.

Unawqi burst into joyous laughter at the spectacle, calling his new friend, the condor, his silkworm. For the first time he felt the true meaning, the ecstasy, of being a hunter. It had nothing to do with killing, only the desire to subdue fear.

Seeing this, Aakti grew afraid, retracted his heat, and ran west. He saw Mama Killa and hid behind her, turning the sky dark in the middle of the day, and foiling Unawqi's chase.

Aakti's strategy worked, and the condor began to feel tired and lost his stamina to climb. Instead, he sailed gradually to the ground, but he had traveled so far with Unawqi that the place they came to rest was many days' journey from where they had begun. They landed in the jungle, in a distant land, far north in the territory of the Sikuani.

Fortunately, upon encountering Unawqi and the condor, a band of Sikuani hunters believed they had surprised a pair of gods, for the red boy in a white smock with a bird of that size at his side was nothing they had ever seen before. The hunters fell to the ground and pleaded for mercy for seeing what they should not have seen, and asked Unawqi if there was anything they could do to help.

"I am Unawqi, and I and my silkworm are hunting the Sun! Can you show us where he is hiding?"

The hunters were stunned at the boy's laughable premise, but dared not laugh. They told the boy that the Sun was not their prey, but they knew where it traveled. They took him and the condor where the River Meta broke open the forest canopy, and Unawqi saw the pink tail of Aakti running into the horizon, with the stars looming close behind. Now he knew which way to go, and he was determined not to let the yellow dragon elude him again.

6 UNAWQI AND THE THIEF

Unawqi and the condor planned their attack. The best time to fly was in the pitch of the night when they could hear the night animals rustling in the bush for their food, and they would fly in the dark and set themselves down upon Aakti where they saw him go to sleep.

As soon as he heard a khirkinchu sniffing through the fallen leaves, the condor pushed himself into the night sky with Unawqi on his wing.

They flew west, using the stars on the horizon as their guide, and looked below for Aakti as he slept. In due course they spotted many flickering lights below them, which reminded Unawqi of the emerald-studded walls deep inside the stomach of Antisana. He thought this must be the Sun, even though the Sun appeared to be made up of a million, tiny suns. So he pointed the condor to descend toward the lights, quietly and swiftly, right into the heart of the sparkling mass beneath.

The condor shot downward as quickly as a falling star, so that Aakti would not have the time to prepare for what was about to pierce his heart. As they came closer, Unawqi could see the lights had walls around them, and some lights were many stacked upon the other. Still some others moved along trails cut through a forest of trees with no branches, only stone and lights.

It was a bizarre landscape, this back of the Sun, the likes of which Unawqi had never seen before, and for which Moche had given him no education.

With the grace of a falling leaf, the great condor of Reventador landed upon the back of the Sun, and Unawqi jumped off his back to claim his prize.

It was quite different than what he'd imagined.

Even though it was night he could immediately tell he was not the first to arrive. Many people came out of the lit-up trees and more were dancing on the trails. In between them were horses pulling boxes with wheels, with even more people inside each box. The spine of the Sun was like all the villages of the Quijos Canyon combined, coming together to celebrate a great reunion.

Unawqi looked around his feet for where he might grab some flesh of the Sun, but in truth some of it was just grass and earth, no different than that of the forest or páramo. Other parts of it were measured and cut into unnatural shapes, made of a substance so smooth and yet as hard as the walls of a mountain. Unawqi grabbed this strange flesh at his feet, but it would not yield to his hand. He bit into and nearly broke his teeth. It tasted cold and coarse.

Unawqi felt this beast of his might be impervious, as it did not even rise to its own defense. He thought he had perhaps found its scales, but not the skin, and that he should search elsewhere for Aakti's soft belly. Around him, on every horizon, all he saw were millions of tiny lights, like the eyes of bats across the cavernous flues of Antisana. He could only leave his direction to chance, and set out walking.

He walked for hours. It all looked the same, and Unawqi wondered how the Sun could be so dark, when it was so bright in the sky. Eventually daylight appeared around him, and the lights in the trees began to fade and disappear. This confused him all the more, for daylight came from the Sun in the sky, and this made him think the emperor had escaped from underneath his feet, or that what was under his feet was not the emperor at all.

He squatted in a patch of grass to rest and think, watching the horses pull the boxes past him in increasing numbers. He listened for the condor to call from where it soared above him, hoping that together they might spot a sign to help them set a better course.

Not so far away, Titu Ilumán slept, slumped over his laboratory desk, surrounded by his calculations and diagrams, beakers and boiling tubes, and chemical concoctions smoldering in petri dishes. In the center of it, Aakti Amurugana, the primordial seeds of the Sun that were his life's obsession, sat securely enclosed in a crystal jewel case, where since the time he had stolen them, had yet to show him their power.

While Titu's eyes were still closed, the seeds began to tremble and glisten. They sensed a missing bond nearby, and were restless to reunite with it.

Unawqi lifted his head. His stomach, groin, shoulders, back and feet all burned at once. He was looking around for what might be taking hold of him when the condor swept low, pointing his wing at one of the large square boulders behind Unawqi's shoulder.

There, radiating from a cave in the boulder, a stream of golden rays spilled into the daylight. When Unawqi saw them, he was sure he had found the elusive belly of the Sun. His heart surged as he raced toward the hole in the boulder, assured he would, at last, strike his prey.

Jumping through the increasing parade of horses, Unawqi made his way to the boulder where the golden rays grew more brazen. He tried to scale the escarpment, but it was too smooth to get a grip, so the condor came to lift Unawqi to the portal, and he jumped in with his eyes lit up red, his arms raised up for the catch.

Titu awoke at the same moment, startled by the trembling of the table. He leaned back, both in terror and awe, at the freakish, half-naked boy, with arms raised over the seeds which had, at long last, burst open.

"Stop!" Titu commanded.

The boy froze, for while the seeds still shook and shone, they now made the whole cave tremble. This did not look like the belly of the Sun, either.

The man in front of him was like a mirror, and the seeds between them like his eyes. A feeling overcame Unawqi, the same feeling he had when he encountered his mother with a dead goat between them, standing on the precipice of something forbidden and sacred.

Titu reached forward to protect the seeds, but it was too late. They shattered the crystal case and flew into the air towards Unawqi, entering his nostrils and mouth, flooding his eyes with a diamond luster, and changing his arms and chest from those of a boy into those of a young man. His hair tightened around his head to a coarse mat, and he grew a bit taller with each second that passed.

Titu stepped backward in fright at seeing this dreaded transformation take place in front of him. He remembered very well the rightful owner from whose hands he had stolen the seeds, and to whom they had now returned.

Unawqi's eyes had grown as arresting as the dead black goat caught in the tarapacana. The father was looking at the son, but the son was looking at a very small thief.

Unawqi now had the power in him to destroy. He felt it. He was the hunter Moche had fashioned him to be. Was this cornered man in front of him Atama, the thief he had been seeking? Even if he could not be certain of it, Unawqi was tempted to kill him while he had the chance, and fly back to Antisana to tell Moche of his victory.

But the seeds within his body pulled him back, compromising his obligation, and blurring the line between the vengeance and desire he was feeling.

Titu could not come to confess what he knew, that Unawqi was his son. His lust for the seeds was stronger, and if there was a way to get them back, it would not come from telling the truth. Instead, he cowered at Unawqi's feet, and wept for mercy.

Quite the opposite of assuming the role of foe, Titu promised to help the boy, to provide him shelter, food, and rest before he continued his journey.

Unawqi did not trust this thief, and yet the journey had indeed left him famished. Behind him was a burned wilderness and slavery, to which he had no desire to return. He reluctantly nodded in approval of the thief's offer and relaxed his offensive posture.

Titu got back on his feet and led Unawqi out through a door into another room, and then into another room beyond that where there was a bed and a half-eaten dinner of chicken, bananas, and rice. For the moment, Titu closed the door behind him and left his supernatural son, the captor of his seeds, to eat and sleep in peace.

Outside, Aakti broke through a bank of clouds and felt his heart being drained, beating inside the bones of something within his reach.

7 JAQUNQAY

Unawqi didn't sleep all night. The seeds that had flown into him kept him awake. They were exploring his veins and finding places to take root and made him levitate above his bed.

He wondered what end this new power inside him sought. Was he a gift, or was he simply a vessel?

He thought about Moche, festering in the azure underworld of Antisana, impatiently wringing his hands for Unawqi to return with the Aakti Amurugana in his hands.

How would he explain to Moche that the seeds were indeed with him, but not in his hands?

He thought about the woman with the red clay hair, wandering the trails of the cloud forest, calling out Unawqi's name.

He thought of the farmers from whom he had escaped, who were now washing their own plates and tools.

He thought of the thief in whose room he was now resting, and whether this man could really be of much use.

Last of all he thought of his trusted friend, the condor of Reventador, who was probably circling outside, ready to fly Unawqi away.

This, to fly, was the only thing that gave pause to the train of Unawqi's thoughts. It was the only thing he really desired, to have his thighs wrapped tightly around the breast of the great bird, his chest against the wind.

He sprang to his feet and moved toward the door to leave. At the same moment, Titu opened the door and entered, carrying a variety of contraptions in his arms, appearing that he himself was also ready to embark upon a journey with Unawqi.

From around his shoulder, Titu unburdened a large leather bag and laid it on the floor. Out of it spilled metal and glass devices mixed between stacks of corn cakes and figs wrapped in brown paper.

From his other arm, he set down on the bed a pair of trousers and a shirt, a pair of shoes for Unawqi to wear, and a tight roll of paper money.

But the largest thing in his cache was what looked like a tarantula made of silver, or the Sun with its rays bent like knees. In the middle of the object was an orb, that when Unawqi set his face up next to it, it was like he was looking into one of the dark and motionless pools in the caves of Antisana.

He could see his face staring back at him and was surprised how different he looked than from when he arrived. His jaws were more squared off, his shoulders were broader, and there was a small bit of hair growing over his lip. But most alarming of all was the steely glow in his eyes that the seeds were lighting up from within.

Unawqi had not acquainted himself with the young man he had changed into, and he was frightened and fascinated at once.

Titu interrupted, but a bit nervously as he also was afraid of Unawqi looking into his eyes and finding out too much.

"I thought much last night, and decided you need to follow the Sun, and find where it's calling you.

"My duty, as it seems, is to help you pursue it."

Titu pushed the clothes toward Unawqi, but Unawqi didn't know what they were or what to do with them. So Titu took it upon himself to dress Unawqi in the clothes.

To Unawqi, the material smelled of tobacco and coffee, enough to ward away a bear. They felt like a cloak of armor with which he might better shield himself from the Sun. They made him feel somehow bigger, but heavier, and he pushed himself up off his heels to try and keep the clothes from weighing him down.

Titu began removing items from the leather bag, showing Unawqi their levers and dials and explaining how to use them to measure the Sun, trap its heat, predict its path, and so many other things. Unawqi did not know if he could remember it all, or why he should even try. To him, it might as well have been in the language of the forest monkeys, the one they use when entertaining each other when they are drunk.

Eventually, Titu picked up the silver tarantula, which rattled and jangled as he moved it through the air, and placed it in Unawqi's hands.

"Now, you must promise me to protect this very well, and never to let it stray far from your side. This is my invention, I call it a phototeledar, but don't you worry about the name. I made it to be the ears and mouth of the light that is now inside of you. It will tell me where you are at all times, so that I can know if you are well, or if you are in trouble."

Unawqi touched the orb in the middle, and it gave him a shock.

"Oh, yes," Titu warned, pulling Unawqi's hands back.

"Be careful of getting too close or the power will come right out of you, destroy what's in your path, and then flee, leaving you very weak."

The great eye of the condor peered in through the window next to the bed. Titu lifted the sash and motioned for Unawqi to mount himself and all of his provisions onto the great bird's back.

"Go! While the Sun is still waking, go!"

And with that, the bird and Unawqi pushed off into the sky, tethered to Titu via his metal trappings.

Smelling the brine of the sea to the south, the condor flew in that direction, over the spine of the Andes. Unawqi held on, confused as to whether he had been lost or found. He wasn't sure anymore whose undertaking he was serving: Moche's, the thief's, or the seeds that now possessed his flesh. Was he his own hunter, or was he a soldier under everyone else's command?

A passing Black Solitaire, so small and insignificant of a bird in the shadow of the condor, cast a pitiful look on Unawqi, as if the youth and the bird were slow. It made Unawqi feel dense, less nimble than he used to be on his feet, and doubtful of his own power.

That morning, the sky was owned by Puyo Supai, the cloud spirit. Her blanket of clouds spread over the land, hiding Aakti from being seen. But the condor flew further south through the avenue of the volcanoes, and past the great deserts farther south.

They eventually saw fishers in their boats at sea, and followed the coastline south some more, though the waves and wind grew more fierce. It gave hope to the condor that he would be able to find the edge of the clouds under which he might pass to see the fleeing Sun.

The rains came, and tried to discourage them, but the Aakti Amurugana inside of Unawqi were enough to keep both him and the condor warm and fortified.

At last, over the Jaqunqay islands in the Chiri Sea, the clouds broke their reach, and the condor soared out into open sky where it spotted the emperor, no longer veiled from Earth.

There, in the bracing clarity between the blue heaven and the watery deep, Aakti halted his run and glared down at the condor's garnet eyes. The metal orb in Unawqi's pouch sizzled like fat on a fire, and the seeds in his body surged into his shoulders, forcing him to stand up tall, like a man, almost leaping off the condor's back.

The wide expanse over Jaqunqay and her rocky cathedrals was to become the long-awaited arena for the battle Unawqi had sought.

The emperor fulminated, sensing his progeny buried in the chest of the earthling on the condor's back, and he circled the islands, his rays dripping fire like drool.

From a thousand miles away, Titu could see the standoff unfolding in front of his eyes, channeled through the phototeledar at Unawqi's side. He stood at attention over the receptor, desperately hoping to witness the true power of the seeds, or if necessary, to coax them to unleash the greatest physics display of all recorded time.

"Boy!" Titu called through the orb. "Defend yourself! Take the long crystal needle from the bag and point it directly at the Sun's flares. It will extract the Sun's serum and weaken his energy."

Not having much time to think, Unawqi reached into the bag at his side and pulled out the needle, even as Aakti turned inward from his circle to launch his assault. The needle gleamed as Aakti's rays hit its sapphire tip, and Unawqi watched as the needle's interior flooded with a blue-green gas, dimming Aakti's light.

Titu exulted. "Yes! The extraction is working!" He insisted Unawqi get closer and extract some more.

The Sun's power, however, was overwhelming, and started to burn the hair on Unawqi's arm and the tender down beneath the tips of the condor's wings.

"Closer! Closer!" Titu bellowed through the orb, delirious with his growing success. The gas in the needle changed to bright green, intensifying its volatility, condensing itself into a vapor that slid down to the hilt, which in turn made space for more energy to enter the tip.

The seeds reacted exactly according to Titu's predictions, gravitating toward the Sun through the infusion of gamma vapor held in Unawqi's hand.

It was a dangerous chemical reaction that Unawqi was not prepared for, as the seeds surged up through Unawqi's shoulders to his wrist, turning his hand into bronze metal and burning away his flesh.

"Don't stop now, child!" Titu urged. "Fly right into the heart!"

Unawqi had become the unwitting conductor of material transformation for the benefit of Titu's experiment, in a process through which the seeds would leave his body and turn him into a material byproduct.

Soon, the Sun, the needle, and the seeds had become a virtual forge, spinning Unawqi's arm, part of his chest, and half of his face to a precious metal that many prospectors spend years digging to extract from the earth.

More of Unawqi's body would suffer the same fate if it was not for the condor, whose wings could no longer withstand the blazing heat, and so he broke the snare. His wings set aflame, which forced the great bird to lose the current and hurl downwards toward the sea like a fiery comet.

"No, no, no, don't stop now!" Titu bawled through the orb as he watched his gold drop toward the sea.

The condor could not regain control and plunged into the broad waves east of Jaqunqay. Hitting the surface, the needle burst into an immense ball of fire, large enough to be seen by a lone fisherman on the other side of the island. The fisherman turned his sails and moved as quickly as he could toward the other side until he was able to see the bird and the young man flailing in the waves in the distance.

The saltwater had short-circuited Titu's channel through the orb, and he fell to the floor wailing, so close to achieving the golden trophy before it all went down, burning through the clouds. All his life's hopes and work were lost somewhere in the sea, rewarding him but a few brief moments tasting the fruit of his glory.

The fisherman held out his oar to pull Unawqi, the condor, and their belongings into the boat. It was enough weight to nearly capsize the small craft, but the fisherman had an unlucky day without catching a single fish, so he was graced with room to spare.

Like Titu, Aakti had lost track of his contender, and had to carry on with his perimeter patrol of Earth, hoping for another match on another day.

The fisherman set his sails homeward bound on the beach of Jaqunqay, somewhat confounded, yet enchanted by the half-golden youth and the condor with garnet eyes crouched together in the helm of his skiff. He had set out that day in search of some mackerel, or maybe a tuna if he were truly lucky, but catching a young man made of flesh and gold, as well as an avian legend, was beyond the wildest tales of the sea he could ever dream to tell.

They sailed with the current, letting the gentle waves rock the boat as if it was their baby. When the fisherman came to a kelp bed, he reached down, pulled up as much as he could hold in both arms, and then laid the cool, gelatinous mass over Unawqi's burned arm, the one that still had flesh on it. At first, the salt stung sharply, but just as quickly, the silky part of the weed licked his skin, feeling like the red clay the woman had bathed him in.

The kelp calmed Unawqi, and so did the tenderness of the fisherman. The fisherman couldn't have been more than fifteen years older than Unawqi, still in the prime of his years, with strong shoulders from pulling nets, and fit for fighting. Yet his eyes, as caramel brown as the bright leather of Unawqi's pouch, seemed to be finished with fighting. They smiled without the aid of his mouth, alive, not so much with ambition, but with heart.

He hovered over Unawqi, meticulously caring to make sure every part of his sore skin was covered with kelp. Then he turned his eyes directly into the eyes of Unawqi. He looked curiously, not fascinated by the dancing diamonds, but by something else, something he saw, more desirable than diamonds, and both he and Unawqi wondered together what that might be.

The fisherman placed his cool hand on Unawqi's brow to calm the sting of the Sun's fever. "Do not worry. Only sleep," he said.

Unawqi started to drift off to sleep as he watched the fisherman turn his attention to the condor, giving it the same medicine of tenderness.

Unawqi was caught up in something he had never felt before. The fisherman, this stranger, was the only man Unawqi had ever met who had no desire to lord him, to use him, or to enslave him. In fact, despite Unawqi's battered state, the fisherman seemed charmed by Unawqi's striking looks and brave spirit. Unawqi felt the urge to reach his hand out to touch the fisherman's arm, but his hand was buried under such a heavy amount of kelp, that he did not know where it was. All he could help but do was give the fisherman his attention, who, as he tended to Unawqi and the condor, smiled and sang a song to himself he had composed at that very moment in his head, but felt as if he had been singing it for all his life:

"I will not let you go;
I will not let you go
until you take me in your arms.
I will not let you go until you love me."

The kelp medicine worked well, and soon Unawqi succumbed to sleep.

Having finished the dressing and cooling of the condor, the fisherman leaned back against the boat's gunnel and looked toward the looming mountains of Jaqunqay, sitting beneath the haze of the fading rose sky.

The Sun fled. The seeds slept. And from underneath the northern clouds, the faintest outline of the Moon appeared, on her own quest from Moche to find where the stray hunter had fallen.

8 STORM WITH A VIPER'S TONGUE

Over the course of the next several months, I returned to as many of St. Rita's breakfasts they would allow, hoping for the odd chance that Unawqi would be there to tell more of his story. It was wrong of me, of course, to expect anyone to be a regular for charity meals, but I didn't know where else to find him.

It happened in early June. The lilacs were starting to bloom. The soggy air had begun to dry out, and you could feel the energy of the people in the streets as they were eager to venture beyond the pavement. The project this time was cleaning fish down on the pier, not in the kitchen, and it was there that Unawqi also showed up, this time to volunteer himself.

I jumped up from my station to embrace him. The past months had done him well, and he looked stronger and sure-footed.

He explained that he had found a good string of gardening jobs that kept him busy, but that he was still hunting. He was not giving up hope. He felt certain he was in the right spot, and needed to keep paying attention.

We put on some heavy rubber gloves and gutted fish, a messy job at first, but once it became routine we were able to turn our minds back to unfinished conversation. I wanted so badly to hear what had happened after he fell into the ocean at Jaqunqay.

However, Unawqi was disturbed by the Sun's brightness, so we agreed to find some shade under a nearby alder tree. I asked him if that was still the effect of the Sun's burning him, if there was some leftover damage to his skin and body. He said, no, it was actually because he was fatherless, and the sunlight only made him feel sadness for it.

"I came here today," he explained, "because the sea, these very fish, are the closest I can get to loving the father I never had. Fish, of all things, remind me of someone who gave birth to my second life, and made me want to be a hunter for all the right reasons, even though he was not a hunter at all, but a fisherman."

As if the story Unawqi had told so far had not already made me intrigued, now I was doubly captive, and I didn't notice my hands settling in the innards of the poor bass on my lap.

He continued by explaining that there used to be a ritual in his lands, and one not confined to human beings alone. It was so primal that even the beasts partook.

It happened around the time of year when the emperor Aakti, the Sun, gave his greatest attention to the happenings on Earth. Seeing they had the greatest of all audiences, older males sensed they were being called to present themselves and renew their manhood, particularly to their sons, while the golden emperor had his gaze upon them.

The sons knew the pattern, and they mostly stood by and humored their fathers as the older men talked louder than they had in a year, lifted heavier objects than they had lifted in a year, straightened their spines, and shook the muscles that had sagged for a year. This was all to make sure they had not become invisible to the younger men because the light was at its greatest for them to account for themselves.

All creation under the Sun had their manners of familiarity with this ritual, and the condor of Reventador was no exception. He awoke one morning on the beach of Jaqunqay next to the fisherman's shed, and could feel by the brightness in the air that his own father must also be preparing for the ritual, and looking for his son to observe.

Now the condor's father was not just another condor. It was Reventador himself, the wild and reclusive mountain god of the East whose explosive temper rages often but is rarely witnessed. The absence of his son the condor would, of course, bring him disgrace in front of the emperor, causing Reventador to hurl poisonous rock and smoke into the skies to vent his distress. This in turn would result in great damage and death to the many innocent living things surrounding Reventador.

Therefore, the condor needed to hastily make his flight to Reventador's side to allow the mountain, his father, to spew his fire and shake his rocks only for his son to witness, giving his father assurance that Reventador was still as powerful and virile as ever.

So, without any noise to wake Unawqi or the fisherman, the condor lifted off above the shore and into the current, disappearing into the northern sky on his return home.

Moche, who had raised Unawqi as a surrogate father and only for the purposes of making him his instrument, also felt the cramp of the annual light, but was troubled as to what to do.

The ritual was one he used to oversee as a priest, but because he was not a father, he never needed to practice the ritual himself. But now that he was for the first time absent from Unawqi, Moche sensed some responsibility, some need to prove himself a man that he had never demonstrated to Unawqi.

There was a further complication.

Moche did not want to be called to account by Aakti, given their contentious history. He was no longer a servant of the Sun, instead he was now the Sun's chief stalker. As such, Moche was deliberate about staying undercover.

In essence, Moche's second life obligated him to be a fugitive from the annual father's rite, and hence forfeit the masculine role that creation now afforded him this opportunity to defend. The situation in which he had put himself forced him to take an exemption from the rite of passage of other males.

So, Moche used the time of the ritual to continue to hunt for Unawqi through the eyes and ears of Moon, Mama Killa. But he was not indifferent to the rest of creation and their preoccupations. Indeed, he silently wished to be a part of it, to have Unawqi at his side to ratify his paternal role.

This begged the question that I put myself to Unawqi: "But what of Titu? Isn't he your real father?"

Unawqi snickered a bit at the toughness of the question. "I wonder if I'll ever know the answer to that question, but I know he feels it."

Titu, having seen Unawqi in person, and with his very eyes witnessing him transform from a boy into a young man, was now terribly bedeviled at his own incapacity to participate in the masculine ritual.

The light of Aakti beamed so hot and bright through Titu's laboratory windows, that even drawing the curtains closed was not enough to drive back the intense rays piercing through, like sabers reaching for his throat. They streamed in through every crack and seam until they burned an impression onto the curtains of the head of the dead, black goat he first saw when fleeing his son's birth.

"What kind of man are you?" the apparition hissed. "Where is your son, Titu? Why does he not stand by your side?"

Titu clung to the wall at the opposite end of the room, pulling at his hair and rubbing his eyes, sore with grief. He could hear old men outside making their loud noises, boasting to their sons of their power and conquest, hitting sticks against stones to demonstrate their virile strength.

But Titu had no such audience. He was so proudly a modern man living among the people of pale skin, and he thought he could emotionally distance himself from the old ways of his village, three hills away.

Now that he had encountered his own son after having abandoned him at birth, it was a very different feeling that haunted him. He felt as much a man as a mouse hiding in the walls, and even the mice in the walls were making more noise than he. It came to him the absolute irony of how, after all these years of coveting the Sun's power, now all he wished was for it to go away and leave him alone.

So why did Unawqi need this shade of the alder tree? He was not a father. Why did the Sun's light bother him? He grew up in a cave, protected by Moche from being conditioned to these traditions, and Moche would not participate.

Unawqi and the fisherman carved out a different life for themselves on Jaqunqay, and they were happy. They had taken to sharing the same bed, for since he had arrived on the island, Unawqi had been bothered by the sounds of the sea, and he found warmth and solace, not just from the fisherman's spirit, but from his body as well.

Likewise, the fisherman did not know why or pretend to care why, but it was instinctual for him to want to protect Unawqi; to show him that manhood came from the ability to touch and be touched; to be moved by others and ensure they receive your care. He would always raise his arm to shade Unawqi from the Sun when they were out in the boat, and he laid out illuminated jellyfish in the sand to make trails for Unawqi to follow in the cool twilight. The feelings for each other came so easily, and they worked with each other in unperturbed contentment.

There they laid sleeping together that morning the condor left, submerged under a grass blanket, the spiny edges quivering in the shore breeze coming in through the half-opened door. The fisherman's arm was crossed over Unawqi's chest and had been that way all night, sealing their two bodies firmly together.

Some particles of sand blew through the pile of the grass blanket, dusting the tongue in Unawqi's open mouth, waking him to see the light of earliest morning streaming in.

Usually, the condor would be there standing in the doorway, but that morning he was gone.

Unawqi rose and stretched his neck out the window, looking up and down the beach for any sight of the condor. A fear rose up from his stomach, one that gripped him so strongly he left the shed without thinking to put on any clothes or raise the fisherman for help.

He walked out to the beach. His stomach felt upside down, as if it were just as frantic as Unawqi's eyes, restless and dizzy. Still there was no sight of the condor.

From the time he strode by Unawqi's side at the edge of the cloud forest, the great bird was a gift, and Unawqi felt indebted to him.

And that was what led him to take refuge under the alder tree. The shame was still too hard for Unawqi to bear the pain of light, because light forced him to remember the empty door.

The fisherman had made Unawqi realize how good it felt to be cared for. Unawqi was the fisherman's to watch over, to keep, and protect from harm.

Who was Unawqi's to watch over then, if not the condor? Caring for the condor was Unawqi's way of being grateful to the fisherman, and now something had snatched his bird away under the cover of night.

Was it the Sun?

"Oh, the cunning and cruel Aakti!" Unawqi thought, tears welling in his eyes, his head boiling with shame. And while he was not aware at that time of the traditions of fathers, at some level, Unawqi felt he was a father to the condor, and he had failed to give him protection and care.

Unawqi ran in every direction on the Jaqunqay beach, spinning himself into a delirium of anguish. His chest was so tight with shame for losing his condor, he could not get himself to cry out. He ran by himself until he was parched dry.

"What would the fisherman, who never lost anything, think of me now?" Unawqi lamented. "Is a hunter not as able as a fisher to watch over his own mount? What kind of man am I?"

Exhausted, his feet shredded by salt and sand, Unawqi tripped over a washed up log, and rolled and wept in the sand. He had never felt less a man, and he curled himself into the shape he was in the womb before he was born. In desperation, the only word he could utter before crying himself to sleep was

"Máma!"

The power of that word must have been great, for Mama Killa, who had long been searching for Unawqi on behalf of Moche, was just about to leave the sky when she heard Unawqi's voice. She turned around and moved back toward the beach, challenging Aakti for his appointed hours of the day.

Only on rare occasions does the Moon stand in front of the Sun, and certainly not during this most sensitive period of ritual when the Sun is most worshipped.

This came as a great affront to both Heaven and Earth. The impulsive cry of a half-golden young man for his mother caused the whole Earth to fall into shadow, and all the fathers making their rituals with their attendant sons stopped in awe at this most surprising cosmological interruption. They wondered if they had done something to gravely upset the emperor, failing their displays of virility, and causing Aakti to retract in disgust.

Aakti broiled in anger at Mama Killa's contemptuous offense. She, in turn, ignored the emperor and carried on with her duty to find and retrieve Unawqi.

When at last she spotted him, unconscious on the shore of Jaqunqay, Mama Killa blew her breath into the sea, causing a gale to quickly rise up and send its waves to shore and seize Unawqi. They did as she commanded, and pushed onto the beach, dislodging Unawqi and the log next to him from the sand, washing his naked body out to sea.

The commotion scrambled him from his blackout, and he grabbed hold of the log, screaming for the fisherman to come and save him. He readily remembered when he was drowning with the condor, that the fisherman had found him then. Surely the same would happen again.

But neither the fisherman, nor the condor, nor the thief, nor the thief's gadgets, nor the woman with the red clay hair, nor the chinchay, nor even old Moche was in sight.

Unawqi was alone, surrounded by crashing surf, with the faces of white vipers falling down on him from every side.

The fisherman awoke upon hearing the fierce sound of the gale, and saw that his lover was gone. He bolted out of the shed in a panic to hear Unawqi's curdling screams. The fisherman ran for his boat to rescue Unawqi from being further tortured by the open water, but the high waves were too close to shore, and only pushed him over and back to the beach, no matter how many times he tried to get past them.

Eventually, Unawqi's voice faded away, and the beaten fisherman, humiliated by the sea, could do nothing but stand helpless on the shore and cry.

The fisherman, who had always preferred silence over words whenever possible, broke his custom and raised his voice to the sky to curse Sun, Moon, and Sea.

"Curses are upon you, you heartless monsters of heaven! Why have you fouled my home with your careless quarrel? You, stench and stain upon us all, you denizens of life, you have taken my youth away yet again! From this moment, you are all the fish at the end of my spear! I will chase you down until your breath fails, and you are begging for mercy, until you return my love to my side!"

The Sun, blocked by the Moon, heard nothing of the fisherman's curse.

The Sea, however, who had always been the fisherman's friend, heard it well, and reacted angrily, spitting up a tremendous breaker that crashed on shore to sweep away the fisherman's shed and boat as effortlessly as a broom dusts a floor. Then it came back, and swept the fisherman himself off his feet and out to sea, until he crashed up against the cathedral rock offshore. The sea vipers whirled around him, trying to finish him off for his blasphemy, calling up a school of giant lobsters from the deep to thrash at his legs and frenzy themselves in his blood.

But Mama Killa, seeing how she had caused offense to Aakti at her back, caused ruin to life and love of a human affair below, and was herself the instigator of the ocean's tempest, could only feel regret for her actions, now too late to undo.

She lifted her silver belly from above the shore to call the sea to calm its temper, and she returned to the Sun its throne of day. Hers was a broken heart for the fisherman, for she never intended to leave a tragedy in her wake.

When the gale subsided, Mama Killa sent some debris to the cathedral rock, so the fisherman could float on them back to the island and put the pieces of his shed back together.

She didn't stop there. From her luminous white mass, she released a sunflower that floated down through the clouds and ocean spray, finally coming to land on the beach precisely where Unawqi had been taken. She left the sunflower there as a sign of her mindfulness that this child of the Sun was also a man, beautiful in his own skin, and loved for his own life.

When the fisherman found the sunflower laying on the beach, he instantly knew what it was, for no such flower could ever be found on Jaqunqay. He picked up the sunflower and held it like a newborn child, bathing it with his flood of tears.

Every night from there on, he would lay the sunflower next to his head, cover it with the grass blanket, and cross his arm over it to shield it from harm, while the Moon stood like the condor, gleaming through the open door, pleading for a fisher's grace.

9 INSTRUMENTAL DESIRE

Mama Killa had washed Unawqi out to sea, and the white vipers of the sea buried him underneath their stormy surface, where he stayed submerged.

But this was not the end of Unawqi. It was not an act of murder. Mama Killa was well aware of Unawqi's power, for neither the Sun nor his progeny can be drowned by something as petty as the Sea.

The seeds swelled up inside Unawqi's lungs to protect him from the deep, creating a breathing membrane around his body. All sorts of fish, turtles, and dolphins came to witness the sight of him in his pearlescent dirigible, attended by a caravan of box jellyfish. Together, they floated under the water like a royal procession, the Moon pushing them north and east where Moche's hands could retrieve Unawqi again.

A few nights into the journey as Unawqi was sleeping, Mama Killa drifted his body into the mangroves of Balao, where he beached in over some stilt-roots near a collection of bamboo crab cages.

As he was gathering his cages in the early morning, a crab fisherman spotted Unawqi's shimmering, golden body, picked him up, and carried him into town to his house where he could be washed and clothed.

The town near the mangroves, Balao, was a port for trading bananas, cacao, shrimp, and gold! So, the fisherman attracted a lot of attention around the village, as the others were quite curious about the golden armor Unawqi wore. They picked him over, trying to find the edges of his golden armor so they could pry it off and sell it. But the harder and closer they looked, the more they realized it was no armor. It was welded to his skin, and this made them all the more in awe of him.

Seeing the commotion around the house, a cousin of the most powerful trading family in the town went to the crab fisherman's house to investigate. Upon seeing the golden man, she demanded he be taken at once to visit the house of her cousin, Naira.

Naira was married to a modern, foreign man that the people of Balao affectionately called "Qayqa huk'ucha," which means "crazy mouse." He told the people of Balao that his real name was Ernest Heatheridge.

But he had his nickname for a reason.

Ernest was a rather obsessive man, fascinated with all manner of creatures that swam, crawled, or flew. He had an endless assortment of books, half of them of his own pen, in which he documented and drew every species he'd observed on his many travels at sea.

After one voyage, Heatheridge decided he had his fill of sailing. But neither did he want to go home. What he really wanted was to quietly disappear from history while he remained in the area to continue doing what he loved: finding the oddities of Earth, undisturbed by the pressures of empires.

Heatheridge was still very young, and an only child whose antecedents had passed away. He was very alone in the world and anonymous except to his shipmates.

So, he made a deal with a fellow sailor named Charles Darwin, where he would transfer all his discoveries under Darwin's name in exchange for Darwin claiming to be the only witness to see Heatheridge lost at sea.

Darwin agreed, as he was very envious of Heatheridge's mounting research.

The two set out in a skiff on a scouting expedition together one afternoon. Hidden from the main ship behind an atoll, Heatheridge and Darwin assembled some driftwood washed up in the rocks, enough that Darwin could use them to float back to the ship. Heatheridge, meanwhile rowed away on the skiff toward the mainland, covering the skiff over with other debris to keep from being detected by searching telescopes.

When Darwin got close enough to be seen by the ship, they recovered him, and he told the captain that the skiff cracked open on some sharp rocks, and Heatheridge went down with the skiff.

Darwin's story was accepted, Heatheridge was free, and neither of them looked back in regret.

Here in Balao, Heatheridge would survive by buying and selling gold, using his profits to finance his ever-growing collection of undiscovered nature, beautiful and bizarre alike.

Heatheridge's library was stacked high on every side with drawings, taxidermy, and nautical instruments, so his eyes grew large when Unawqi was brought in. He scrambled for pen and paper with which to record this magnificent, metallic mutation in front of him.

As he drew, he asked the crab fisherman many questions: Where was the creature found? In what condition? If there were more than one, and did it travel in groups? Were there any unique behaviors to note?

He took all of this into his brain as fast as he could to give further shape to his depiction on paper.

As soon as the drawing was finished, Heatheridge asked the crab fisherman what price he would accept to sell the golden lad. The crab fisherman had to think carefully, because he knew this find had a shell of gold worth more than all the tortoise shells in Heatheridge's collection combined.

Eventually, the crab fisherman worked up his nerve, and told Heatheridge:

"Qayqa huk'ucha, you know that I am a poor fisherman and am growing too old to feed my family. I will give you the creature on one condition: that he become my slave during the day when we go out to sea. When my eldest daughter is wed and has someone to take care of her, on that day I will return the creature for you to possess forever."

This was a bit of an unusual proposal, but to Heatheridge it seemed acceptable and he was no stranger to crazy schemes. Plus, it required nothing of immediate or material sacrifice. And so, it was agreed--Unawqi would belong to the crab fisherman by day, and to the house of Qayqa huk'ucha by night, and when the daughter of the crab fisherman was married, Unawqi would become the property of Heatheridge's collection in entirety.

For the second time in his life, Unawqi was set to work as a slave. The brilliant sheen of his body was the perfect lure, and fish jumped out of the water into the slaveowner's boat as Unawqi leaned over the side to pull up the crab traps.

In the late afternoons, Unawqi would walk up the sandy trail out of the mangroves to Ernest and Naira's home. There he would bathe himself, feast on bananas, rice, and crab, and then retire to the library where he and Heatheridge would engage in long conversations into the night about their extraordinary adventures.

It had become clear to Heatheridge that Unawqi was quite human, not a specimen at all, and yet in possession of something beyond human reach. And so, over time, Unawqi became less a subject of study than an absorbing companion, so much so that Heatheridge began to consider Unawqi as his own son.

The affection was not lost on Naira. She and her husband had a daughter named Qina, about the same age as Unawqi. Naira noticed that Qina was charmed by Unawqi's ruddy looks and brave spirit, and she approached her husband to tell him that it would be good for Unawqi to truly become their son by marrying their daughter. Ernest marveled at the idea, and set it on his mind to persuade Unawqi to court his daughter.

But the crab fisherman was no fool, for all the while he had another scheme that was .cleverly planted into the agreement with Heatheridge.

Heatheridge made the mistake of not to ask who and who not might be the groom of the crab fisherman's daughter. He assumed it would be some other fisherman's son.

Not at all.

The crab fisherman planned to force Unawqi, his slave, to wed his eldest daughter, thereby nullifying the ability for Unawqi to become Heatheridge's exclusive property. That way, when Unawqi was to be given back to the house of Qayqa huk'ucha, Heatheridge would have to take the crab fisherman's daughter as well, and furthermore share his estate with the fisherman's family by right.

But that would come when the time was right, and for the moment Heatheridge spoke to Unawqi about courting his daughter and how proud he would be to make him his son-in-law. Heatheridge beamed with satisfaction as if he had awoken to a new creation.

But Unawqi was terrified. He had become endeared to Ernest and could not find within himself the courage to tell the truth. He was not attracted to Qina, indeed, not to any girl. He could not bear to break Ernest's proud heart, at least not now, so he summoned the Aakti Amurugana within him to pour some light into his eyes so that he could falsify some pleasure for Heatheridge's plan.

For the nights following, Unawqi and Qina would take walks through the mangroves, each asking the same questions of each other multiple times over, at a loss to think of something authentic to say.

Unawqi's mind was completely elsewhere. His heart was heavy and his face pale with worry. All he could think of was his true love in Jaqunqay.

Every step he took alongside Qina, and every word to her he was able to utter, seemed like a dagger thrust into the back of his lover, the very one who had plucked him from the snatches of the sea and carried him to safety, never asking for anything in return.

Likewise, Mama Killa overhead, distraught for her part in bringing this lie to life, covered her face in a blue veil to express her malady, and resolved to herself to do something about it.

The people of Balao were curious as to why the Moon was blue, and thought it might be smoke, drifting from harvest fires burning far away. But the air smelled clean, and so they could not understand.

The fisherman of Jaqunqay, broken by his lover's absence, gathered all the instruments, clothes, and a pouch of provisions that Titu had given to Unawqi, and put them in a palm basket.

When the tide was low, he carried the palm basket out on a reef, and then walked into the sea with it as far as he could go, where the water was up to his neck. He was near the very spot he had first pulled Unawqi and the condor from the water, and there he pushed the basket out over the waves when the wind was moving away from the island.

When the basket disappeared from his sight, he was satisfied he would never be reminded of the love that was stolen from him, and he floated himself back toward the shore.

The current moved the basket in the same direction in which it had taken Unawqi, toward the mangroves of Balao. As Unawqi and his master were fishing one morning, Unawqi noticed the basket floating in the waves, and he dove into the sea to fetch it.

Upon seeing what it was, Unawqi's breath stopped, for to him it was a sign that his lover had abandoned all hope of his return. He sat paralyzed in the water, torn with what to do with the basket and what it meant. He had never been so afraid and uncertain.

The master's boat came near and pulled Unawqi back on board, inspecting the strange findings. He cursed the basket as junk, except, of course, for the roll of money. He told Unawqi to throw the rest back out to sea, but Unawqi, visibly troubled and shaking, begged his master for permission to keep the belongings as mementos. Feeling merciful, the master agreed, and they returned back to the town for the day.

Unawqi took his repossessed belongings back to Ernest and Naira's house but hid the basket underneath his bed before anyone could notice.

After a shortened conversation with Heatheridge that evening, Unawqi returned to his room and drew the basket out, reconnecting with all his memories of Titu, of the condor, of his lover.

He was saddened by the one thing they had in common, they all abandoned him.

These things were the conduit of too much sorrow, but Unawqi did not know how to extract himself from the sadness, neither could he understand why he did not want to.

These things were the only tangible channel to his past, his adventure, his youth and manhood, and he couldn't let any of it go.

10 TOMÁS

Naira had still not gone to bed. Everyone else was asleep, but she stayed up to finish mashing plantain so it would be set for the next morning's breakfast.

As she worked at the kitchen table, she looked across the room to the where Unawqi was sleeping. He was laying with his arm over the side of the bed, the same position that her son lay when he had slept in the same bed so many years before.

She stopped looking, not wanting to stir up the sadness. Bringing up his name was forbidden in their house, so it was better to not even think of it.

Where her son went, nobody knew. Why he went, everyone knew too well.

His name was Tomás, and he was destined to guarantee the legacy of Ernest Heatheridge.

Heatheridge wanted to go way beyond the predictable babble of history. He loathed the stuffiness of his fellow naturalists and the drivel of their diaries. The way they would squabble over test tubes and such. He just plain hated scientists altogether.

He wanted to be an artist, a John the Baptist in the wilderness, a complete disruption to the established order of science, the initiator of an entirely new epoch of thinking about the natural world and our place in it.

Tomás was the promise. He was born in the purity of the mangroves, unadulterated by academic prejudice and laboratory methods. Heatheridge's project would take more years than he had, but Tomás could finish it, free of the pressures of his celebrity name, with no social status ladder to climb, and no preoccupation bringing glory to a queen in a far-off land. Tomás could walk right out the jungle into civilization like a messiah, startling the world that the jungle was more civilized than they imagined.

In his boyhood, Tomás grew exactly as his father desired. He was brilliant in an original way. He went down to the shore every day, like all the other fishers of Balao, but his father did not want him to learn too much from the fishermen. He wanted Tomás to learn what the sea had taught him, and adapt; to learn how to fish based on the same instinct to survive as any other predator.

So, Tomás watched the sea, and was not allowed to come home until he could provide for the survival of his family.

Naira remembered the many nights she had spent awake, worrying for her son all alone on the beach, having yet to catch anything. To her, he was just a boy, hungry and alone.

This didn't bother Ernest in the same way, as he fiercely believed that such deprivation would serve to motivate Tomás to work even harder. "Take away a child's bread," he would say, "and soon he will become a great baker."

Heatheridge insisted the boy was fine when Naira protested, and that Tomás should not be rescued from his task, for that would only weaken his instinct.

Not wanting him to starve, Heatheridge made the first challenges easier, like to find an urchin and bring it home. This was followed by the challenge of finding a crab, then a shrimp, then many crabs or many shrimp.

But the test that caused Naira to fret the most was when her husband had raised the bar and challenged their son to catch a fish. Tomás was not prevented from watching how the other fishermen did it, only that he could not ask them for their advice nor could he borrow their tools. He could only watch, and figure out his own way to improvise.

This made Tomás's early years very solitary, and full of long periods for pensive thinking. He spent his days alone, thinking not just about surviving the hunger that ached in his stomach, but surviving loneliness. Tomás had no friends.

There was a stretch of near three nights that Tomás did not come home. The only thing that prevented Naira from leaving her husband and going out to rescue Tomás from this cruel madness was the observation of how much praise Ernest heaped upon Tomás when he did come home with a catch.

Heatheridge felt it was natural for one creature to appreciate another creature's gift, indeed, that bonding could be defined as the byproduct of animals that share their food and belongings. Therefore, he was not reticent to express his thanks for, and pride in, Tomás, as long as Tomás understood this gratitude was an evolutionary behavior in a long scheme.

But that third night on the beach was just as excruciating for Tomás as it was for his mother. He was in serious trouble.

He fashioned a line out of palm fiber and dangled from it a piece of gold, fairly easy to come by in Balao. After all, Balao was a gold trading port.

He made a spear so sharp he hurt his own feet when he missed a fish swimming between his legs. On his own, he figured out how to make a net, and tried several types of bait, from banana to crab, even a piece of his own skin.

Still, nothing was working, and his head began to pound from hunger. He was getting more desperate to find the key to survival. The young boy sat on the beach in the dark, crying over his shame of failing to pass his father's test, feeling helpless to provide. The lack of a fish was a judgment that Tomás did not have the capacity to love his family, or to show he was evolved enough to be able to bond with them.

"Won't someone help me?" he sobbed, looking out off-shore with the hope that some fisherman would be late coming in. "I just want to go home. Please?"

No one was there. Tomás was truly by himself, except, of course, for the sea. Tomás had only it for company, listening to its waves lapping against the shore.

But the Sea could not feel for him, nor could it respond, for it had no aptitude for pity.

The sea did have one thing, though, and that was the persistence of its serenity. Its patterns of motion and rhythm pulled Tomás in. He looked long and hard at the gentle waves, how such a great ocean, as far as the eye could see, could diminish to a tender trickle of water by the time it reached his toes.

He made an observation: the waves were always coming toward him instead of moving away from him. In fact, they were the only thing coming to him and for him. The only thing! Over and again, they did not arrest their coming to him. They were there for him, and generously so. All he had to do was accept them, give himself to them, and they would hand him their gifts.

Tomás knew he was allowed no friends, but who would deny him making the sea his friend?

His headache faded, and he stood up, walked into the surf, and sat down in it, allowing the waves to embrace him. As he sat there, he did nothing but let his arms drift in the waves, blending them in with the seaweed floating by.

It was then the fish came to him, kissing the tips of his fingers, tickling his back, and causing him to laugh.

"Thank you, brothers," he said. "Thank you for hearing me."

From that moment on, Tomás understood he was different from the other fishermen. The sea belonged to him, only because the sea took him in. When he grabbed hold of one of the fish, he knew it was not a victory, for he had conquered nothing, and that they were just being generous, having been born for this very moment. The fish did not regret sacrificing their lives for their friend's survival.

When Tomás arrived home with the fish, his mother and father were ecstatic, and leapt up into the air to greet him.

Ernest exalted Tomás in the usual way, but not Naira.

Naira noticed an unusual look on Tomás's face, one that did not equally exalt his father.

Tomás ate his meal and went to bed exhausted, hanging his arm over the side, the way Unawqi was now sleeping.

As the years went on, Tomás proved himself to be the town's most masterful fisher. He didn't need a boat, or even half the tools of the other fishermen, which caused the others to gaze upon him with both amazement and resentment. It seemed Tomás didn't struggle as they did, and it made them feel inferior.

He had so many fish in his catch that he would stop at other houses on his way home to share his bounty with neighbors who had not been so lucky that day. The rest he brought home to please his father.

But Tomás had grown indifferent to his father's adulations, no matter how ebullient. His sense of obligation was now to the sea, and he wanted to pay it back for it being there when he needed it most. Tomás never felt he had been generous enough, because the sea kept giving him more.

As Tomás was on his way home one day, he noticed he had just one net of fish left, which he would ordinarily give to his mother, Naira. But when he was close to his front door, he remembered a strong, young man who had not had any success fishing for near two weeks.

All the other fishermen laughed at the man, calling him an idiot, saying he was dried up and too lazy for his own good.

But Tomás entirely disagreed. He knew what it was like. He had been on the dark beach on an empty stomach. The man was a good man, and in time, the sea would be good to him in return.

Tomás knew if the strong man would only let the sea help him, he would also regain his pride, and brush away the scorn.

An even more solid feeling emerged, which was that Tomás was no longer just a friend of the sea. In this situation, it was clear to him he *was* the sea. He *was* now one of the waves, who could just as persistently come ashore bearing gifts.

Tomás turned around from the approach to his house and went toward the strong man's house. Ernest noticed Tomás walking away and followed him, curious as to where he was going, for the father and son had become estranged and Tomás had told his father fewer stories each and every day.

When Tomás came to the man's house, Tomás said with a most beautiful smile, "I really have too much catch today, and this will spoil. Will you help me put these to good use?"

The man took the net, full of fish, and thanked Tomás sincerely, for he was famished as a result of his bad luck. He said "Only if you promise to help me eat it tonight."

Tomás accepted rather quickly, as if he were just waiting to be asked. The two carried on talking and joking as the daylight faded into dark. At the end of the meal, the strong man thanked Tomás for showing him a kindness his other friends were reluctant to afford for fear of appearing weak.

The strong man told Tomás that even if he could not bring him another fish for the rest of his life, the man would still be eternally grateful for this single meal. He said that he would be sure to look out for Tomás and give him everything he needed. Even if Tomás should ever be the last fisherman on the beach in the dark of night, the strong man would not forget him out there to be alone.

Ernest was watching the event unfold, from a distance. He reflected on how his son never laughed that way in their conversations between father and son, nor did he linger that way to keep the talk from ending.

Then, through the candle-lit window, Ernest watched as the man reached out his hand to shake Tomás's farewell. But instead, Tomás took ahold of the man's arm, looked at it, feeling the tendons and muscles up to the bottom of his biceps, and then snuffed the candle out.

For Tomás, no one had been on his mind more than the strong man. His strength was not so much there in his body as it was in the man's bravery and self-confidence. How, in spite of his poverty, he had made such a generous oath to Tomás. Ernest's son wished he had learned that kind of confidence, for it would have helped him get through those three nights on the beach with less terror of dying. It only served to make Tomás want to fish harder and better, in order to bring the strong man a bigger catch every day.

Fortunately, the strong man's luck returned, but that didn't matter. Tomás still wanted to give more back to him.

Tomás spent fewer nights coming home, and more nights having dinner with the strong man. They cleaned each other's fish, which led to mending each other's nets and cleaning each other's clothes. Tomás and the strong man loved each other, that was for certain. There was nothing they wouldn't do for each other, even though they could not agree on the better way to catch a fish.

They were drifting off to sleep another night as they lay next to each other on the floor, staring at the ceiling. Tomás was the more asleep of the two, but before he drifted off he said,

"Ah, you are a fool, but I don't care. As the sea gives everything to me, everything I have is yours. Never worry for anything."

The strong man, moved to tears by the words, turned his head to see Tomás had already closed his eyes. Nonetheless, he reached his head over, and kissed Tomás on the mouth. Then he drew a blanket over their bodies and drew him closer in.

Their romance would not last long. There came a day when Tomás came home, but home was no longer with Ernest and Naira. The strong man's house felt more his home, and there he arrived to find it empty. The fire was cold, the walls were bare, the tables and chairs and the bed they had come to share were gone.

It felt like that third night on the beach, years before, when Tomás felt the world had left him to die.

He stumbled out of the house in a daze until the man's neighbor came out of her house and explained.

Ernest had come to the strong man in the early morning, banishing him from Balao unless he could immediately reimburse him for all the fish Tomás had brought, that would have otherwise gone to Tomás's own family.

The man, feeling guilty that he had caused such offense, also knew he could not pay back such a debt, and was therefore escorted out of town by the fishermen who were jealous of the man's happiness, despite his being a mediocre fisherman.

The story the neighbor explained made Tomás angry and sad, doubly more than he had ever been. He knew his father cared nothing about a debt, and that it was an alibi to conceal his jealousy. Ernest could not tolerate that the love between Tomás and the man was stronger than that between himself and his son. Ernest wanted not just for the man to suffer for the offense, but for Tomás to suffer in equal measure.

Tomás would not be so gullible with his father's game, and he refused to offer penitence. Neither could he bring himself to turn his anger on his father, as he felt it would be wasteful. Instead, he longed for the comfort of his sea, and he retreated to the shore.

Naira, who knew what had happened, worried for Tomás, and went to the man's house. Unable to find Tomás, she asked the neighbor if she had seen him. The neighbor told Naira she had seen Tomás running toward the shore, and Naira hurried her way there behind him.

Tomás, having reached the shore, went into the sea and sat down as he always did, asking for the sea to explain to him why he always had to be left to be alone. Was this world really so cruel, that no one cherished him enough to fight for him? That instead, they preferred to leave him?

The sea, in its usual form, said nothing, but it picked him up and floated him away, far away, far, far, away from Balao where Tomás and the sea could have a fresh start.

Naira arrived at the beach to see her son floating away on the waves. Convinced he was taking his own life, she screamed out for other fishermen to come and help.

None of the fishermen would come, as they had all gone home for the day, and Naira was left alone on the beach in the dark. She was delirious in her grief, pounding on the sand as she begged for the sea to send Tomás back. There on the beach, she sat among his crude tools, not knowing what to do save to grab hold of them and attach herself to the only things he had left behind.

His body was soon out of her sight. He was gone. Irretrievable. The only company Naira had was Mama Killa overhead, to whom Naira cried out, pleading,

"Please, Mama, look out for him, and bring him home."

Naira immediately halted her crying, for she was startled by a stirring in the sky.

At first, she thought it was the tears blurring her eyes, but when she cleared them from her face, she saw what appeared to be the Moon, turning and drifting out to sea in the same direction as had her son.

The Moon left Balao that night, and Naira was the only one who saw it. Tomás would not truly be alone.

People say that the Moon is so large because she has seen too much. She remembers everything, takes it inside of her, and never lets it go.

11 THE MOON'S WHISPER

When Unawqi reclaimed his possessions from the sea that he thought were a symbol he had been spurned by his lover, the blue-veiled Mama Killa knew time was short before any number of unalterable events would make his life even more tragic. So, she pushed her body high up into the black sky.

She was so high, that the stars were disturbed by her unusual visit, for she was not of their kind. She wished to get higher so that from one spot she would clearly see both the fisherman of Jaqunqay to the south and Moche roaming near Antisana in the north.

She turned in each direction and blew a whisper through the skies. "Hurry and come to Balao!" she said. "Unawqi needs you urgently!"

The Moon's whisper landed on each of their ears at the same moment and entered their dreams as they slept.

Inside the dream, the Moon's whisper created a window through which Moche saw the fisherman, and the fisherman saw Moche. For Moche, he interpreted that perhaps the fisherman was Atama, the thief of his seeds, who had been putting Unawqi's journey in peril. The fisherman interpreted the foul-looking creature that was Moche to perhaps be the embodiment of the white vipers who had kidnapped his lover, and was keeping him prisoner in Balao.

Mama Killa could not control how the two interpreted their dreams, but she knew it was enough to motivate them to take action.

Neither the fisherman nor Moche were able to sleep for the rest of the night, and made haste to Balao instead, directed by the shafts of blue moonlight in their paths.

As the dawn broke, Unawqi gazed at the silver phototeledar, wary of and yet intrigued by its mystery. He looked into its shining surface, saw his reflection, and felt the machine to be a strange passage into his interior, where so much remained of what Unawqi wanted to deeply understand, but which no one had given him any answers.

He decided to take the phototeledar to the high point east of the mangroves where the trees cleared and one could see the stars and sky. He laid the phototeledar down there on the ground, and waited for daylight to find them.

But he was not as alone as he thought, for Naira had heard Unawqi leaving the house, quietly followed him from a distance, and watched him from behind a buttonwood tree.

Sure enough, even before Ernest or the crab fisherman had noticed he was gone, Aakti found Unawqi as he spread his wings over the mangrove, attracted to the silent hum of the phototeledar and the stirring of the seeds inside Unawqi's chest.

In the same moment, Titu awoke, and through his receiver saw Unawqi's slumbering body lying next to the phototeledar. Overcome with both joy and remorse, Titu called out to Unawqi, letting him know he was there, calling for him to wake and speak; to please not leave him again.

Unawqi clearly heard Titu's voice calling through the instrument, but Unawqi was despondent and just stared at the phototeledar, confused what to do with the words he was hearing from the man who had previously sent him into the fire.

Meanwhile, Aakti, seeing the revival of an elusive opportunity, turned his angry face at Unawqi and bore down on him with great force.

Unawqi, lost in a daze between the voice of Titu and the sudden assault of the Sun, had nothing with which to separate love and power except this emotionless, silver contraption. He reached out, took the phototeledar into his arms, and embraced it as if it were his desperate means of grace.

"No, no!" Titu pleaded. "Don't touch my phototeledar!"

But this only made Unawqi want to hold it harder, to break the mystery denied him.

At first, the phototeledar began to tremble in Unawqi's arms and warm his chest like a bath of morning milk, but then it rattled harder, as if trying to escape, and the hunter in Unawqi clutched even tighter. He could feel Aakti Amurugana burning in his chest, like frustrated tears waiting to burst into a scream.

The intensity and passion he felt drowned out Titu's voice and the onset of the Sun, but soon, unbeknownst to Unawqi, the phototeledar's tentacles had themselves wrapped around Unawqi's chest and would not let go.

Aakti threw his energy into the phototeledar, which turned from silver to a blazing orange and violet, searing into Unawqi's chest in an attempt to grab the seeds and pull them free. In turn the seeds spun and thrashed their way through Unawqi's tissue and ribs, leaving in their wake a poisonous residue of radiation on their way out of his chest.

Passing from his body through the phototeledar, the seeds entered the Sun's rays that were the shoulders of Aakti, creating an explosion that could be heard through Balao and beyond.

Aakti screamed with a curdling glee as he withdrew into the sky, leaving Unawqi's blackened body smoking on the ground next to the smoldering phototeledar. Unawqi was so racked with unpitying pain, his eyes reddened with poison, that he could neither see nor raise himself to walk. He could not even cry for help.

It wasn't long before the whole village had gathered around him. Qina fell to his side, and begged for mercy to be made.

Unawqi seemed so much smaller now, a charred shell of his former nature. His golden skin was still there, but it looked now more of a rusted bronze.

As Ernest and the crab fisherman lifted his limp body to carry him away, rain fell from the sky, washing his body clean. Everyone looked skyward, for the rain was hard and peculiarly sudden, and they beheld that it was not rain at all—it was the blue-veiled Mama Killa directly above their heads, weeping upon them with the weight of her memories.

She was so close, they could reach out and touch her, which they did. They touched her body, holding up the Moon, the inconsolable Moon, the heavy-hearted Moon, the blue Moon that came on that day to lay her head on the mangrove, and bury her tears in their hands.

12 THE GREAT MANGROVE GATHERING

The irony is the very same day when Aakti had finally reclaimed his progeny, thus saving his future, was also the beginning of his darkest hours.

Even though he had spun around the Earth, exulting in his recovered riches, he did so alone.

Nothing on Earth could hear him, see him, or congratulate him, for in protest, Mama Killa had abdicated her seat in the sky and settled herself over the mangroves of Balao, blocking out any sight of the Sun.

The days of Earth were too dim for mariners to sail. Beasts could not hunt, and people could not work. Without the light, there was only paralysis and fear.

This made Aakti terribly angry, for with Mama Killa in his way, there was no one to whom he might boast his treasure or glory. It became instantly clear to him that if he had no audience to spectate at his victory parade, the Aakti Amurugana were worthless to him after a millennium of hunting them down.

These days of the Moon's entrenchment were likely the most profound days of all time, the days that ever since have been called the Days of the Great Mangrove Gathering.

We call them that name because right under the belly of Mama Killa in the mangroves of Balao where she cast her exclusive canopy of light, many events occurred, many forces collided, and many stories met an unexpected fate in a short season of time.

Around Unawqi's dying body hovered the many characters of Balao. Like a flock of buzzards, they eyed which piece of flesh to claim as their keep.

Unawqi felt very afraid, seeing the blurry outlines of their frames through his nearly blind eyes. He felt no one touch him. With a fading hope, he strained to look for something that might break through to comfort him—the condor, the woman with red clay hair, the chinchay, and yes, most of all, the fisherman of Jaqunqay.

It was like being swept out to sea all over again. Nothing came for him. He heard only squabbling. He felt only the cold chill of the open air around him and the menacing pain of his broken bones.

The crab fisherman and his daughter turned up their noses, for now Unawqi's golden breast looked not much more than a scrap of tin, and the other fishermen debated whether he might be of some use as bait, or a lure for bottom-feeding fish.

Ernest shook his head in disappointment to see such a promising specimen slip through his fingers by way of a cosmic accident. He had so much hope for Unawqi to become useful to him as a second son, of sorts, but now he was explaining to the others his plan to add Unawqi's cadaver to his collection for continuing research.

Naira held her head in her palm, worried for the shattered future of her daughter, Qina, who clung to her mother somewhat ashamed of her association with the shriveled mutant, wondering if, should Unawqi die, someone might actually accuse her of some fault in the whole affair.

Mama Killa could not do much more than shed light on the drama, and let it play itself out.

And that is when they noticed the leaves of the mangrove trees begin to shrivel and ice over. The stench of sulfur and mold formed in the air around them, and they saw a small, bizarre-looking goblin approach them from the eastern edge of the clearing.

It was Moche, the legendary sorcerer of Antisana, his face embittered with anger as he hobbled closer to the crowd, trying to get a better position from which to speak to Unawqi.

"Stand back!" he spat, "or I'll fill your lungs with the same ice that halts the breath of your trees."

Huddled under the sinking roof of Mama Killa bearing her pale belly down upon their backs, and shivering from the creeping ice Moche had strapped round their arms and feet, the people of Balao shuffled aside from the stack of banana leaves Unawqi's body was lying upon, allowing Moche to get close.

Ernest was most uneasy, for not only did the sight of this demon and its seeming connection to Unawqi stir up the wonder of an overlooked biological realm, but he worried what Moche might do to further damage what was left of Unawqi, his property. He took two steps towards Unawqi, but Moche growled and raised his hand, sending a gaseous flash of fire and ice at Ernest's feet, freezing them where he stood.

Then Moche placed the same smoking hand over Unawqi's mouth and leaned his rotted teeth over to Unawqi's ear so he could whisper. The people held their breath in suspense, waiting for a spell by this demon to revive Unawqi and make him walk again.

But Moche was not bent on salvation. Instead, he hissed into Unawqi's ear,

"I have done everything for you, and all you have brought me is disgrace. You were to bring the seeds to me, and instead you gave them back to my enemy. You are no hunter of mine. You are no longer Unawqi. You are nothing now but finished!"

And as simply as that, Moche raised his head up, turned his eyes away, and clenched his hand firmly over Unawqi's mouth, suffocating the young man of his last breath.

The people of Balao were aghast. They had not even a chance to reason or bargain with Moche. They had witnessed Unawqi's murder with their own eyes, in the same moment they were expecting a resurrection. And yet they stood still, fearful of what Moche might inflict upon them next.

This is when a most chilling sound came from within the fog behind Moche's back. It was more a cold shock to him than the frost over the faces of the people around him. It was the sound of a bleating goat, and not just any goat, but a certain black goat he had not heard since the day he took Unawqi from the hands of his mother.

Moche turned, eyes wide open in fright, to see the eyes of the freshly killed goat staring right at him. He tried to turn away, but it was too late, for once you looked into the eyes of a dead, black goat, your curse is sealed, the eyes will never leave you, and it takes possession of your mind.

Emerging from the fog behind the goat, Unawqi's mother, Tamaya, came to stand not ten paces from Moche. Her eyes were red with rage, no less damning than the goat's, for she remembered well the sorcerer's deeds against her family and had arrived to witness this latest and ultimate of his crimes.

Unlike the rest, Tamaya had no fear, and only resolve.

Moche had not a moment to close his mouth or cast a spell before the machete thrown from Tamaya's hand like a hunter's spear thrust into the center of his chest, throwing him backwards off his feet, and over to the other side of Unawqi's body.

As Moche lay dying, his blood melted the frost on the ground, thawing the leaves, the trees, and the frost from the flesh of all those around him.

Although there was so Sun, the people felt warmth on their skin and faces again. They looked at Unawqi's mother who looked back at them.

It was eerily silent as Tamaya stood there in a solitary pool of watery moonlight, saying nothing, only breathing. Then she turned toward the body of her son, fell over him, and wept. She wept for all the years of love that had been taken from her, and for all the future years that had now been denied to her son.

Tamaya's tears flowed over Unawqi's chest, mixing with the sorcerer's blood, staining Unawqi's back from the ground. The mingling created an aroma, much like when the wood of sacred piquna trees are burned in ceremonies to cleanse the air of spirits. The people took it in, and it made them feel this bitter occasion was no less sanctified as they held their heads down to mourn.

In consolation, Mama Killa lifted her heaviness from their backs, for she knew she could not waste any more time in self-pity. She needed to make some room for the people to grieve on their own. Her mission to bring love and power to this uniting of men in the mangrove seemed a failure now, for laying beneath her belly was nothing but death and despair.

If she disliked the emperor before, she hated him now and more. Feeling she could no longer put the weight of her own sorrow upon the people of Balao, Mama Killa raised herself up and ascended into the night sky. This would allow the Sun to return in the morning, if only for a while.

She knew a new mission was upon her: to find Aakti and confront him on Unawqi's behalf; to become a hunter herself, not to vanquish the Sun, but to show him there was a power greater than his throne.

It was as the dark of night fell into the void where the Moon once hung, that at last the fisherman of Jaqunqay arrived through the trees on the edge of the clearing.

The darkness in their eyes prevented the people from seeing him, but he followed the scent in the air to its source until he was standing at the feet of Unawqi's body.

It wasn't so much the aroma in the air that excited him as it was the scent of Unawqi himself, for the fisherman remembered it well from their nights lying next to each other under the grass blanket. Unawqi's scent coated the fisherman's tongue, brought tears to the back of his eyes, and overwhelmed him with happiness to have found his lover again after having lost him to the sea.

"My love?" the fisherman called tenderly. "I am here. I have come for you."

He knelt down and fumbled around to find Unawqi's leg. "Are you sleeping, my love? Wake up! I am here to take you home now."

"Who are you?" Tamaya's voice asked through the dark from the other side of Unawqi's body. "And who is your 'love'?"

The fisherman juddered back, startled and confused. So did the others nearby, for Tamaya and the fisherman's exchange seemed to precipitate more conflict to come.

"This is my son," Tamaya continued, "who no longer lives. Leave his mother to her sorrow, for you are looking for some other."

The fisherman could not have heard more damnable words. His body shuddered with anger, helplessness, and deep sadness. How could this be? Even unable to see his face, the fisherman knew Unawqi's smell, the shape of his body, and the features of his feet, legs, and hands. He touched what was beneath him and he was certain this could be no other than Unawqi.

Holding his hand over Unawqi's mouth, the fisherman felt no breath. He took Unawqi's hand, but felt no heat.

He spoke more solemnly. "Please, wake up, my love. The ocean is not as wide as the gulf of your silence right now. I am here. I came for you. Do not leave me alone yet again."

All of this talk was unsettling for everyone, for a man to be talking to another man with such words, and on an occasion following his murder at that. It was also disturbing to them that the woman did not know the other voice who was speaking to her, which made it seem to them she was in a mistaken place, grieving over a mistaken man.

Ernest felt it was his place and the right moment to intervene, and he stepped forward between the fisherman and Tamaya, whose faint outlines he could barely discern in the dark.

"I regret to bring you both more sad news, but this young man who came to us from the sea, was a member of my family. This is his home, where he lived and died, and where he will never leave. He was to marry my daughter, Qina. I beg of you both, please leave us and our son now in peace."

What Ernest said was enough to make their hearts stop cold. The fisherman and Tamaya were without words, for nothing else with which they had ever been confronted could be more a betrayal of their life's purpose than those few stinging words.

Townsfolk took Tamaya and the fisherman away in separate directions, putting them in nearby houses to sleep for the night with the plan to send them away from the mangrove in the morning.

As they were taken away, they gasped and wailed. They looked back, desperate for Unawqi to awake and look back at them and tell the people who they were, to tell them his real story. But of course, they could see him no more.

Before dawn had broken over Balao, Naira had stolen her way to the house where Tamaya was being kept, and Qina did the same where the fisherman lay. It was a pact between mother and daughter to set a new course; to not allow the Great Mangrove Gathering to end in this way.

Naira sat down on the bed beside Tamaya, holding a candle over her eyes until Tamaya woke. Naira wanted to see her eyes, for a mother can always see a truer tale in another mother's eyes. Tamaya did not speak, for she seemed to know what Naira was looking for. She only looked back, brown eyes meeting brown eyes, breath meeting breath, until they were in unison.

With the tenderness of lifting a feather, Naira took Tamaya's hand, looking at them and the stains of forest soil, the anguished creases only a mother separated from her child could possess. She held her hand and moved it to her breast so that Tamaya could feel the beating of Naira's heart to engender a trust. Tamaya looked back at her directly, without blinking.

Naira put the strap of Unawqi's leather pouch into Tamaya's hand. In the pouch was the phototeledar.

"Never forget," Naira whispered, "who truly took your son, and who still reigns over us both. Take this, for one day, you will see each other, face to face."

Then Naira left just as quickly as she entered.

Over in the crab house where the fisherman of Jaqunqay was sleeping, Qina climbed in through a back window and made her way to his room, not wishing to wake him.

She saw that his hand was hanging over the side of the bed. Qina crawled on her knees toward him, reached into her pocket, and pulled out the golden ring her father, Ernest, had kept for her wedding with Unawqi.

Qina looked at the golden ring, which shone as gloriously as the sun-forged armor of Unawqi's chest. She kissed the ring, slid it onto the sleeping fisherman's finger, and then crawled back out of the shed the way from which she came.

It was a simple band of gold, but it illuminated the dark room like the light of the Moon, and the fisherman smiled in his sleep.

The crab fisherman, who owned the shed, came in the morning to banish Unawqi's lover from town, saying to him, "Go now, for you will find nothing here."

The fisherman sat on the edge of the bed, weeping and smiling at once. "Yes," he said back to the crab fisherman, "that is because somehow, he has found me."

13 ATAMA'S JOURNEY

"So…that is how I died."

Unawqi looked at me out of the corner of his eye as he threw a gutted fish into his bucket, knowing I would appreciate the dark humor. At this point, it seemed insulting to ask the obvious question about his being very much alive, so I didn't, but I held the silence and continued working. I knew he had to have more story to tell.

He broke the silence and chuckled on my behalf and said,

"Surviving is just about how stubborn you are, or how stubborn others are for you. We always presume to think we are the only ones in control of our body, but that is such a lie. Your brain, your heart, your lungs—so many people have their hands holding on to them, and only when they all let go are you truly dead."

He leaned back, poured some clean water over his hands, and explained how the world came to know of his death.

Word came first from Unawqi's mother, who sat on the side of a dusty road on her return to the cloud forest, crying into her lap as mosquitoes bit her neck.

It was then that the phototeledar in the pouch next to her began to transmit the sounds of her grief to the receiver on the other end; that is, to Titu Ilumán.

He did not say anything back to her, for he was still afraid of the black goat, and of Tamaya's memory of what Titu had done to her. As he listened, he understood why she was crying, and he opened his laboratory windows and angrily cursed the sky.

Puyo Supai, the cloud spirit, was sitting over the sky and heard Titu's curse. She drifted eastward, to tell the condor as he flew over Reventador.

The condor sailed with the southern current until he saw the chinchay of the cloud forest, and the chinchay then brought the news to all the monkeys of the cloud forest.

The monkeys of the cloud forest then announced everywhere that Moche, the sorcerer of Antisana, would not be returning to his throne, for he had died at the hands of a goat herdess as vengeance for Unawqi's murder.

The chinchay walked somberly through the paths of the cloud forest until he found the woman with the red clay hair. She was digging up an ailing Huasquila tree and putting some strange seeds underneath it to give it more life.

The cat approached her and rubbed its side against her arm, causing the woman to stop and listen to the grave news. It made the woman shake her head in disgrace, for she knew the culpability went beyond Moche.

"This is my father's doing," she mumbled through a sigh, "and he knows what he has done."

The chinchay looked at the woman in confusion, for she had never seen the woman's father nor heard anything from the condor about such a man's involvement in the story.

The woman lamented upward to the canopy of green overhead, for the leaves of the trees seemed to understand the things she said more than others did.

She then started to climb the largest of the trees next to her. Even though she was blind, she knew exactly where she was going and bore no timidity. Indeed, as she climbed higher, the younger limbs of the tree bent themselves under her feet, lifting her even faster through the growth.

When she reached the top, she burst her red clay head through the last leafy green veil to point her eyes toward the Sun. Only in this moment did the retinas of her eyes and the lids around them transform from dead to living, for on top of the canopy, she could see!

In addition, her hair changed from red clay to silken black, as black as a brook of oil seeping through the crevasses of the earth. Because her changed state only occurred at the treetops, no one on Earth knew that the woman with the red clay hair could transform herself this way, and that she was not entirely blind, and not entirely human.

She then reached up her arm above her head as high as she could, until she was able to grab hold of a passing sun ray, which she clutched like the handle of a sword, swinging it around in the sky until it snapped from the Aakti's body.

The dislodged ray was the exact shape of the needle given to Unawqi by Titu, the one Unawqi had used in his duel with the emperor over Jaqunqay, for unbeknownst to Unawqi at that time, he was using the same thing to extract the Sun's energy that the woman with the red clay hair was now pulling from the sky.

The woman with the red clay hair shook the sun ray until its energy turned into small solids inside the ray, like diamonds on fire. These were Aakti Amurugana, the seeds of the Sun. They were the same kind that Unawqi was born with in his hand, which Titu stole away to his laboratory, and which then later flew into Unawqi's chest, only to burst again from his body on his fateful day in the mangroves of Balao.

The woman with the red clay hair could recreate them!

The woman withdrew back into the canopy, taking the ray of seeds with her, and as she descended, the tree glowed, as if a torch was tumbling down its spine.

The woman's hair became red clay again, and by the time she had touched her feet to the ground, her eyes had become blind once more, and the ray had dissipated to a pale haze around her body. The only thing about her that was different from when she had climbed up was the pouch around her waist. It was nearly empty when she went up, but now it was full of the thousands of glowing seeds she had been planting underneath the fallen Huasquila tree.

Whenever the woman with the red clay hair pulls a ray of seeds from the Sun, it is like pulling a hair from a man's body—it grows back again, but it stings when it is removed. In the same way, Aakti felt the sting, and he turned to spit at the woman, but as always, she was too quick for him to see where she was, so he gave her his usual curse.

"Atama! One day I will catch you, my daughter, and bring you back to the skies. Then you will no longer be able to steal my seeds."

Most earthly beings and creatures of the forest knew her as the woman with the red clay hair, but among gods and sorcerers they called her "Atama," for she had the power to take the Sun's seeds and sow them into the earth, spreading life that could flourish like weeds, and allowing a part of her and her father, Aakti the Sun, to be everywhere at once.

This is why when she was talking with Tamaya in the forest, her voice could be heard so many places at the same time. Atama is always growing like a weed, so they say. She cannot be contained, and this infuriates Aakti. Even if the world knew her real name, they would be reluctant to use it, for calling a woman a 'weed' would only bring them scorn.

On all occasions except one, Atama planted the Aakti Amurugana beneath dying trees, in clefts of rock, or at the edge of the forest, to make it grow further.

But one day, when Moche, the sorcerer of Antisana, found her sleeping in the forest, he stole a handful of the seeds from her pouch to take with him for safekeeping in the depths of his mountain lair. Atama knows every one of her seeds by name, and all of the growing things they create, so it didn't take her long after she awoke to discover she had been robbed!

She hunted for 888 years to find her stolen seeds, asking every little lemon ant and blade of grass where they might have seen the feet of the thief pass.

Eventually, Puyo Supai, the cloud spirit and mistress to Moche, confided to her what had happened to the stolen seeds. Atama, still then a young and seeing woman, trespassed into the thief's mountain and confronted him.

They wrestled for possession of the seeds, but Atama was the stronger, and seized them from Moche's hands and broke one of his legs. Moche, on the other hand, had smashed a bottle containing a potion of molten rock and sharp diamond dust over her head during the struggle, which burned her eyes until she was blind.

Without sight, Atama had to feel her way out of the mountain and back to the forest, and that journey was how she learned to survive without being able to see. Direct sunlight is the only thing that can temporarily remove her blindness, which she rarely risks for fear of being captured by her father and removed from Earth.

Knowing Moche would eventually come after her again, and even more so for the seeds, she decided for the first time in all her years to not plant them under a tree. Instead, she planted them in a human being, inside the womb of her friend the goat herdess, Tamaya, because Tamaya had shown such kindness to her.

While Tamaya was sleeping, Atama put the seeds inside of her friend. Atama knew the gravity of what she was doing, for in such a planting, she was conceiving a life more powerful than anything on Earth--a child, and a human descendant of Aakti, a rightful prince for the dynasty of the emperor the Sun!

Atama would never tell Tamaya what she did, but the act would bind their common fate of being fugitives of Aakti.

Back to her sitting at the base of the Huasquila tree some thousand years later, Atama thought back on the history of events. Even though she was no friend of Moche, she was bothered that the sorcerer would receive the blame for regicide, when in truth, the world did not know the full story. Moche had unwittingly played into the hands of someone more powerful--the very god he once worshipped and now despised: Aakti.

She did not know how long it would take to right the wrong, but she knew her time to hide in the cloud forest was over, and that it was time to set her life on a new journey.

The chinchay approached her again, this time holding in her mouth the eucalyptus punchu that Unawqi had received from Moche to hide himself from the Sun, but which he had lost in the forest. The woman with the red clay hair felt it and immediately sensed its power.

She smiled at the chinchay with gratitude, telling her, "Come with me, my dearest friend, and in thanks, I will make you the mother of a new generation beyond your kind."

Atama left the forest, with the eucalyptus punchu and the cat to protect her. They headed north through the Quijos Canyon, destined for the Valley of the Iraca, the birthplace of the Sun. They would seek some intervention from her grandmother, Bachué, mother of the universe.

She travelled like a hermit, rarely letting herself be seen by creation, lest they advise Aakti of her location. But wherever she went, she planted Aakti Amurugana along the way, encouraging them to spread quickly and imitate her presence, confounding the emperor's ability to find her.

14 THE MEETING WITH THE MOUNTAIN

It was a cloudy afternoon. The fisherman drifted in his boat somewhere between Balao and Jaqunqay, brokenhearted by the loss of his true love, Unawqi. He was going back to an island that would only serve to remind him who was not there to share it with him.

The sea was absolutely still, as if it was at a loss what to do with him, so it didn't cause him any commotion. He hung his head over the stern to gaze deeply into the deep. Its infinity seemed to match his immeasurable questions. He noticed the creases in his face, and was reminded that he was getting older, which made him resigned to die a lonely man.

In the reflection of the clouds on the water he saw a large bird soaring overhead. Even though at that height all birds look the same, for some reason this one seemed familiar. He turned his head up and saw it was the condor of Reventador: Unawqi's condor.

Was the bird looking for Unawqi, too, having not heard the news?

The fisherman stood up and waved his arms at the condor, so eager to reconnect to the only living extension of Unawqi he had shared. He jumped higher and harder in the boat to try and get the condor's attention. His jumping stirred up the fish in the sea around him, and they, too, jumped out of the water to create a noticeable scene.

The great bird spotted the froth of the fish beneath him and the boat in the center, and spiraled down to investigate. The fisherman thought the condor had been looking for Unawqi, but no, the condor was looking for the fisherman. As he landed in the boat, the bird hung its head over the side, just like the fisherman had been doing, for he was bearing the same sadness.

The fisherman felt different now, no longer sad for his own state, but for the welfare of Unawqi's companion. He reached over to comfort the bird, picking up some kelp from the sea and stroking it over the bird's back.

The condor turned and sunk into the boat a little lower, extending its huge wingspan out, inviting the fisherman to mount on his back.

The fisherman had never flown on the back of the condor before. In fact, from the day he was born, the fisherman had his hands in the sea. But what else, he thought, should he do?

So, he climbed on and embraced the bird's frame, burying his face in its neck as it lifted into the sky.

The fisherman brought nothing with him except for a fishing knife and the sunflower Mama Killa had given him. For the first time, he was detached from his world and his responsibilities, wholly dependent on the creature upon whose back he rested. He felt like a small child again in his mother's arms, and he held even tighter, weeping like a baby. He could not stop weeping as he remembered his mother, and that she, too, would carry him to the moon if she had been given the chance.

The condor was not bothered at all by the grief, in fact it gave him purpose and fueled his determination to climb higher into the sky. They eventually came over the top of the clouds and felt the brush of heaven's breeze on their backs.

The condor then flew north. He was on a mission he could not much explain to himself, let alone to the fisherman. It was aimless energy, to run and to cry until his breath was dry.

But after hours of flying, that is when his destination became clear. He was going to fly home.

Something in the bird's innermost being knew that if this tragedy was to be broken, it must be broken by something strong and shattering, and nothing was more than that as Reventador, the angry hermit mountain of the eastern cloud forest.

The condor wasn't sure it would be a success. Reventador was not kind or comforting in the least. He was a fierce and cruel character. He had no patience for the world and its complaining. The human condition was, for him, the badge of their weakness.

Humanity was trifling and pathetic. The only thing that mattered to him was his own creation around him, his son, and the stature of his brother and sister mountains. They were the superior lives who need only concern themselves with the world of the gods.

So why the condor would risk bringing a human being to Reventador, a sad and broken one at that, the condor did not know. He had no plan. He only had instinct.

They flew over the mangroves, then the central highlands, past the barren Antisana, and over the Quijos Canyon.

Finally, the bird began to descend into the smoking shroud of a land few ever dared to venture. It was an unnerving place. Everything hushed for fear of waking the hermit. The only thing they could faintly hear was the distant mumbling of Reventador himself, spitting and swearing in the dense forest ahead.

At last they passed over the black ashen ridge and could see ahead of them. There was Reventador, the solitary mountain, fuming, and boiling blood red.

The fisherman sat up and recoiled, for he was afraid of the hellfire sight in front of him, and yet he did not doubt the condor knew what it was doing. It circled in the upsweep currents around the mountain until it found one that would allow it to set foot on the rim of the crater.

Seeing the man on his son's back, Reventador reacted defensively, and spat at him. The bird blocked the fireball and pleaded for his father to calm himself, as bringing the fisherman was his own idea. The condor reminded his father that they were too strong to be afraid, and that men could never harm them.

The condor then began to tell the story of the fisherman to his father. He had never summoned such courage and frankness before, and it made the fire in the hermit's belly stand still. The condor told Reventador that this humble fisherman standing next to him had a story that so moved the Moon, she grieved over it by blocking the Sun, casting the world into darkness. The fisherman's power in doing so was not made by fear or force, but by love.

"Love" was a word Reventador loathed and it made him angry and start to boil, that is, until the condor explained what love meant to the condor.

This plain fisherman, who asked for nothing, was the one that plucked the condor from the sea and saved him from drowning, and that there were places in the world that Reventador could not reach out in order to save his son.

Then the condor talked of his deepest hurt, of how the gods, not the world, had failed him. When it was time for the condor to return home to take part in the rite of fathers and sons, he left Jaqunqay. It was during this absence that Moche's scheme severed the fisherman from the one he loved and devastated his home. For this, the condor was greatly ashamed, and said he had failed his duty to protect those to whom he owed his life.

Shame was not an emotion Reventador knew, and he was surprised to hear it coming from his son.

"Since when do you have a duty to men? I gave you no such liking for them."

"No," the condor replied, "you did not."

The condor then asked the hermit mountain,

"What greatness do gods and wizards amount to when they conspire to ruin innocence? What power do we gain," he asked of his father, "by trampling on the powerless who toil on the same Earth that is our home?"

Reventador listened to his son, impressed with his passion, and yet perplexed by things yet unexplained. The condor hung his head down in defeat, hoping some silence would help him know what to say next.

But then the mountain spoke. "Who is this…'love' of which you speak?"

The condor, knowing his next words could be his last, paused for a while. But he was reminded of Unawqi's fearlessness on his back to hunt the champion of the sky, only to be washed out to sea. The great bird inhaled deeply so his chest swelled large, raised his head, and spoke with a voice as bold as his father. "His name was Unawqi, Hunter of the Sun, Warrior of the Quijos, and my friend."

"His?" the mountain spat back. "*His* name?"

The bird's garnet eyes, just as fierce as his father's, heated with a new strength. He stretched out his massive wings, so wide that his golden down sprayed light over the whole frame of Reventador's towering body. It was the first moment the hermit realized the condor was no longer his son, but the greatness of a god.

"You, my son, have never showed me such splendor, but all the more you do it for the defense of men?"

"No, father," he replied, "I do it for the defense of love. Love that even if you don't know it, you have never failed to give me, and love that must never fail the universe again. Help us, please!"

Reventador had never been asked for help, let alone from his own son. This was the moment he wished for, in front of the emperor, in the rite of fathers and sons. He wanted to show the emperor something extraordinary about who he was as a man--not as a mountain, not as a god, but as a man. A man, he thought, is only a man if he comes to the aid of his son. It did not come on the day of the annual rite of fathers and sons, but here it was, now. It was what he had always wanted, but never knew how to explain it.

Reventador stood up. Boulders fell. Steam broke from vents and shot into the air. A proud light raced around the peaks and valleys, embracing the strength and wisdom of the condor. Flocks of thrushes and wrens sprung into the air all at once, for they felt this was no ordinary tantrum of the hermit, this was an altogether extraordinary event and something big was about to happen.

Reventador called out to the sky for an audience with Puyo Supai, the cloud spirit, for she stood in between the mountains and the heavens. Puyo Supai came, and sat down over the mountain, cloaking it in an impenetrable fog. Reventador and Puyo Supai consulted in private for a good long while, for Puyo Supai knew many other parts of the tragic tale that the condor had not yet explained, and the hermit was greatly moved by it.

He fumed and steamed over the emperor's cruelty, expressing his marvel that his son played such an important role in this epic with so many lives involved, far beyond the realm of Reventador. He was saddened that his son could not have told this all to him before.

For the first time, the great hermit was stunned to silence as he withdrew into himself, thinking on his behavior throughout the years, growling instead of listening, neglecting instead of caring. Like his son, he felt terribly ashamed and could not speak. All the creatures surrounding the mountain came to a complete stop, never having known such a solemn mood of their master.

Puyo Supai then bent her veil back a bit to give the hermit a sight of the condor standing on his rim, strong and fearless, but who would not live a life longer than the days of the mountains. "Who am I?" Reventador said to himself. "Who is my son?"

Reventador then did something no one had ever seen before. He wanted to send a different message to everything around him. He stirred up pools of azure water from his belly that spilled themselves down his crater, mixing with the lava to create a vapor that had a fragrance of balsa and jasmine. It filled the air above and around the mountain, calming and soothing everything it touched, making them lose their fear of the mountain, and instead, leave them with a feeling that his beauty when let out was far greater.

The hermit mountain then spoke directly to the fisherman. "Go on my son's back, and with my blessing. I will lift you as high as my force can muster so you can rally to the side of Mama Killa, for she is your justice."

Reventador inhaled deeply, then inhaled some more, and the fisherman held fast to the condor's back, for it was clear the mountain was going to blow in a very big way.

The first boom came from deep within the earth, and the condor burst into the air to catch the imminent vent. A second boom then came from beneath the surface of the crater and split faults in the rim, a sound so great it could be heard all the way to Balao.

Finally, the hermit hurled a massive plume of ash and steam into the air, dispersing Puyo Supai's thick cover and vaulting the condor high, high into the heavens. The condor was higher than he had ever soared before, so high that he could see all the lands of his journeys in one glance, from the Meta River in the north, to the Chiri Sea in the south. Above him, he saw the Moon not so far away, and thrust himself through the black and soundless sky toward her.

The condor shrieked in the hope Mama Killa would hear him and stop her advance. Out in the vastness of space, there was nothing for the condor to land on for rest, which made him fly with all the more haste and fury toward her.

Mama Killa noticed the unusual sound of a bird in space behind her and turned her face to the most startling sight. She smiled widely to see her old friend, and turned back to give him her aid. She smiled even more to see on his back reaching out toward her was the one over which her heart had broken.

She lowered herself beneath them and the condor landed on top of the Moon, spreading its golden wings wide like a royal crown on her head, for this most certainly was the beginning of a royal campaign.

The reunion of Mama Killa, the condor of Reventador, and the fisherman of Jaqunqay required a great passing of time. Many stories needed to be told, and many tears needed to be shed. In time, the three came to understand they belonged together for the good of Unawqi. They resolved to go together to confront the emperor, for they knew that despite their lack of Unawqi's power, they had, nonetheless, acquired his courage.

15 THE BUTTERFLY INTERVENTION

Until you know the whole story of Unawqi, it will be a mystery to you why they call Antisana "the motherless mountain," or why to this day all the great mountains and rivers of these lands are such a fierce tribe to be reckoned with.

They weren't always that way. Like Reventador, they each led solitary lives with their own paradises to watch over.

But the age of Unawqi changed all that.

With the death of Moche, the fearsome sorcerer of Antisana, the mountain became a desolate place. The goddess after whom it had been named did not reappear, the bats had left for lack of company, the blue pools of lava had stopped stirring, and the caverns had grown damp with mold. It would gain a new master, in time, and through most unexpected circumstances.

To the west, Tamaya was making her way back to the cloud forest to pick up the pieces of her broken life and assemble them back together again. To create what, though, she did not know. She did not want the life she had. She did not want to be reminded anymore of what she had lost.

But on the way, she continued to be distracted by sounds coming out of the phototeledar, and it made her wonder if it had been given to her to lead her in another direction.

As she came around the edge of the Pasochoa Forest, where she would normally turn east in the direction of the Quijos, the phototeledar let out the clear sound of a voice she had almost forgotten. It was the voice of Unawqi's father, and he was in the middle of some long ramble, as if he was in a conversation with someone.

"Titu?" she called. "Is that you?"

The voice stopped immediately.

"Tamaya?" he called her name in response. "Is that you on the other side?"

Titu was only pretending to hear her for the first time, as had previously listened in while she was crying by the side of the road. Now, due to his own carelessness, he had been found out.

Tamaya was puzzled from where the voice was coming. She thought Titu must have possessed the body of an insect or bird, sitting on a tree limb nearby. "You sound as if you are in front of me, but I cannot see you."

"Tamaya, I am speaking to you through the phototeledar. How did you come in possession of it?"

That was when Tamaya realized it was coming from the metal object in her pouch.

Titu continued, "Don't try to understand it. It is like the wind is carrying my voice to you from far away. Do you also have the seeds? Do you have the Sun?"

Unawqi's mother was all the more baffled as to what Titu was talking about, for she never knew of any seeds, or what they might have to do with the Sun.

But then she remembered what Naira in Balao had told her by the bedside when she had been given the pouch with the contraption inside. Naira told her that one day Tamaya would see the one who had truly taken her son. Tamaya thought that Naira must have been referring to Titu, and that Titu must have had some hand in the whole plot for Moche to take her son from her when he was born.

"Tamaya!" Titu called again. "Bring to me what you possess, and I will explain everything. Hurry!"

Unawqi's mother wanted that: an explanation. To be sure, she wanted even more an apology, and then a judgment, and then a reversal of fortune. If Titu had abandoned her to spend his life at the expense of her misery, creating magic in the manner of this contraption, then perhaps he could be persuaded to bring back her son.

But those were the last words she heard. His voice was disrupted by a crackling and wheezing coming from the device, just when he was trying to explain where she would find him.

Tamaya looked at the trees above and around her to see if his voice would appear from somewhere else, but the birds offered no more than their usual calls. She held his plea, but had no direction as to where to go next.

The source of the disruption was nothing sinister. It was the season of yellow butterflies, when they burst from their cocoons in the Pasochoa Forest and take to the skies all at once, in the millions. The forest was so thick with them, they formed a veritable wall that blocked out the frequency over which Titu had been communicating with his phototeledar.

Tamaya could not see through the butterflies. Their numbers were so great they removed the air she had to breathe. She therefore didn't notice they were forming their own cocoon, wrapping Tamaya's body inside of it, making her, in a sense, the renewal of their collective lives.

Then, they picked her up off her feet, still encased in her cocoon, and sprang into the sky like a small sunrise.

They fluttered over the Pasochoa crater to stabilize their mass, recovered Titu's signal from a northern draught, and turned into it. Like flecks of sun sprinkling the rolling sea, they lit up the clouds that carried Tamaya on her way.

She peered through the open spaces between their wings and could see beneath her the many valleys and mountains as she passed them by: Pichincha, Pululahua, Kayambi, Imbabura, the mighty Cumbal, and many other places so far from anywhere she had ever been she did not even know their names.

At last, the yellow butterflies set her down on the ground again at the doorstep of Titu's laboratory. It was an edifice the likes of which Tamaya could make no comparison except to call it many white mud houses stacked on top of each other.

The butterflies swept into the laboratory and intensified their fury, for the room did not let them move about as freely. It was like a snow blizzard on the side of Antisana, but shining brilliantly with the color of their yellow wings that they blinded Tamaya and Titu's eyes from being immediately able to see each other.

Then the butterflies' climax settled, and they retreated all at once to attach themselves to the four walls of the room, revealing in the middle of them a small, old man neither Titu nor Tamaya knew.

It was the great and powerful hermit, Reventador himself.

His eyes were as yellow as the butterflies he commanded. His wild auburn and gray hair fell over his wrinkled face. Even though he was old, he was tall, and his back was straight. He stood with a composed sense of determination, like an owl on a tree limb, calm but ready to strike.

"Step over the threshold, Tamaya," Reventador said in a voice as bolting as the mouth of his mountain, "and I will give you a new life. Run away, and you will seal the fate of your beloved son."

His voice frightened Tamaya. She did not know him or his part in her life, but what he said scared her even more. It was the same terrible choice she had been given by Moche when he came to take her son away from her, and she could feel the burning in her eyes as she remembered that dreadful day now being thrust at her again by yet another inexplicable wizard whose presence she neither desired nor invited.

Titu was on the other side of the hermit, and no less surprised. He had not expected Tamaya to arrive so soon, nor in this fashion, and he had nothing in his mind that could help explain the interference of the tall wizard appearing between them.

Reventador stretched out his arm to beckon Tamaya to cross the threshold. She was afraid, but the hermit didn't blink. He waited, as unmoving as a barren tree in the windless desert.

Tamaya looked down at her feet. They were covered with yellow butterflies, and their tenderness diffused the tension. She felt comforted by them, like they were her guardians, and would always guide her to wherever she wanted to go. She lifted her foot, and the butterflies did not scatter. She put her foot back down across the threshold, and the butterflies did not abandon her. They were her raiment.

She moved forward toward the hermit, examining the laboratory around her with all its instruments and bottles. They seemed like shapes made of clear water underneath the falls, but how Titu could create such a bizarre collection added to her puzzlement as to whether he, too, might be a wizard.

Reventador took her hand. His hand was firm, but not tormenting; nothing like the gnarled knot of a tree it appeared to be. He waved his other arm a single time at the walls of the room, and the butterflies came and covered her body to form a silken, cream-colored robe with a long trail. They brought an iridescence to her olive-colored eyes, and showed her to be the same, beautiful woman that had so many years before been the object of Titu's desire.

"Titu," the hermit turned his head toward Unawqi's father. "If you truly wish to know your son, you must start anew by knowing his mother as your wife."

"Son." It was the first time that word had so directly confronted him, and coming from a stranger, it shamed him all the more in front of Tamaya. Unawqi was his son, too, and he had always known it, but was afraid to hear it or admit it.

Reventador noticed the scientist's eyes glancing over at the pouch under Tamaya's arm, from which the phototeledar was protruding.

The hermit shook his head in disappointment and said, "Allow me to erase your distractions." He took the pouch from Tamaya, threw it into the air, and blew a flame from his mouth, igniting the pouch into a ball of fire, that when it fell back to the ground, set everything else in the lab to immediate smoke and ashes.

Everything in Titu's laboratory was incinerated so immediately, the scientist had not a second to agonize over it burning.

The only thing of value in the room was Tamaya, and she could not be avoided.

With that, Reventador left the room, leaving Tamaya and Titu alone, surrounded by ashes floating in the pale light.

Titu approached Tamaya, looking small in comparison to the grandeur of her vestment, so alive, and shimmering as the Sun.

"You are too radiant for me, Tamaya. I cannot ask anything of you, for I have done nothing but cause you harm."

Tamaya looked at him, bolstered by the confidence of her butterflies.

"And I do not wish to have you, Titu."

She took another step toward him.

"But whatever is happening to us, it is much more than us now. We must do something for our son, together. Return with me to Antisana, for buried within its walls are the memories of his past, the foundations of his youth…the ghosts that will tell his story."

She turned toward the door, and the butterflies with her. To Titu it was clear she was no longer a woman, but a crowned queen who had more wisdom and power than all the years of his learning could explain.

They left the incinerated shell of his laboratory, and Tamaya picked up the pouch as they left, for despite Reventador setting it ablaze, it lay on the floor unscathed with the phototeledar inside.

Together, they went out into the open air, and greeted what felt to them a completely different world than the one they had inhabited just moments before.

They had not taken twenty paces further before they encountered the woman with the red clay hair, heading in the opposite direction with her chinchay, and wearing Unawqi's eucalyptus punchu.

16 BACHUÉ: MOTHER OF THE SUN

To see the woman with the red clay hair so far from her native cloud forest chilled Tamaya to the bone, for an old woman to travel that far and alone was impossible. It was equally as chilling for the woman with the red clay hair to see Unawqi's mother dressed with living butterflies–a magic that could only be wrought by sorcerers.

Because her eyes were exposed to direct sunlight, the woman with the red clay hair had no blindness, and she beheld the wonder of Tamaya with both delight and astonishment.

They both knew that meeting like this was neither by coincidence nor chance. It could only have been brought about by forces beyond comprehension. They were aware they were being moved now, not by their own feet, but by a story of which they were a part and to an end far in front of their knowing.

Unawqi's father, Titu, standing at Tamaya's side, still appeared somewhat disoriented with his new place in the world, dazed by the loss of his laboratory that had given him both hope and failure.

The chinchay, the woman's companion, walked up to and passed through Titu's legs, rubbing up against one of them, flicking her tail, and batting her paw at a passing butterfly. It helped turned the initial surprise of the meeting into a blush of tenderness, reminding them that despite the occasion, they were among friends, there for each other.

"Well," the woman started, "I didn't expect to come across you on this road, but now that I see you, there is no doubt in my mind we are on the same journey."

Tamaya didn't understand. "But you are going north, my friend, and I am returning home to Antisana. It must be that you cannot see that you have gone astray."

The old woman was less inclined to explain that she could actually see. What really caught her ear more was noticing a single word in Tamaya's sentence, the single word that changed everything, for Antisana had never been Tamaya's "home." It had always been for everyone a place to avoid at all costs. Yet now, and quite intentionally, Tamaya was claiming Antisana as her abode?

The woman with the red clay hair took Tamaya's words, along with all the ominous signs in front of her, to mean that formidable things were happening on a higher plane of the cosmos. Tamaya and Titu were not comprehending these things because they were mortals, but they were central to the drama, nonetheless.

Tamaya was supposed to come with her. The woman with the red clay hair shook her head with confidence about that much.

"No, Tamaya, do not go back to Antisana, not yet. Come with me first to Suamox. I am sure you have a part to play there, for I am going there on account of your son."

Tamaya knew nothing of the place to which the woman with the red clay hair was referring. However, Titu's face grew large with awe, for he knew it well.

"Suamox," he said. "Of course, it makes perfect sense, the city of the Valley of the Iraca, the birthplace of the Sun." Still, he was puzzled. "Then again, the Sun is not there, for he now travels the heavens."

The old woman laughed.

"Oh, we are not going there to seek the emperor. We are going to look for his mother!"

Titu's eyes grew even wider with excited agreement, for while he did not understand the old woman's plans, the authority to which she was appealing was a wholly enlightened idea, at least according to the legends he was beginning to validate, now that he had seen so much of the old myths come to life.

"Yes, Tamaya, yes! I do not know who this woman is, but what she advises is wise. If what we want is answers to be found somewhere on this earth, there is no better place than Suamox."

Seeing Titu and the old woman in consensus, Tamaya concurred, and they continued together walking north, climbing to the high and windy plain of the Hunza before turning east even higher to the villages of the sacred Tota lake, and finally arriving to the great gates of the Sun temple in the Valley of the Iraca, Suamox.

If one is going to arrive in Suamox for any business at all, making a pilgrimage to the Temple of the Sun as a first stop is compulsory.

The temple was a round and stately edifice, with a conical roof made of reeds and held up by twelve tall columns of mahogany around the circumference. Twenty men would have to stand on each other's head in order to reach the ceiling.

Titu marveled at the immensity and grandeur of the temple from the outside, but feared the energy emanating from what was inside and tried to hold Tamaya back.

But the woman with the red clay hair was unafraid and told the other two that the temple was as much her home as was the cloud forest, and they were welcome to enter as her guests.

Inside the temple sat the governing priests, who possess authority over mediation with the world that surrounds the world, that is the world of the Sun. As such, they transit in two different dimensions of existence, giving their skin and the gestures of their hands an extraterrestrial appearance.

When the priests saw Tamaya was obviously endowed with some type of extraordinary power in her vestment of butterflies, they were eager to receive the trio into their audience.

The high priest was regally dressed and particularly beset on formalities, moving his priests in liturgical processions around the temple. They burned all manner of herbs for a good long while before they all sat down again, at which point the high priest addressed Tamaya directly.

"Welcome to this highest of holy places, the nexus of adoration of our celestial emperor, on whose behalf we receive your tribute..."

The high priest was about to go on, but the woman with the red clay hair had no patience for it, and interrupted.

"Our tribute," the woman with the red clay hair said, "I assure you will be enough to extend beyond the walls of this house, but first we seek an audience with Bachué."

The priests were taken aback by the old woman's insolence, and muttered words between themselves before the high priest gave her a clear and utter refusal.

"No one is permitted to speak to the great and powerful Bachué, not even the most esteemed of our sacred valley. Your request is impudent in the least. We will not grant it."

But of course, the priests did not know the real identity of the person to whom they were speaking. Indeed, neither Tamaya nor Titu knew as well. They only knew what they saw: a woman with red clay hair, in a eucalyptus punchu.

The woman with the red clay hair sighed, shook her head, stood and then removed the punchu. She opened her pouch to reveal Aakti Amurugana, thousands of seeds of the Sun.

Titu instantly recognized them and ran to the corner of the temple, for he knew of their volatility, as did the priests, who retreated behind their altar to hide in the shadows. This left Tamaya confused as to why everyone was fleeing. The priests noted the woman dressed in butterflies had no fear and were impressed.

The woman with the red clay hair took a handful of seeds and cast them on the floor, where they burst into all manner of creation: huasquila vines, precious gems, pumas and condors, fish jumping from ponds of water, lemon and papaya falling from leafy trees, grasses growing, and bright flowers blooming, all bound by a crystalline light so luminous they all could feel it vibrating in their chests.

"It is she!" the chief priest exclaimed, his knees shaking. "It is she, Atama, the emperor's lost daughter, in front of our very eyes! At once, open the forbidden doors!"

The high priest shuffled against the back wall to the deepest part of the temple where he felt for the iron lock on a small door, into which he inserted a rusty key.

As the door cracked open, a soft, lime-colored light danced into the temple. The door led to a beautiful garden, filled with the same verdant life that the woman with the red clay hair had created inside the temple, garden connected to garden, life connected to life.

In the very back of the garden, behind the temple, they could see a humble cottage around which floated the same yellow butterflies that adorned Unawqi's mother. This reassured Tamaya that it was safe to move toward it.

They entered the garden together, except for the priests, who would not put their eyes upon it, but bowed in reverence to the woman with the red clay hair as she and her companions passed through the door.

As they came nearer to the cottage, a woman appeared, even older than the woman with the red clay hair. She was dressed in a black gown. Her appearance was meek, that of someone who held no authority except over the flowers in front of her house, but as she peered out to the group approaching her, she held up her walking stick and motioned them to come closer.

The garden woman noticed that with every step the woman with the red clay hair took toward her, wild orchids of every color sprang up around her feet, and the woman smiled widely.

"Come closer. Let me take a look at you."

Even though the rest of her body was very old, the garden woman's eyes were the most handsome brown, and rejuvenated youth into all who looked into them. Her gazes were captivating and kindly, bringing Titu to awe-inspired tears, even before the woman had said anything to them. In her presence, they felt little need to explain much, for she seemed to already know everything; she was a mother in every sense.

She looked most intensely at the woman with the red clay hair, as if seeming to remember, but unable to locate the exact time and place. "Now, where have I lost you, child?"

Child. Lost. They were two immaculately chosen words that broke the woman with the red clay hair's impenetrable self-confidence. Tears streamed down her face, and her chin shook, making it difficult to speak.

"I…am…your granddaughter. The one they call, 'Atama.'"

The older woman raised her back and widened her eyes in amazement, staring at the woman with the red clay hair intensely for a moment, then she softened again, and opened her mouth with a grand smile, tilting her head at the pity of it all, and covering the woman with the red clay hair's mouth to stop her from saying that word again.

"No, you are *not* Atama! You *are* my long-lost treasure. It is me, Bachué, your grandmother!"

Bachué opened her arms and embraced the woman with the red clay hair and kissed her sobbing cheeks. She reached out to Titu and did the same, without reservation or formality of introductions. "Welcome, son!"

Though the butterflies would have seemed to be an impediment, they were nothing to Bachué. As she reached over to Tamaya, all the butterflies jumped into the air, a torrent of happiness, turning the light around them as bright as gold.

Bachué led them inside her cottage and served them chicha, a sweet drink of honey and fermented corn. The more they drank, the more it removed any apprehension from the stories they were about to tell.

The woman with the red clay hair explained to all of them why she had been forced to hide from her father, Aakti, for the past thousand years, for she feared he would abandon Earth and take her with him against her will.

She told them of her stealing the seeds of the Sun and planting them in the earth to make it more difficult for the Sun to forsake his creation.

She told of how she had planted some seeds in the womb of the woman sitting beside her, Tamaya, who had then given birth to Unawqi.

Up to that point, Bachué never interrupted and never broke her sympathetic smile. But when she heard that the seeds had produced a child, the gravity of it bore down on her countenance, and she stood up, trembling.

Bachué walked around the room to try and settle her heart, and then turned to look back at her granddaughter and Tamaya in an attempt to extract a confession.

"Tell me, if what you are saying is true, granddaughter, was the child born with the seeds in his hand?"

Titu's face turned white with terror, for only he knew the answer to that question. Bachué noticed, and her eyes pierced into his soul, causing him to shake and sweat.

"Tell me! Tell me the truth!" she demanded.

The power from her penetrating eyes was so strong, it lifted Titu to his feet, and pulled him toward her until he knelt at her feet.

"Yes, yes, your majesty, Bachué. He was born with the seeds, and I…took them from his hand and ran away. Have mercy upon me!"

Bachué then looked at Tamaya and said, "Do you know what this means?"

Tamaya shook her head no, for this was the first time she had ever heard of the seeds having been put inside her, and the first time she heard the reason why Titu had run away so abruptly. It was too grand a confession for Tamaya to absorb so quickly. She was just a goat herdess, grieving the loss of her son, and wanting some higher justice.

"It means," Bachué continued, "that you have given birth to the end: the end of the Suamox era and the dawn of a new era. It means that my house shall now pass to yours, for you are the mother of the new emperor, heir to the throne of the Sun!"

Before it could all make sense to Tamaya, Bachué asked, "And where is your son? Why did he not accompany you? Why is he not here to present himself to me?"

Tamaya bowed her head in grief. "My son, my son who I could never know…my son is dead."

The woman with the red clay hair continued, for Tamaya could no longer speak.

"It was Moche of Antisana that took his life, grandmother, the same demon who held him captive in exchange for sparing Tamaya's life from Aakti's torture."

Bachué now turned her face to the opposite wall so they would not see her horror. After holding her breath for what seemed an eternity, she exhaled a deep and bitter sigh, noting her comprehension of the tragedy.

"Now I see it, and how terrible this story goes on and on! Moche first used Amaru to try and supplant my son and rule Earth in his place. When that failed, he waited all these years for my grandson to be born, for the sole purpose of using him as bait for a second chance."

"Yes, grandmother. You tell yourself the whole truth."

Bachué shook her head and wept at the terrible crime, and the victims making victims along the torrid path.

As Bachué held her head in her hands, night came to fall, and the story she was told went on, revealing it was even deeper and wider than what she had already realized.

The priests left the temple, for it was now transformed into something so different, beyond their ability to master. The city hushed itself, as if the mountains around it were gossiping of the day's events and not wanting to talk any louder. And when the night descended to its deepest hour, Mama Killa arrived to Suamox, carrying upon her back the condor of Reventador and the fisherman of Jaqunqay.

Unawqi's revolution was about to begin!

17 THE DAY THE SUN RETURNED HOME

It was a day that began most simply, which is surprising when considering it would end as a chapter in the history of titans.

Bachué was sweeping her porch with a chamomile broom, muttering words as she went. She was edgy and perturbed, and every once in a while would stop and flick her fingers at a dead leaf or dusty corner to cast a spell on its negative energy.

"Lazy you!" she spat, trying to wake up every void and get it busy.

A bracing wind was also sweeping through the garden, imitating Bachué's chore upon the rest of nature outside her reach.

The woman with the red clay hair awoke, felt the chilly breeze, and saw her grandmother's uneasy commotion outside.

After watching for a moment, the woman with the red clay hair recognized what was going on. It was a procedure that she herself had done in the past, usually to prepare for a sacramental occasion, like the wedding of two mountains, or the death of a forest.

Exactly what Bachué was preparing for was a mystery, so the woman with the red clay hair asked, "Grandmother, I was not aware. What has happened and how can I help you?"

"My young girl, is it not obvious?" Bachué shot back bitterly, releasing some of the negative energy she had collected while doing her chores.

"I am very disappointed in you! You should have never planted Aakti Amurugana in Tamaya to germinate this terrible chain of events. Have you not seen what you did to her? She has had nothing but a life of fear, being punished for our wrongdoing. You put our house to shame by using your power in such… human ways."

"But grandmother, I never--"

"Silence!!" Bachué's face ruptured into a thicket of thorns, and her eyes and tongue smoldered like black coal before fading back again as her temper subsided. "What is done is done; we cannot reset the past. But today we must do something nearly as impossible: to unbreak Tamaya's heart, and give the keys to our house to its rightful owner."

Not one to challenge Bachué or question her judgment, the woman with the red clay hair said nothing more, and went about the garden, and even the temple, casting the same spells as her grandmother had, until the entire scope of view was clean and alive with the positivity of creation.

Titu and Tamaya could immediately feel the difference as they came about. There was a sense of completion in the air, as if nature was embarking on a wholly new idea. The trees and even the stones were bathed in a nectar that smelled of tangerines and jasmine after a spring rain. Insects and birds were not in their usual hurry. All life was lingering, as if it were groggy after a fine meal, content with its surroundings, ready to listen, and then listen some more.

Bachué went into the temple. She had not set foot in it for many hundreds of years. She looked around her and saw that everything was in order and to her taste. The roof had collapsed to the ground and was covered with vines. Only the walls remained, and barely, at that.

But she was not there to clean or inspect.

She sat down on the ground, turned her head up to the open sky, and began to chant. Her voice was strong and sure of itself.

She sung in an ancient dialect even the priests nearby didn't recognize, but when they heard it, they knew it could be no one else but Bachué singing. The fact that she was singing from inside the temple grounds made them all the more amazed. It further confirmed to them that Bachué's granddaughter had come to initiate an epic occasion they were powerless to stop. To them, she would not be remembered as the woman with the red clay hair, but the woman who was able to draw Bachué out!

The chanting continued without pause all throughout the day, and as she sang, all creation grew more silent, as if holding its breath. The air grew hotter, and the Earth started to tremble, like the sound of many horses running down the sides of the hills. Streaks of gold and blue gamma rays shot through the air, like arrows flying between the foes embroiled in a celestial battle.

And then, at last, a loud clap broke over the temple, shattering the flying gamma rays into a billion fragments, sending everyone on the ground running for cover, all except for Bachué, who held out a single loud, high note, without taking a breath.

It was then that he appeared.

He came over the top of the mountain where the sacred Lake Tota lay, moving with regal dignity until he was positioned directly over the temple. Everything was still; nothing was moving. Even the leaves on the trees dared not tremble for fear of being noticed. The only thing that moved was the steady, high pitch from Bachué's throat.

It was Aakti, the emperor too magnificent to lower himself to Earth, there, hovering above the Suamox temple for an audience with the only one on Earth who could summon him, the almighty Bachué!

Unable to bear his heat or blinding light, living things took cover and buried themselves within their houses or deep in the trees. Bachué inhaled some clouds from Puyo Supai and blew them back out around the temple to create a cover for her companions.

The woman with the red clay hair escorted Titu and Tamaya out to the garden and into the temple grounds near to Bachué. Titu was terrified, so much so he could not walk and instead he crawled on his knees under the shadow of the woman with the red clay hair's eucalyptus punchu. Even though this was an encounter that he had toiled his whole life to see, now that it was here, it was too overpowering for him to compose himself as a man.

Tamaya, however, was not afraid. The goat herdess from the Quijos valley was caught between curiosity and the blood of vengeance wetting her tongue. She could sense this was the moment she was waiting for and thought of little else than those whom she would be given to confront as she firmly grasped the hand of the woman with the red clay hair.

Because of her punchu, the emperor could not see his daughter at his mother's side, but he noticed the two others and hissed at them in disgust at their mortal presence.

"Bachué! Who is this you dare let contaminate our company?" Aakti cried out, breaking the chant of his grandmother.

"My son," Bachué replied calmly, "our meetings are indeed uncommon, so you should expect uncommon company. We have a grave matter to discuss, and everyone here has a purpose in it."

She then stood up from the ground to stretch her neck a little closer to his face, and look him more squarely in the eye.

"Our time has come to an end, my son. Our days are over, for it has come to my attention this woman you see before you dressed in a thousand butterflies is the mother of your son, who was born from her womb with your very seeds in his hand…"

The Sun interrupted his grandmother, "What foul nonsense have you given your higher mind to swallow, Bachué! How dare you fester our holy hall with trivial lies. Let me burn them now for defiling us before we waste another thought on them."

The emperor boiled in the sky and stirred up fire within him to throw down on his accusers, but Bachué countered, and holding up her small hand, hurled a spray of Tota's cold water up on the mountain and into her son's face.

"There will be none of that today, my son, and you should be ashamed for mistaking your mother as a gullible fool. I have lived twice as long as you.

"Besides, we have a witness."

Bachué beckoned for Titu to get up from his knees. He was trembling all over and could not bear to look upon the great emperor's countenance. Tamaya helped him up, steadied him over her shoulder, and urged him to speak of what he knew.

Titu mustered every last bit of courage left within him to utter his confession, which trickled out of his stuttering lips.

"Yes, I s-s-saw the seeds in the h-hands of the boy c-coming from Tamaya's womb. They glowed like d-d-diamonds. They did. I stole them and kept them in my lab-b-oratory for many years until he came. The s-s-eeds, the amurugana, flew right to him, as if they belonged to him."

"Silence, you weak and thoughtless liar!" the emperor shot back. "Your story is nothing but imagined in order to rob my mother of her senses."

Titu shrunk back to Tamaya's feet and covered his ears, too terrified to say any more.

"What a stupid old woman you have become, Bachué! How can you know any of this to be true?" Aakti said to his mother.

The woman with the red clay hair then removed her eucalyptus cloak, revealing herself.

"Because," the woman with the red clay hair said, looking for the first time in a long time directly into the eyes of her father,

"I put them there."

The emperor fell backwards in shock, not only seeing his daughter who had always eluded him, but here, in his mother's company.

He was speechless for a long pause, for the testimony of his daughter was the one thing he knew he could not dispute. She was the only one on Earth who could possibly do such a thing.

"Why?" the emperor exhaled after a length.

Bachué intervened.

"Why is a different issue altogether, my son, and for a different day. It has been proven. My house now belongs to Tamaya, and her son now inherits the heavens."

"The heavens are mine," the emperor fumed, "and will be mine forevermore. I leave Earth to your insane illusions, Bachué. But for me, I will take my daughter now, and dismiss myself from the world altogether."

The emperor then stirred up a thick torrent of his fiery body and thrust it downward as a blazing ray in order to seize the woman with the red clay hair.

But Titu, even though he trembled on the ground, shook even more thinking of the disaster about to befall Earth if the woman with the red clay hair was abducted. It would mean a complete cessation of light, because the Sun would leave. It would mean the end of the subversive creation of life that was solely dependent on the hands of the woman with the red clay hair. Titu had never confessed to be a believer, but neither could his instinct allow for her extinction.

Titu believed, in her!

He jumped from his shadow and threw himself in front of her, intercepting the emperor's bolt. It burst upon impact squarely on Titu's back and consumed his flesh and bone in a gruesome flame and smoke, bringing Titu's life to an end.

It even took Bachué by surprise, throwing her and the others to the ground.

Seeing he missed his target, the emperor stirred up another bolt, but the woman with the red clay hair, who could still move faster than her father, dove into her eucalyptus punchu and disappeared from view.

The emperor screamed in rage and blasted his furnace all across Suamox, desiring to melt the entire city to an end.

Bachué fought back as much as she could, throwing clouds in his way, but the Sun was so determined to have the final say, he burned his way past her defenses.

It was from behind him that the salvation of Suamox came, and from a most unexpected helper!

Even though it was the height of day in the brightest of light, Mama Killa thrust herself onto the scene, and sailing down from her side flew the condor of Reventador with the fisherman of Jaqunqay on his back.

Though tiny in comparison, the condor's talons had the greatness of a volcano in them, and he set them down upon the crown of Aakti's head and pierced them into his skull, swinging the emperor around in the sky like a writhing rabbit in his clutches.

The emperor screamed in terrible pain, but the condor refused to let go.

Then the fisherman pulled from underneath his shirt the last remaining gift he had of Unawqi's power, the faded, but still graceful sunflower Mama Killa left behind on the beach of Jaqunqay.

With the precision of a skilled fisherman who knew what he always had known since he had met Unawqi, that only the fearless can conquer force, the fisherman threw the soft sunflower onto the surface of the Sun.

As the sunflower landed, its own seeds burst open with all the colors of the rainbow, covering Aakti's body until the emperor had been enveloped in the sunflower's embrace.

The seeds sang Unawqi's song as they opened:

"I will not let you go; I will not let you go until you take me in your arms."

They sang the ultimate desire of both hunters and fishers, and why Unawqi and the fisherman understood each other so well. They sang in anguish for the Sun, too, to join them; for him to know in plain and simple terms: *"I will not let you go until you love me!"*

18 WEDDING FOR A NEW EARTH

The combined determination of Bachué, the fisherman, the condor, and Mama Killa had brought about the shunning of Aakti, the Sun, from the heavens.

The condor had cast the emperor so far away into space that Aakti would never be able to return to his own orbit, at least not without a great deal help, and the emperor had no friends of the kind that would help him.

It was no glad occasion in Suamox. With Aakti exiled, Mama Killa carried a double burden. It was now upon her to give light to the world, both day and night.

Because of this, Bachué carried on with her chanting as intensely as she had sung the Sun down from the sky.

The priests interpreted her chant as a lament for Mama Killa, who was going to be draining herself to death, but in truth, they were wrong. Bachué's chanting was actually a conversation with Mama Killa about another event soon to unfold, and Mama Killa had a long story to tell.

Tamaya was sincerely stricken with grief. She wept for a man she had not yet had time to forgive but had hoped to at some point in time. She looked at the pile of ashes that was Titu Ilumán, wondering how this man--who had been so cruel to her–had in an instant, sacrificed himself for her friend whom he never really knew.

This was neither the revenge, nor the justice Tamaya wanted. It was yet another episode of her hope being robbed when she hadn't been looking.

At the same time, it allowed her to search inside of herself for buried memories. She counted the presence of the people in her life and how they had brought her here, needing, again, to imprint them on her mind to understand why she kept losing them.

"What have I done," she thought to herself, "to let my loved ones slip away from me?"

Her mind brought her to Titu, to her son, to the woman with the red clay hair, to her goats, to Naira–to everyone and everything on her journey. She was grateful for what each had given her, but never got her chance to tell them.

All she could do was to shake her head and try to rid herself of feeling so damned, but even that was a futile effort. Lost, gone, taken, alone–these were the words that seemed to be stuck to the insides of her eyes.

But if she could not sense the moment herself, the butterflies could on her behalf. They left her body to make a yellow shroud over Titu's ashes, giving him Tamaya's homage.

The woman with the red clay hair listened to Bachué's lament, and watched the butterflies' memoriam, noting how death was their union.

"How is it," she thought, "that one's plain sadness and the creativity of nature work together so miraculously like this? They are one, even though they're not speaking to each other. Or are they?

"Perhaps some other thing in creation is a mediator? Like the chinchay, or something invisible, like the breeze, taking its cue from the grieving to direct nature with a response of wonders and signs?

"Death and birth brush past each other so unnoticed, unaware they have touched each other's hand on the way."

The woman with the red clay hair wanted to share what was happening in front of them, but Bachué and Tamaya were so inconsolable, she could not find the words to bring their attention to it.

Her own life had been spent preventing the Sun from leaving Earth on his own accord, but now he had been involuntarily cast out by forces beyond her control, and the wake of it left even more things unresolved for her.

Was his crime of masterminding Unawqi's death his crime alone, and was it worth the punishment? How could the world go on? How would things grow instead of die?

She understood this was why Bachué was wise to resist her earlier on; that justice might only be served at the expense of a long darkness.

Her pondering was interrupted at the sight of the condor, floating down to the blackened field around them, the fisherman on his back.

The fisherman dismounted and stood before all of them in a way he hadn't stood before. He appeared taller, braver, humble, but not weak. He knew something they didn't, perhaps. He had the presence of command in his shoulders, and he walked between them like a General among the wounded, respecting their suffering while anticipating something better was in store.

He went over to Tamaya, the same woman who had contested him over Unawqi's dead body at the Great Mangrove Gathering in Balao, and he stood over her to guard her as she grieved.

Then the other priests of the Suamox temple came, along with their most loyal and faithful, to attend to Bachué and their new surrogate, Mama Killa. They spread their robes and gold and sweet-smelling food all around on the ground, relinquishing their excesses of wealth to support anything that might be asked of them.

Finally, into the scene walked a complete surprise. It was the great hermit from the south, Reventador.

He surveyed the scene with some regret that it had come to this, and looked up at Mama Killa, so heavy over his head. He then looked over and saw the fisherman and how he was mourning so differently from the others, so calmly, and Reventador admired the fisherman.

"This," Reventador thought, "was the mark of a man, and the seed to save the world."

Reventador would be the one ordained to abruptly change the scene.

In a move that was a stark contrast to the quiet melancholy, Reventador drove his walking stick into the ground in the middle of the crowd, and like a bang coming out of the crater of his mountain, it called everyone to immediate attention.

"People of Suamox," he bellowed in his deep and vibrating voice, "have no fear. I am Reventador, and I come to share your loss, for this malady is not yours alone.

"The mountains, the oceans, everything under the sky, we have all seen what has just come to pass, and we join our loss with yours.

"But the world is watching and waiting for Suamox to answer, and if you answer by standing up, so will the whole of Earth stand with you.

"Before another hour passes, we must set a new path. Let us prepare to turn this funeral into a wedding, and not one wedding, but two!"

Everyone was bewildered at this wild wizard in their midst, only the eldest of whom knew him by name, for his home was far to the south and the subject of forgotten legends.

But a glimmer emerged in the back of the eyes of two: Tamaya and the fisherman. As they turned their heads toward Reventador, his eyes met them directly in return.

Like a waterfall falling upwards, the butterflies leapt into the air, bringing the ashes of Titu Ilumán with them in the draft. They circled the Moon to give it a golden glow for the occasion.

Reventador looked at his son, the condor. He gave him a nod, and the condor swelled his breast with pride and spread the breadth of his wings.

The condor needed as much space in his lungs as possible, for out of his throat came a trumpeting sound that called all the spirits and gods to stand at attention. It got everyone on the ground to their feet as well, raising their hands to Mama Killa above.

The hermit then bid the fisherman and Tamaya to come over to his side, and then behind them, to stand the condor and the woman with the red clay hair.

It seemed clear to most everyone that Reventador was going to bind the fisherman and Tamaya as husband and wife, that this would be the best compromise to heal the broken cosmos.

But Reventador, as fearsome and commanding as he was, had something revolutionarily different in mind.

He beckoned Bachué to stand with him at his side, and the high priests of Suamox behind him. He wanted to leave no present authority unaccounted for, and for all of them to have their hand in sealing this juncture.

"Surely, Atama," Reventador said, winking at the woman with the red clay hair, "you can spare us a seed?"

The woman with the red clay hair could very rarely forgive the use of that name, but this was one of them. She smiled, took a seed out of her pouch, and dropped it on the ground to the side of the hermit.

Up sprung a spectacular peach tree, hanging heavy with fruit, giving them a verdant canopy. A breeze reappeared, having been sent by Puyo Supai, reviving the scent of jasmine and tangerines, all of which calmed everyone again, and they came in closer to watch the ceremony unfold.

Reventador took a gold ring from his own finger, one forged from the fire of his mountain. He held the ring up to the Moon, for he wished for Mama Killa to bless it, as the ring was half hers.

Mama Killa rolled her brow down in agreement, and Reventador took Tamaya's hand and slid the ring on her finger.

"Tamaya, fair daughter of the Quijos: to you we give the union of Moon and mountains, for today we beg you to be our queen.

"Return to Antisana, and make it your throne. Revive it to be Earth's palace again, the seat of the princes of Napo, Coca, and Pastaza.

"And with all the solemnity we endow, take Titu Ilumán as your beloved, the one we lost to the Sun. Someday, he will return to you in the flesh and go with you into the silken sky."

"Titu!" Tamaya cried.

Her eyes flooded with tears as the years of their youth raced through her mind, the spontaneous dances to the howls of the woods, bathing naked in the Duende falls, long laughing nights drunk with chicha.

The woman with the red clay hair embraced Tamaya from behind, kissing her tears away.

"My queen! My queen! I hail you, my queen!"

Tamaya wiped her tears away. She didn't know what to say, and just knelt on the ground before Reventador.

"How can I be a queen without a king? I only have my goats to love me."

Bachué lifted Tamaya from her knees, looked her in the eyes and smiled widely.

"We have the world in you," Bachué said. "Show it how to be beautiful again." She pointed up to the glowing circle around the Moon. "Look! Titu is there to help you!"

The high priest of the Suamox temple brought Tamaya a long and flowing crown, and he set it upon her head. It was succulent, sweetened with the best gifts of the soil, made of lilacs, sun roses, and purple clover, and held together with yarrow and inebriating verbena. A dappled willow branch rose above the crest, growing and shedding leaves as every moment passed, making Tamaya the very image of the tree of life herself.

"Welcome into our company, Queen Tamaya," Bachué said as she took Tamaya's hand, and escorted her to stand between herself and Reventador.

Reventador reminded the crowd: "Now, I said today would give us not one wedding, but two. While crowning Earth with a new queen is a grand enough occasion, my honor is incomplete--my heart is still empty."

Bachué agreed and took over, for this was the fruit of her conversation with Mama Killa.

"People of Suamox," she announced.

"You have served your family of the Sun so well. It is true, that our new queen of Earth does not resolve who shall rule the sky, now that our emperor, and my son, is gone.

"But as all of you have heard today, the emperor has an heir, a prince whose ascent was cut short, but whose defiance lives on. You cannot see him in the flesh, but he is standing in front of us now. With your blessing of this union, together we will reclaim our dynasty and celebrate on the shores of Lake Tota before the hour's end."

Bachué then presented the fisherman to Tamaya to explain Mama Killa's tale but so that everyone could hear.

"Tamaya, learn now what you have never known. Your son was given the name 'Unawqi,' for he was the anointed heir of the emperor Aakti, the Sun.

"Unawqi was not only your son, he was my grandson as well. My granddaughter, your friend, is his sister, and your half-daughter.

"But even more profound than this, is that Unawqi lived! He ran as a boy, he hunted like a man, and like you, he knew the happiness of love. Never do the gods get as much an indulgence as that!

"This fisherman gave your son happiness; and when Unawqi was lost, this fisherman, like you, searched the sea and land to find his beloved, and went even farther, flying to the Moon on his bid to face down the most powerful being of the universe. This fisherman, my dear Tamaya, is not only your greatest ally, he is as much deserving to be cherished by your heart as Unawqi himself. Will you receive him as your own?"

Tamaya looked up at the fisherman. Even though she could not see him that night they were side by side in Balao, she recognized him by her other senses. She noticed his eyes were so richly brown, just like she remembered her son's eyes were when he was born. He resembled both the innocence and the audacity of her own blood, and still seemed so unfinished a man, his eyes wanting to recover the diamond of his life that was stolen from him. He clearly needed Tamaya to restore what had been lost to both of them.

The corner of Tamaya's eye then caught something moving in the crowd. She looked out and saw, one by one, the children of Suamox raising their hands in blessing, urging others to join them. Their mothers soon joined in, raising their hands, too, admiring this new and joyful liberty at hand. And yes, even then the men of Suamox could not stop themselves from the contagious spirit of happiness in the air, and they added their own raised hands for what was clear to them a victory of a new kind.

Tamaya looked behind her, and the priests who had once been so prohibitive, were raising their hands as well.

But when she turned to her left to see Reventador's reaction, he was missing. He had moved his place to stand at the fisherman's side where he waited for Tamaya to agree; to raise her hand as the final sign.

Tamaya knew she was being asked to do something she had never done before, to bless the union of two men to each other, and even more, to wed the living with the dead! This was, at once, so incomprehensible, and yet the world and the world that surrounds the world were right there, together, urging her on.

She reminded herself that she had just received much of the same blessing, and it caused her to look up to catch sight of her now-husband. There, the yellow ring of butterflies glowed brighter around the Moon. It was as if Titu was at peace, and raising his hand, too.

She looked back, directly into the eyes of the fisherman, and let her next words glide from her tongue as easily as rain falls from the sky:

"I say, yes! We say, yes! We all say, yes!"

19 ON THE ROAD TO ANTISANA

A little blue jay hopped along from one side of the trail to the other in front of Tamaya. It was the new queen's only companion as she walked home to Antisana. She had no soldiers or attendants, and the jay distracted her from thinking too much about her solitary condition.

She did, however, have Titu circling the Moon above her, and he would be there constantly, since there was no Sun to light the sky.

Her thoughts turned to how she might govern creation without daylight. She felt the same burden that weighed upon her friend Mama Killa. They would have to work together.

The woman with the red clay hair had stayed behind in Suamox, for on the night of the great wedding feast on the shore of Lago Tota, Bachué, the mother of the Sun, had fallen ill from the lack of light, and needed her granddaughter at her side.

"What would happen to the woman with the red clay hair," Tamaya wondered, "for she is also fashioned from the Sun?"

The priests of Suamox considered becoming Tamaya's servants and establishing a court in Antisana, but Tamaya refused to hear it, for it was not their home, and she wanted them to continue to serve Bachué.

The hermit and the condor returned to their mountain home in the east.

And the fisherman? He had disappeared amid the celebration at Lake Tota. Tamaya looked for him, for she hoped he would join her on the journey south, until someone told her they saw him walk off on the darker side of the shore, but he never returned.

She worried for him. There were still too many who would put a high price on his head, or see him as a disgrace and want him dead. But then the gentle chinchay came in from the bush and pressed up to Tamaya's side, which of course, made the blue jay fly promptly away.

The Moon flickered in the sky like a candle with only a limited time to burn. Tamaya had so much on her mind, she hardly even considered she had been walking for an entire day without rest.

As they came around a turn in the road in the shadow of Urcunina, there he was. The fisherman was standing in her path, holding the mane of an auburn horse.

That's where he had gone: to find the queen a horse and bring it to her.

He held out his hand and helped her climb onto the horse's back. He divided a bushel of sweetgrass in two, gave one to the horse to eat, and put the other behind Tamaya's back to support her. He then draped the eucalyptus punchu over her shoulders, the same one shaped into being by the hands of Moche and passed on to Unawqi, only to be lost in the cloud forest, and eventually rediscovered by the chinchay and the woman with the red clay hair. The leaves had grown supple with age, and comforted her as much as the memory of the journey they took.

"The night will grow colder," he said, "but trust me; our friend here will help you reach the gates of Antisana before dawn."

"But wait!" Tamaya stopped him. "Aren't you coming with me? I was hoping –"

"No, my queen, I cannot. We are united in that our redemption of Unawqi is not finished. I must bring him home, and I promise you, I will."

He then kissed the nose of the horse and whispered in his ear, and the horse leapt forward and galloped away at lightning speed, disappearing into the night toward Antisana.

When the tail of the horse had vanished, the fisherman was alone again in the night…or so he thought!

He looked down at his feet to realize the chinchay was still there, having had no intention to follow the queen. She stood at attention in front of her new companion, the fisherman, who looked back at her with instant admiration.

The fisherman sat down by the side of the road and the chinchay came over to him.

"Hello, my friend," the fisherman said. "It seems as if you are the friend of us all."

As he stroked the chinchay's back, he pulled a handful of sunflower seeds out from his pouch and let the chinchay eat them out of his palm.

The two of them sat together and rested in the dark of the wilderness, two small specks in the sea of forest, thinking for the moment of nothing but the joy of each other's company and the feast of sunflower seeds.

And yet, they were not alone. Mama Killa was watching over everyone, and the ring of Titu Ilumán around her was stronger than ever before.

20 THE DEMON ON THE WALL

The time of the great Bachué was coming to an end. Without the Sun in the sky, her strength had been greatly diminished, and her granddaughter, the woman with the red cay hair, was left to tend to Bachué and the remains of the temple.

As she was doing her cleaning and sweeping one day, the woman with the red clay hair's broom hit a heavy object underneath the bed Tamaya had slept in. The same sound of her broom hitting the object echoed in the sky above her like a thunderclap.

She pulled the bed aside and saw there the leather pouch Tamaya had brought with her to Suamox, and must have simply forgotten. Inside of the pouch was the phototeledar, the metal and crystal invention Titu had fashioned to be a conduit between himself and the bearer of the phototeledar, whomever that might be. He had used it to stay close to Unawqi on the boy's travels. It was the instrument that had allowed him to make contact with Tamaya, which in turn had brought her to him in his laboratory. And here, now in Bachué's house, it throbbed as it had before…listening.

The woman with the red clay hair picked it up and hung it on the wall to get it off of the floor, but it gripped onto her so forcefully that it was difficult for her to get her hands back. When she did, her hands stung, but she let her puzzlement subside and continued on with her chores, for she did not know of the object's story or its power.

But when Bachué passed by the room, her weakened spine arched up as she felt the Sun's power coming through the phototeledar. Her eyes wandered around the room looking for the source of energy until she spotted the bizarre object on the wall. As she came closer to it, blue gamma rays danced through the room reacting to the friction between her and the object, which made Bachué all the more curious, but cautious.

"Granddaughter!" she whispered. "Quickly, bring me some buried stones."

The woman with the red clay hair went outside, pulled up some stones from underneath the garden, and brought them to Bachué.

Buried stones are devoid of energy, and therefore useful for blocking it. Bachué took them and held them up in front of her as she approached the phototeledar. The gamma rays did not detect her movement. She then placed the stones on the phototeledar and it turned pale when the stones short-circuited its transmissions.

At last, she was able to speak freely, and she asked the woman with the red clay hair,

"What demon is this that you have brought into my house, granddaughter, that possesses such a strange magic in its heart?"

"I do not know, grandmother. It belonged to Tamaya."

"Tamaya? The girl could not possibly have knowledge of such a thing. This comes from somewhere else, from a wizard, or a god."

Bachué then removed the stones, one by one, placed them in her pockets, and put her hands on the phototeledar. Its color revived, warming Bachué's hands, and making her heart liven. She felt younger again and looked into the surface of the device. Seeing her reflection in it, her face softened.

"Tamaya," she said. "What have you brought us?"

Listening on the other side was not Tamaya, but Titu!

The phototeledar was not just a conduit to Titu, but to the Sun's power. It mediated Heaven and Earth, requiring only some storage of that power on the other side of the instrument in order to ignite.

Unawqi himself had provided this ignition, as did the yellow butterflies, and of course, the very lifeblood of Bachué and the woman with the red clay hair.

Now that Titu was consumed by the Sun, he was not separate from such power, but vested with it, for he now lived in the same dominion of Aakti, the qanaq'wa makuyhana, or the "palace where they forever struggle."

What is this palace, you may ask, and why is it known by its struggle?

That was the same question I posed to Unawqi in our conversations at St. Rita's. It would take a long time to explain, and in many different ways at various points in his story, but the best way to start is to explain it like this:

When the Sun vanquishes life, that life does not entirely become extinguished. It is consumed, removed as earthly matter, and brought into another astrophysical dimension. More simply, it goes into the house of the Sun.

What you are probably realizing is indeed correct: Unawqi…did not die.

Neither did Titu Ilumán.

They were swept up, never to return to Earth, and instead, were transferred to the guild of stars where they live with the emperor Aakti.

But as you know, Aakti, Titu, and Unawqi each had their own kind of investiture of the Sun's power, and each had their own agenda with respect to what should be done with it!

So even in the celestial realm, the three carried on their struggle with each other, using each other to their own gain. This is why they call it the qanaq'wa makuyhana, the "palace where they forever struggle," for there the three are locked in a match of wills, and no one knows when it might end, or who the ultimate victor might be.

Now vested with the Sun's power, Titu could uniquely hear the voices on the other side of the phototeledar without the need for a receiving instrument.

He heard Bachué's words, "Tamaya, what have you brought us?" and he leapt up from where he was sitting and said, "Tamaya, I am here!"

This made both Bachué and the woman with the red clay hair jump backward, for they recognized Titu's voice, but did not expect it to be coming from the demon on the wall.

Bachué clarified that she was not Tamaya, and because Bachué and the woman with the red clay hair were part of the Sun's family, they understood where Titu was speaking from, but never had they possessed a tool like this to channel their very words directly to the celestial palace.

The magnitude of the phototeledar's power quickly set in upon Bachué. She realized, for the first time, she would be able to also hear the voice of her grandson Unawqi, who must have been nearby. And she thought that the emperor himself could speak to her without needing to return to Suamox, or anywhere close to Earth. The thought was, quite literally, a deadly thing. Finally, she realized that she, too, could be on the listening side. That is, she could hear things she was not meant to hear! But this matter she kept to her own thoughts.

Bachué placed the stones back on to the surface of the phototeledar, and then spoke to her granddaughter in a serious tone:

"The people of Suamox must never know of this demon, for they could use it for all manner of evil. Not even the queen, Tamaya, must know of it. See to it you never mention it again to her, and let it be forgotten."

The next day, Bachué rose early in the dawn before her granddaughter was awake. She went into the phototeledar's room, removed the stones from its surface, and listened until she could hear Titu speaking to himself.

"Let's try it again," he mumbled. "Nitrogen. Hydrogen, of course, but not too much. Sulfur carbonate, yes, that's a given. Argon, Selenium. Radium, Bismuth. That should be it, but something's still missing. Well, not to worry, I'll find it here in this palace.

"It won't be too long, now that I have access to the emperor's kitchen. I will find the missing ingredient when he is distracted with one of his preoccupations. Little does the fat yellow-bellied king know I am growing as smart as him.

"The day will come when I will find his weakness and put him on my chain for once. The very Sun will become a horse in my harness, and I will make him the Earth's eternal slave. The tables will turn and we on Earth will be kings of the universe, and Aakti, our subject…it's only a matter of a little more time and the discovery of my missing element."

Titu had not changed. He was as conniving as he had ever been.

Bachué listened quietly on the other side of the phototeledar, closing her eyes with a heavy sadness. This was, after all, the groom she herself had blessed to Tamaya, queen of the earth and mother of her legacy, a man whom Tamaya had let herself love again. And now, Bachué was witnessing a plot to undermine the very order of the heavens, replacing the sovereignty of the Sun with that of humankind.

It was horrible to her ears, and she knew she had to do something about it, and quickly. Titu's mere presence in qanaq'wa makuyhana was even greater than Bachué's power on earth, and Titu was therefore completely capable of achieving his catastrophic goal.

21 TUNGURAHUA AND
THE BALAO PROPOSITION

The once teeming port of Balao, where traders of gold, fish, and fruit all crossed paths, had become a foul-smelling place in the absence of sunlight. The mangroves rotted in their place, the crab pots were full of sludge and dead fish, and overgrown vines pulled down the walls of houses and let water find its way in. Even Ernest's house fell into decay, and his books and bottled specimens rolled off the shelves onto the floor.

No one visited Balao anymore. It was too dark to find one's way there, and too dangerous to be on the road in such conditions. The fishers did not go out with their nets or pots, as the sea could not be trusted if you couldn't see what was in it. Instead, they turned to raising pigs and chickens, and burning the mangroves for light.

Little did they know what their small village was about to become. Even as they slept, their dreams could not imagine the soil underneath their beds was already kindling the embers of a planetary revolution.

Despite his being thrown far from the Earth's sky, Aakti was lucky he had one follower left on Earth who was fiercely loyal. He had lost his political capital or illusion of partnership with Mama Killa, or with Puyo Supai, or of course with the dynasty of Suamox.

But there was one everyone preferred to not talk about or be reminded of, and that was the dreaded Tungurahua, the Black Giant, Southern Warlord of Fire.

Tungurahua belonged to the same clan as Reventador, Cumbal, Antisana and others, but had long been ostracized from his kin for his reckless nature. He had a reputation of a psychotic assassin, killing indiscriminately without cause or warning, and throwing raging tantrums similar to Reventador's, but that would go on for days. Reventador, at least, cared about the balance of nature around him, creation and destruction. Tungurahua, on the other hand, only considered living things an accident, waiting for him to come around and slaughter them.

So, no one dared go near him. Indeed, it was better to avoid him altogether.

It was the terrible Tungurahua who rode into Balao one day, riding his ashen gray horse and bearing a message from his lord, Aakti, the Sun.

He was draped in a hooded black cloak, but his hands were as pale white as fresh fallen cinders. Out of his horse's nostrils spewed smoke like a burning volcano. The Black Giant was indeed very tall, and as he dismounted and walked through the town, he towered over everyone he passed.

"Qayqa huk'ucha", he growled at a pig trader in the town square. The pig trader dared not lift his eyes to meet Tungurahua's, and instead just pointed the direction to the house of Ernest Heatheridge.

Tungurahua would not even tolerate the burning fires of mangrove to challenge his authority, and as he passed by them, he snuffed them out and turned them to piles of stone, and Balao grew darker by the minute.

Despite his irritable reputation, he walked slowly and deliberately, his boots leaving treads that smoldered behind him.

Tungurahua did not knock, but pushed the door open of Heatheridge's house, as if it were willow brush in his path, and went inside. Upon seeing the Black Giant, Ernest was terrified into silence, and he fell backwards in his chair.

Naira, Ernest's wife, was returning from catching frogs for the evening meal. She had not had much success, so her basket was fairly quiet. But she had seen the tall, hooded figure from a distance as he entered her house. She didn't recall him being a previous guest, and certainly not one that would be welcome to come in so brazenly. This made her curious, and she put down her basket and approached the side of the house, ducking her head beneath the window to listen.

Tungurahua's voice hissed and crackled like fire splitting wood.

"I bring you word from Aakti, the emperor. He wishes to make you an offer that will bring light back to your village, life back to your waterways, and make here a capital of trade many times over what it has ever been before."

"The emperor was cast out, sir—I don't believe I caught your name."

"Not gone forever. He will return with the aid of your hand."

"I don't understand. My only knowledge is trade and science."

Tungurahua maintained his short wick of restraint by pacing around the circumference of Ernest's room, peering into bottles and cracking open books as if to be conducting an investigation.

"Quite the contrary, Ernest Heatheridge. I am no fool. You have knowledge of something greater--or someone greater--than yourself. Someone who trusts you very much: Unawqi!"

"Then you must know that Unawqi also died here. We buried him on the edge of the mangrove."

"Died? No. Your pitiful burials serve no purpose. What is beneath the ground is not Unawqi. He was removed. And you can see him come back, just as you can see the Sun come back in the sky."

"But this is not possible. There is no such power."

Tungurahua raised his voice in protest.

"There is one you overlooked. It is the bond between Unawqi and a certain fisherman. The bond is very strong, so strong that in order to protect that fisherman from harm, Unawqi will burn a path through what you think of as the death of time and space. This path is all the emperor needs to find his way back to Earth, and then he can establish a foothold here to regain his dominion over our skies.

Ernest cringed at hearing of such a bond. He did not think it was the crab fisherman and Unawqi's temporary slave master. Instead, it reminded him of the affair between his son and the strong man. Ernest had found that bond so abominable he had broken it apart, only to then see his son react by drowning himself at sea. The whole saga still drove a bitterly emotional wedge between himself and Naira, and now this hooded figure was asking Ernest to bring together the same kind of union he had previously put asunder. Had that strong man plotted some revenge by now bonding with Unawqi?

Tungurahua did not know that old story, nor that it was the particular fisherman being recalled to Ernest's mind.

"Qayqa huk'ucha, bring us the fisherman of Jaqunqay, and not only will you be the savior of your town, you will open the door to a whole new world, a new creation under the victorious Aakti. Balao will be his new temple, and you his high priest upon whom he will bestow all the knowledge of creation you still have yet to discover!"

"Jaqunqay!" Heatheridge said with a sigh of relief, seeing now he was not being asked to repatriate the strong man he had banished. The details of the Jaqunqay fisherman were sketchier, but finding him, while not simple, seemed a less complicating task to be done and over with.

"Well, I do seem to remember this fisherman. He arrived seeking Unawqi, but was too late. We kept him for the night and then sent him away. He seemed rather harmless. But from what harm does Unawqi need to protect him, may I ask?"

The space between Tungurahua's breaths were growing shorter, indicating he was growing more irritated with the banality of Ernest's questions. Heatheridge was a scientist, but Tungurahua was an ideologue concerned with a cosmic drama playing on a different stage than what Heatheridge was ready to entertain. He drew the curtain open a bit as if to look for anyone approaching.

"The cloak of the night hides many assassins and they are beginning to surround you as we speak. Chief among them are the mutineers of Suamox, the emperor's former temple. If they are able to snuff out the Jaqunqay fisherman, Unawqi would have nothing left to interest him on Earth. Then it would be impossible for the Sun to come back, and the world would be cast into darkness forever.

"We need you to find the fisherman before his assassins do and bring him back here. I will then create a trap for the assassins by making some noise about the fisherman's whereabouts being here in Balao and let Unawqi fight back when he sees his fisherman is threatened."

Ernest rose from his chair and braved some steps toward the black-robed Tungurahua.

"Even for immortals, this would be a gamble."

"You are a scientist. You don't believe in immortals."

"What if it doesn't work? What if Unawqi fails to notice and doesn't come?"

Tungurahua's patience had run out and he pinned Ernest up against the wall, respiring smoke into his face.

"Look around you, Qayqa huk'ucha. Your town will sink into rot before the year is out, and you and your people here will become the food for roaches and snakes. Unawqi knows this place. He will listen to what happens here."

While he didn't know him, Ernest could see by Tungurahua's presence he was a powerful influence not to argue with, and he didn't have any other options near as promising as this one to get Balao back on its feet.

Tungurahua then turned and left through the same door. As he went out, Naira scurried around the corner of the house. Tungurahua heard her movement and looked to his right and left to see who was there, but at the same moment, a frog jumped out of Naira's basket. Tungurahua wanted nothing to be a witness to the conversation he had with Heatheridge, not even a frog, and he lifted his pale hand and shot an arrow of flame out of his sleeve at the frog, incinerating it on the spot. He walked around the corner of the house, but Naira had hidden behind a barrel.

Seeing no one, Tungurahua walked away and mounted his gray horse. Just as unhurriedly as he had arrived, he ambled back into the mangrove road, casting a blood red shadow on the underside of the Moon.

22 TAPAIPI

Tamaya's horse slowed its gallop as it started to scale the canyon of Antisana, climbing the hairpin turns and crossing rock slides moistened with mountain streams. The canyon was dark enough, she couldn't imagine how the cavernous interior of Antisana would be any better. Even more, it was much too impossible a place to be a practical home, let alone a royal capital.

After riding some more on a thin ledge, the trail widened and came into a hollow. At the back, an open hole bore its way into the mountainside. This was the rather unremarkable gate of Antisana, doorway to the empty lair of Moche, and the new throne of Earth.

Tamaya sighed as she dismounted her horse, and Mama Killa cast a silver light onto the entrance, encouraging the queen to go in.

Into the eerie silence she went. It was so bone dead, even the bats had left. All she could hear was the faint boiling of magma and drops of water, deep down in the caverns below.

She would only be on her own for a moment, for just then, from behind her came the welcome rush of her most loyal brigade, the yellow butterflies of Pasochoa, their luminous wings lighting up the vaulted chambers. he smiled and raised her arms to them in gratitude.

"My faithful friends, how honorable are you to light my way. Let my first act as queen be to make you the knights of Antisana, for you are stronger and swifter to come to my aid than any army a kingdom could muster!"

She could now see the great halls that Moche had carved out with his hands over the course of a thousand years around and beneath her. She saw the legendary crystal blue lakes, the bubbling cauldrons of white lava called "hell's milk" that she had heard of since she was a child, and there, in front of her eyes, were countless walls studded with emeralds, diamonds, and gold. powerful

But when she came into one room she stopped, for she felt some intense emotion in her heart from standing there. It was warm. It felt as if it had been calling out for her to find it for many years. It seemed as if it had belonged to her.

Over against the side of the wall she noticed a bed of eucalyptus leaves raised above the floor, and she went over to it. She set her face down into the leaves and inhaled deeply. She could smell in them the blood of her womb, as if she had given birth there yesterday. This was where her son lay the day he had been taken from her. This was the very room where Unawqi had been raised.

"My knights! Go no further. Here lies my throne. From this room we shall restore the world."

The room grew tenfold in resplendent golden light as the butterflies concentrated their energy around her, such that they made the interior of the mountain a brighter place than the brightest moonbeam outside of the mountain.

Birds flying in the air, panthers and monkeys in the forest, and the people in the villages of Quijos, all could see the light glowing out of Antisana that night, heralding a new age. That is when they dropped the ploughs in their fields or left their places in the forest. They streamed to the mountain to pay homage to their queen, and take comfort in the warm light of their beloved and reborn mountain.

They brought their feasts, they shared their gifts of wool and fired clay, they built bridges and reoccupied abandoned homes. Thanks to the yellow butterflies, Antisana hurriedly became a shining beacon, as it had not been for near a millennium, lined with rich and colorful villages of proud people singing cheerful songs all through the night.

But none of this could bring as much joy to Tamaya's eyes than the sight of a completely unexpected guest from the north. It was Bachué, who despite her infirmity, had traveled all the way from Suamox without any companions, not even a horse to carry her.

Tamaya rushed to embrace her as if Bachué was her own mother.

Bachué had no sack on her back or provisions, but her right hand was clenched tight, holding something so precious, she feared letting it slip through her fingers. It would be her only gift to present to the queen.

Tamaya lifted Bachué's hand and opened her fingers. A soft rose light bloomed from her hand, and there in her palm was a single peach kernel that pulsed in and out like a beating heart.

"Never lose it, my dear girl, for this is Tapaipi, the precious link between you and the virtues of the universe. As long as you have it, it will bring you good. The day you plant it is the day you will decide to leave this world, and the day you will set it free."

Tamaya took the kernel carefully and put it in the fold between her breasts, where it was warm and secure, the place she had always saved for Unawqi.

As Tamaya walked the mother of the Sun through the palace of Antisana, Bachué was very impressed, and gave it her blessings, pulling up dust from the path, rubbing it in her hands to become lavender buds, and then blowing them into the air.

But when the queen asked for chambers to be prepared to give Bachué some well-deserved rest, Bachué explained she could not stay for more than a night for she had more grave matters to pursue.

Pulling Tamaya aside to whisper more privately, Bachué's face turned an ashen color. She explained with great sorrow that Titu, Tamaya's reunited love, was plotting to betray her once again, as he was drunken by his own greed to possess the power of the Sun, now that he was even closer to Aakti.

Since Bachué could not stop him in qanaq'wa makuyhana, she felt she must set out to block his path on Earth, and to do that she needed to move quickly and through the shadows.

Tamaya could not understand how Bachué came of this knowledge, but she did know Titu and his weaknesses, and she trusted Bachué like no one else.

Tamaya cried through the night, brokenhearted, even as Tapaipi beat between her breasts. Even though she was the anointed queen of Earth and had the adulation of thousands outside her door, she had never felt so alone and rejected. But the more she cried, the more Tapaipi fastened onto her, releasing its doses of tender affection into her body for greater days to come.

When Tamaya had finally cried herself to sleep, Bachué quietly entered the queen's bedroom and sat by her side, brushed aside her tear-soaked hair, and kissed her cheek. She then whispered into the queen's dreams:

"Live, like the beauty of a peach tree. Flower instead of suffer. When the rain falls upon your world, stretch out your limbs a little wider and let it embrace you for dear life, for the world will never leave you."

Bachué left the sleeping queen's bedside and found her way out of the mountain halls the same way she had come in. Mama Killa greeted her as she came out, and lit her way down the side of the mountain so Bachué would not require the aid of a torch.

Eventually, Bachué disappeared into the cloud forest where the cloak of huasquila concealed the direction of her journey.

23 THE PURSUING SHADOW

For the fisherman, there was only one way to bring Unawqi home. Once again, he needed the aid of Reventador and the condor to lift him to the Mama Killa, the Moon, and then for Mama Killa to be his ship to sail him through the celestial sea to qanaq'wa makuyhana.

The fisherman knew of the existence of Aakti's palace, long before anyone else.

Upon seeing his broken heartedness when he was sent away from Balao, and feeling so deeply pained that it was her fault, Mama Killa came to the fisherman as he drifted at sea, and assured him that Unawqi was alive, albeit not in this world.

This is all the fisherman needed to hear, and why he persisted in his search for Unawqi and his battle with Aakti, all the way to Suamox. It was why he stood so tall in the wake of the Sun's absence when all were grieving in Suamox. He believed in the word of Mama Killa, for she had once inflicted him with the greatest violation, and had lowered herself for his forgiveness. He had ridden to the Moon before, and she embraced him. She would not lie.

Qanaq'wa makuyhana was nothing more than another place to the fisherman. He loved Unawqi so much, the distance was a detail of no importance. All he needed to do was find a way to get there. Surely, Mama Killa could help him get part of the way, if not all of the way. She could carry him to one star, and then that star could bring him to the next, and so on.

To get to the Moon, he had done that before as well. The friends he needed were an even stronger fellowship than before. The hermit of Reventador was not just on his side, he had wed the fisherman to Unawqi, and their union was a commitment--not just understood but witnessed and blessed.

Having secured the journey of his mother-in-law, Tamaya, to her new home in Antisana, the fisherman and the chinchay hurried east to the uplands of Reventador, before the Moon could finish passing over.

As he came into the upland forests, the cypress stands grew thick, the streams louder, and the light of the moon fainter as it disappeared through the treetops.

The chinchay stopped abruptly, lifted her ears sharply, and looked behind her, for she heard something following them.

The fisherman noticed she was alarmed and he pulled his cleaning knife from his belt. Was it a hungry bear? They were still too far from Reventador for it to be the hermit himself.

They pressed on, but the chinchay kept stopping more frequently, and was growing more agitated at whatever was closing in on them, even though she could not see it. She started to shudder and growl, and this, in turn, made the fisherman unsure of what to do.

When at last they reached the base of the mountain, the fisherman was relieved, for they could now get out of the trees and climb the mountainside where they thought they might see better.

But they couldn't. Despite being out in the open, Mama Killa was low on the horizon on the other side of a facing canyon, so only very dim energy hovered in the air around them. And still the shuffle of stones and brush behind them grew closer. They were now practically running up the mountainside, but whatever it was, they could not outrun it.

At last they scrambled over a craggy rock to a wide space and were surprised at what appeared to be the faint outline of a large bird. If only they were one ridge higher, the Moon could shine over and they would be able to see for sure. Still, the fisherman was almost certain it was his friend, the condor of Reventador.

The bird moved its head to the side and lifted its wings a bit to show its bronze breast, and the fisherman sighed with gladness. Yes, it was him. The condor was there to greet them.

But no sooner had the smile come upon his face than a tall, black-cloaked stranger came from behind and threw his cloak up into the air. The cloak remained suspended in the air, blackening out any remaining light. The musty smell of soot permeated the air underneath the cloak, making the fisherman dizzy and short of breath.

He heard a gruff grunting voice behind him, then in front, then to his side – even breathing down his neck for a moment. He did not know in which direction to point himself for his own defense, the stranger seemed to be moving all around him at once.

The fisherman flashed his cleaning knife around in the air in random directions, stumbling over the uneven ground, growing more tired and bewildered.

He heard the condor's wings flapping, too, as if it was going to flee, but then it let out horrifying screams of pain, and continued to jump about in different directions. It sounded like it, too, was as trapped as was he.

The chinchay yowled and hissed, adding to the panic of the scene, and all together they crowded closer together, like fish being pulled up in a net.

The black-cloaked stranger started to laugh as he focused his voice more squarely on the fisherman, and the fisherman responded by thrashing his knife about with all his might.

But as his breath left him, so did his knife. He fell to the ground on his back and the impact knocked the wind out of his lungs and he began to pass out.

The next few seconds told a story in sounds so perplexing, he would spend the rest of his life trying to understand what truly happened.

There was first a silence, a pause in the commotion. The chinchay, the condor, and the stranger all stopped making noise simultaneously. Then there followed some trundling of feet, presumably that of the stranger. It sounded measured, like the stranger knew exactly where he was going, almost as if it were a choreographed dance. And then, the condor made the most eerie and slow shriek.

It was a blood curdling sound, starting low, then going higher in pitch as it beat its wings faster and faster still. It let out bursts of crying in pain, interrupted by gasps for breath, then screamed again, with longer stretches of silence in between each burst of desperate sound. It finally stopped beating its wings, and then stopped its screams, leaving only a silence, so long and cold it was like the noiseless interior of a tomb.

The fisherman lost consciousness, and when he awoke it was from a foot pushing against him to see if he was dead. He opened his eyes and wiped the blood and dust out of his mouth. The moonlight had returned, but it was now behind him, so he knew it had been several hours since he had passed out.

He looked up the leg pinning his body down to see the form of Reventador peering down at him, robed in a black cloak!

The fisherman's eyes scanned the scene around him, but the chinchay was nowhere to be seen. Perhaps she was hiding, or maybe she had found a way out.

Against the mountain wall, the fisherman caught sight of such a dreadful thing, he almost passed out again. The condor hung, strangled on a rope, its chest flayed open and its heart removed, and at the base of its feet lay the fisherman's cleaning knife, covered in the bird's blood.

The first thought in the fisherman's head was that the black-cloaked Reventador had killed his own son, and had for some reason, yet to kill the fisherman.

But why? What kind of warped tale had the fisherman walked into? Certainly, Reventador was known to be fierce, but the fisherman had also seen him to be just the opposite, a defender of higher virtues, of the best good, a merciful father, loyal to his family, and not a wanton slayer.

Something terrible must have happened between Reventador and the condor, and unfortunately the fisherman had unwittingly roamed into the middle of it.

Before he could think much more or let a word leave his mouth, Reventador lunged his foot into the side of the fisherman's head, knocking him unconscious once again.

Reventador picked up the fisherman and threw him over his shoulder, leaving the plateau by a narrow path going up the mountain.

"I would not give you the honor of rotting on the ridge of my mountain," the hermit said as he made his climb. "I will see nothing less than your flesh boil in my fire, and then dissolve into dust at my feet."

24 KUKANIBO

She darted from behind one bush to the next and stayed off the main path, for Bachué knew she was in a forbidden place and there were watchers everywhere.

Forbidden, even though it was because of her the place had any repute.

It was Kukanibo, the jungle of the bridge at the end of the world, the trail of Amaru, from where Bachué dispatched her son, Aakti, to rule the sky.

But now, entering the same place was a promise of death. Tungurahua had long claimed Kukanibo for himself and guarded it jealously. He wanted the world to forget it altogether, flooding it often to erase traces of paths, and planting poisonous vines and insects. What is more, the plants and insects had ears, and were bound to tell their master of anything they saw entering that did not belong.

Bachué moved cautiously, looking for anything that would be looking back at her. She had no choice but to be there. She was the only one who could destroy the bridge, and if she did not, Titu would soon use the bridge to return to Earth and change the order of the cosmos, making Aakti his slave.

The bridge could not be far away, but Tungurahua had made the forest so thick, everything blocked her path. She thought of using her powers to burn her way through, but that would make too much smoke and most certainly get her noticed. All she could do was slide, lean, and crawl, one leaf and branch at a time, and be as quiet as the charapa turtle floating through the lily pads.

Without sunlight, Kukanibo had grown rotten and dank. There was a thin covering of mucus over every stone and branch, and the ponds and rivers were choked with algae. It was no longer the wildly beautiful and sultry place she remembered so many years before, and she was acutely aware it had become the way it was now because of her own decision to confront Aakti that had led to him to being cast out.

For good reason, the bridge was the best kept secret on Earth. Not even the priests of Suamox knew of it, and because of this, it was the missing link in their knowledge of how the Sun rose to the sky. All their volumes in all their many libraries devoted to explaining the origins and shape of the world in which they lived, were absent of any notion of the bridge of Kukanibo. Without it, their knowledge only concluded in questions as to how Amaru could make his transit between the lower and the higher worlds.

Here, Bachué was so near the answer to all the questions they had wondered about for millennia, just a few more thickets away.

She pushed her way through one more stand of towering lupuna trees and rolled her old body down a bank and into a brackish fen.

When she stood back up, she noticed the water around her legs did not move--there were no ripples; she was not even wet. She knew she was no longer in a place of this world.

She turned around to look up the other side of the ditch and had to cover her mouth from her shock being audible.

It was more magnificent than what she remembered.

Towering above her was the crossing to the stars, the bridge so ancient it had been created before time by gods so primordial, no one even knew their names, not even the mother of the Sun.

Bachué beheld its eerie beauty for a moment --- its boney white spires; the massive stone buttresses that stretched out like the wings of a prehistoric dragon and disappeared into black space; the asymmetrical arches underneath the span that together formed no pattern and looked more like the tangled roots of a mangrove cypress; and the span itself, so mesmeric it could drive a man mad, for it was like looking into a million mirrors.

She could not see anything solid to place her feet on, only flecks of stars, reflections of the bodies above and beneath, blinking in and out and moving from left to right as if the universe itself were two halves moving past each other.

She couldn't even discern where the bridge connected to land, so how could she tear it down?

Bachué had put all her hope for that answer in the strange contraption, the demon she had removed from the wall in her home and carried in her pouch all the way from Suamox. She pulled it out, set it down on the ground, laid her head on it like a pillow, and listened.

She listened until she could hear her own heartbeat echoing within the metal orb, knocking on the door to the other side of the universe, waiting for someone to answer. She waited so long that she fell asleep but was then awoken by a voice coming from within the demon.

It was Titu, muttering what sounded like some incantation.

As he spoke, the demon glowed blue and sent out what looked like thousands of snakes lit up with the same blue light toward the bridge. When the blue snakes faded into the morass of the bridge, the demon crawled like a crab back into Bachué's pouch.

The span to the bridge lit up with the blue incandescence the snakes delivered, and the myriad of stars around it pulled together to form beaded pearls of light, making the path across visible and solid.

Bachué thought for a moment. She could walk to the heavens herself. She could cross over, right now, and arrive to qanaq'wa makuyhana to settle affairs. But what if the bridge closed behind her? Who would open it again?

No, she couldn't cross over. There was too much to finish here on Earth where she was needed.

She resolved to burn it instead. It would be for the better if she no longer had this temptation, to let the Heavens and the Earth fend for themselves without a crutch. The time for the bridge needed to end.

She stood up on her feet, arched back her spine, and raised her arms above her head like the shape of a flame. Her eyes turned as black as the back of a beetle, and her skin started to weep like melting wax. There was a snap, and her body ignited into a fire, but she was not consumed by it. She then lowered her arms, keeping her hands together, and directed the flame forward to the arches at the base of the bridge, setting them ablaze.

Given a little more time it would have worked, but just then, Bachué noticed a solid black spot coming up a portion of the beaded span, growing larger as it moved toward her. Perhaps that was Amaru, she thought, slithering back from qanaq'wa makuyhana.

She also heard an increasing array of buzzing insects around her head, and the black circle moving toward her changed into an oblong shape with limbs, and eventually she could discern it was walking and wearing a black cloak.

Bachué was surrounded by the insects, who had the faces of snakes and centipedes, and they hovered in space, entrapping her until the hooded figure broke through their circle.

It was not Amaru. It was Tungurahua!

Bachué looked at him spitefully, neither surprised he had found her, nor allowing him to distract her from what she was doing.

In most places, Bachué had greater powers than Tungurahua, but not here. Kukanibo was so well weaved with Tungurahua's traps and tricks, he could draw up any of them to counter whatever Bachué might throw at him.

This is why he was in no hurry to catch up to her and rather calmly walked around her, his arms folded, studying her technique. He eventually shrugged his shoulders, and from underneath his hooded head, blew some air and smoke combined toward the bridge, extinguishing her fire. The smoke then backed up to Bachué herself, forcing her to fall on the ground, coughing and gasping for air.

As the smoke lifted, Tungurahua stood over Bachué and said, "You appear to be so far from home, old woman, but burning your way out of my garden is a rather harsh measure."

He lifted her up off the ground, and she spat on his feet.

"Your garden? You know very well this is sacred ground and belongs to no one to touch. We are well beyond your mountain."

"If that is so, then why are you touching it so destructively, Bachué?"

"I cannot say." Bachué turned her head away, brushing the dirt from her clothes.

Tungurahua waited a bit for her to change her mind, but she avoided looking at him. So, he countered, "I will make you a deal, Bachué."

Bachué glared back at him. "How dare you? You are in no position to bargain with me, you wayward child!"

"I'm afraid times have changed since you threw out your son, old woman. He now speaks through me, and you are no longer important to him."

"The emperor would never abandon his mother."

"No, but his mother has abandoned him."

This silenced Bachué, and she swiftly swept away the tear he had brought to her face.

"Yes, I understand," Tungurahua continued. "The pain of this situation is heavy on your heart. Your son feels the same. He would gladly return to you if you would only let us know the whereabouts of the fisherman."

Bachué squinted her eyes with suspicion. "The fisherman? What is it you want with the fisherman?"

"His...services, as an aide to the emperor's return, of course."

"I don't believe you," Bachué said, shaking her head. "He is no concern of yours, and he has no more power than that of a mortal."

Tungurahua breathed in deeply. "If you do not wish to take my offer, then--"

"Then what!" Bachué snapped back. "You know there is nothing you can do to me. You are nothing to me but a meddlesome little tyrant. Snuff me out if you wish, or let me continue with what I was doing."

"Neither interest me, spider of Suamox. You are clearly in our way and we need to find you a dark corner to shrivel up in."

Tungurahua then motioned for his flying insects, and they swarmed around Bachué's arms and stung her with venom, causing her to fall asleep. They lifted her off the ground and into the air, sweeping her away from Kukanibo. They carried her over the orchid mountains, west toward the sea, all the way to Balao. There they laid her slumbering body at the doorstep of the house of Qayqa huk'ucha.

Seeing the old woman on his threshold and the ugly bugs that put her there, Ernest Heatheridge knew this could only be the doing of Tungurahua, and he called for his wife's help to bring the old woman inside and put her in a bed until she could awaken.

Ernest then left the room, letting Naira tend to the old woman. Naira lifted Bachué's head up to adjust the pillow underneath, but as she lowered her head back down on the pillow and brushed her hair to the side, Naira gasped.

Out of the pouch around the old woman's waist peeked the phototeledar, the very thing Naira had given Tamaya the night she was sent away from Balao!

Naira wondered how Tamaya could have aged this much in such a brief time. Was this the effect of the Moon, or the lack of the Sun? Was this Tamaya at all?

Troubled deeply, Naira covered Bachué up in a blanket, but left the door open a crack so she would be the first to know when she woke up.

The buzzing insects flew away and the howls of Tungurahua could be heard high in the ever-darkening clouds that challenged the Moon for space in the sky.

Naira feared the worst was coming to Balao, and waited anxiously for the story the old woman had to tell.

25 HEARTLESS

It had been a long time since the woman with the red clay hair had talked with her grandmother, Bachué.

At first, she thought perhaps Bachué had gone foraging up at Lake Tota for seeds to recultivate the temple garden. But it had been days since she was gone, so she asked the priests, who themselves appeared to be packing for a journey.

Ever since the woman with the red clay hair's arrival at Suamox, the priests both feared and respected her, but found her an intrusion upon their authority. Her question had raised suspicious looks on their faces, as if she had found something out she was not ordained to know. She felt they were thinking that she had done something malevolent with Bachué, and her line of questioning was just an alibi.

The priests responded that they did not know the answer to her question, but then asked why it had taken her so long to come to them, and which direction she thought the emperor's mother had gone. The distrustful questions disturbed the woman with the red clay hair, for she was neither accusing them nor inviting them to accuse her. So, she walked away and left the priests to fester in their suspicions.

She then asked the birds, starting from the largest, the noisy chachalaca. The bird had not seen Bachué because she always avoided his bluster, anyway. The woman with the red clay hair then proceeded to each smaller and shier bird, the potoo, the tinamou, the pipit, and the tapaculo. None of them had seen the comings or goings of Bachué.

But then the woman with the red clay hair found the sapayoa, the most reclusive little bird of them all, who because her feathers were so green, Bachué did not see standing next to a leaf of the same shade.

The sapayoa said that it saw Bachué several days in the past, walking alongside the river headed south.

This seemed to suggest that Bachué might have taken the Guayuriba Road on her way to Reventador, perhaps to secure some aid from the hermit. The road was a dangerous one, so why would she decide to go in secret, without telling her granddaughter where she was going?

When she arrived back at the house of Bachué, the woman with the red clay hair noticed that the demon on the wall had disappeared, and she was afraid that perhaps it had kidnapped her grandmother.

With each passing moment, she felt more unsafe in Suamox, and even more, feared for her grandmother's safety. She decided to set out at once to find her.

Not trusting the Guayariba way, the woman with the red clay hair hurried herself through the pampa, and then across the open plains to east of Suamox, before cutting back southwest into the cloud forest.

When she crossed the river Churuyaco, she could hear Reventador in the distance, smoking and blowing steam, which meant he was quite angry about something.

She picked up her pace and eventually ran into a yucca farmer coming the other way, who said everyone was fleeing Reventador's valleys for they had never seen him this angry before.

The woman with the red clay hair asked him if he had seen Bachué there. The farmer told her he did not know who, but Reventador was indeed holding someone as his prisoner, which seemed to be the object of his rage. This made the woman with the red clay hair frantic, and she ran away from the farmer toward the mountain in great haste.

She climbed the side of the mountain, scraping and bruising herself as she went, trying to reach the hermit before he did something terrible. She could not understand what could turn him so quickly from the generosity he had displayed at the wedding. Whatever it was, her grandmother was not deserving of his terror.

When at last she broke the summit to the ridge above the gaseous furnace, she could hear the hermit roaring at the top of his lungs, making heated accusations against, not her grandmother at all, but the fisherman!

Pinned against a rock was the fisherman. The hermit paced around him, greatly agitated and shaking his fist. The woman with the red clay hair climbed down into the crater to get closer. The hermit saw her coming and spat fire her way. She easily brushed it away, for the fire of her own increasing anger was stronger.

She walked into the hermit's camp and knocked him down with her stick, demanding he explain himself for punishing a mere mortal in such a way.

"The blood of my son is on this murderer's hands," Reventador said, pointing his finger at the fisherman. "The great condor is dead!"

The fisherman contested, "No, this is not true. I have told you, I was seeking the condor, but not to kill him."

"Lies! It was your blade that cut out his heart. I found it there."

"It was my blade, but I did not use it."

The fisherman then tried to recount his story, how he was trying to seek the aid of Reventador to reach the Moon, but that a ghost followed him, dressed the same as the hermit.

This infuriated Reventador even more, affronted at the accusation of being the killer of his own son.

The fisherman was sure of himself, though, and continued to indict the hermit,

"Indeed, it was you. Only you could have blackened the night and covered up the Moon!"

The woman with the red clay hair listened to the storm between them, but one thing stuck out in her mind and made her face grow pale.

"Wait!" she commanded. "Did you say the heart of the condor was cut out?"

"Yes, and with the fisherman's knife!" the hermit replied, holding it up to his prisoner's throat.

She pulled the hermit's arm back, and put herself in between the two to set her blind eyes into the fisherman's eyes. "And did you say you were followed until you reached the condor?"

"Yes, and that is when he," he said, pointing his finger at the hermit, "attacked us, both me and the chinchay."

The woman with the red clay hair shook her head in disbelief. She looked as if she were about to faint. She spread the eyelids of the fisherman and laid her hand over them until she could read into his memory and replay the scene of the night, then fell backwards onto the ground in horror.

"He followed you," she said, "to lead him to his prey. But it was not Reventador."

She then turned her face to the hermit. "Reventador, how could you not see it? Only one beast would have need for the heart of the condor. We have company of our own kind…a much worse matter than this innocent man."

Her face sunk with a terrible look of fear, and her hands began to shake.

"Moche has returned!"

26 DEFIANCE

It all started as a small brush fire, but that's all he needed to retake his mountain.

Moche broke open an achiote fruit, let the glistening red seeds catch the moonlight, and then into their membranes he dropped a single bead of blood from the condor's heart. The fruit set alight, and Moche let it roll off his hand and into the fallen eucalyptus leaves at his feet. Each burning leaf rolled down the mountainside, sparking new fires as it went, until they spilled into the Rit'i Siqi Creek.

But instead of the river quenching the fire, the flaming achiote turned the river into oil, which then itself burst into flames and continued spreading the fire downstream like a racing orange snake.

In no time at all it reached the river Quijos and then the river Tamboyaco, setting those ablaze, too, until the entire mountain was encircled in a ring of river fire.

Moche continued scaling the mountain from the western side, sprinkling the condor's blood on thickets and dry grass as he went burning Antisana using the prevailing eastward winds to send the greasy smoke over and around the summit to the interior's main access.

The char stained Antisana black so that its frame could not be seen against the night sky. The villagers encamped on the eastern slope soon caught wind of the noxious smoke and gas. Still more came running up the mountainside, fleeing the river of fire, crying out for Tamaya to save them.

Tamaya heard them and raced outside. She saw everything burning, and the people dying and gasping for air. She called them to come inside, but they would not go because they feared the traces of Moche's evil on the walls within.

It was then that Moche scaled the summit, above and behind Tamaya, holding up the condor's heart in his right hand. He hurled the heart down toward the gate.

As the condor's heart bounced and rolled down the mountainside, huge columns of rock, gas, and ash piled into the air, forcing wild animals to run toward the choking crowds.

It was total chaos. Antisana was besieged on all sides, and Moche had no intention of mercy.

"Run if you will, you fools; you will die even faster," Moche screamed from the mountaintop, swirling black smoke at his back. "You thought you could get rid of me so easily. If you are lucky to get away, your nightmares of today will not, for this is Moche's mountain!"

He breathed in deeply like a dragon and pointed his head towards the sky, exhaling a pillar of fire as red as the condor's blood. When he closed his mouth, he glared down toward the gate with eyes burning with the same heat.

"And for you, the wench who defiles my door, dare not go back inside, for I will burn you out. Yes, I know your name, Tamaya, for it was me who saved your life and raised your child in this mountain. Your debt is not repaid, Tamaya, but three times greater. I have not forgotten that you tried to kill me in Balao, and now you try to usurp my throne! There is only a simple choice for your crime. Become my eternal slave…or die!"

Moche would waste no time waiting for her answer, and as the fire fell back down from the sky like rain, he marched down from the summit in his smoldering black cloak.

He had made just a few strides before he heard a rumbling at his feet. It was not an avalanche. It was not an eruption. It was much fiercer than that.

From behind Tamaya's back bolted the knights of Antisana, so many yellow butterflies that they split open the sides of the mountain and shot into the air, their wings blowing back the burning smoke and creating a towering wall over Moche.

The sorcerer vomited fire out of his mouth in defense, but they were too swift for him and dodged it, or opened a hole between them and let the fire go right through. They kept coming out of the mountain by the thousands, more than even Tamaya knew she had, and they swarmed as large as clouds on the right and left of Moche, forcing him to scramble back up and over the summit.

There on the western side, the butterflies and Moche engaged in battle, a million to one. Still, Moche was a force beyond measure, and the butterflies could not force him back much further. He was cunning and could eventually outsmart them or exhaust them, after which there would be nothing in his path.

As the people started to pick themselves back up and regroup after the initial onslaught, they saw that the rivers below them still raged with flames. There was no way out, and Tamaya did not know how to lead her people to safety.

She looked into the air above her and saw what at first, she thought were falling flakes of ash, but when they landed around her feet, she saw they were the skeletons of butterfly wings. Her army was not invincible and would only buy her a little more time.

The tears from her eyes fell off her cheek, dropped onto her chest and rolled down onto Tapaipi, the peach kernel between the folds of her breast. Tapaipi began to beat and breathe, and then from above her head a single drop of water fell from the top of the gate. She looked up and another fell. She put her hand up, and more drops fell into her hand in a trickle.

It was spring water from deep within the mountain, the head of all the rivers, unpoisoned by Moche's fire and that must have been opened when the butterflies cracked open small faults when they exploded out from the gate.

She let her hands fill up with the stream, and then poured it out into a crease of the mountainside going steep downhill. Her tears turned into laughter, and some old men watching her understood it. They came around her, reaching their hands out into cups to catch the falling spring, undaunted by the equally falling flames, and releasing their handfuls of water into the same channel.

The rest of the people joined in, catching spring drip wherever they could find it, clinging to the side of the mountain and pouring it in handfuls into the channel. Together they built a river of their own, and kept it flowing with their bare hands. Even though it was small, it was pure, it was them, and it was defiant.

Defiance

The hand-made stream flowed down the mountainside until it came to the bank of the Quijos and cut a path right through the burning river, like a knife separating meat from the bone.

It would be just enough to let some of the smallest and frail escape, and hopefully find someone on the other side to come to their aid.

27 CONDOR ROAD

Reventador smelled burning in the air. He wiped his face and then looked at his palm. It came away soiled with ash.

"Hurry with me to the top!" he commanded, quickly setting aside his raging interrogation of the fisherman.

Along with the fisherman and the woman with the red clay hair, the three scrambled up through narrow crags and across thin ledges until there was no higher place to climb. Reventador looked southwest and saw for himself that Antisana was burning.

"Moche!" he said, pointing at the mountain afire in the distance. "We must go before it's too late."

Knowing they would not have enough time to get there on foot, Reventador started digging a hole, clawing at the cold soil with his fingers. When the hole was deep enough, he put his whole arm down in it, feeling around for something beneath the surface.

"Stand back!" he said, and pulled out his arm. He rolled away, and from the hole shot a geyser of steam and hot air.

"Watch me now and do the same."

Reventador took his cloak and stretched it out like a blanket next to the shooting geyser, then curled himself into a ball inside the cloak, pulling the corners over him until he was fully wrapped.

He then shouted at the geyser "Uray!" and the geyser went back down into the ground, at which point he rolled himself over on top of the hole and shouted "Haku!" and the geyser shot up again, firing Reventador into the sky, high into the mountain currents where his son, the condor, used to sail.

Suspended in the sky, he unfurled himself out of the cloak, but held on to the corners until they formed a pocket to suspend the current over his head and glide him downward to the Quijos Canyon, closer to Antisana.

The fisherman went next, taking off his shirt and using it to repeat the same scheme the hermit demonstrated; and then the woman with the red clay hair repeated it with her punchu.

As wind currents are capricious, this one did not carry them all to the same landing place. Reventador landed on a sandbar in the middle of the Tamboyaco River, and the wind carried the woman with the red clay hair into the cloud forest, not far away.

But the geyser shot the fisherman into a whole different air stream, pushing him further west than the others, and brought him down on a grassy plain on the western side of Antisana where the road heads to and from Pasochoa.

When he rolled to a stop, he looked up and could see the raging battle between Moche and the Pasochoa butterflies but saw no sight of the hermit or the woman with the red clay hair.

He thought for a moment about running further west to freedom, for he did not know if Reventador had fully released him from judgment. It was an unsettled issue. However, he couldn't think of any other person to help him with his passage to the Moon, and Tamaya, his mother-in-law, was clearly in trouble.

So, he put his shirt back on and ran toward Antisana instead of away from it, hoping to find the others along the way.

He did not get far.

When he came to the Pasochoa Road and began to cross it, he was struck by a palm whip around his ankles and fell to the ground. Another whip lashed around his neck, and he was soon surrounded by a mob dressed in gold and white robes, a group he recognized immediately but never expected to see so far from their home.

It was the priests of Suamox, and they promptly gagged and bound him, threw him in a cart, and covered him with their provisions. Knowing there were probably others looking for him, the priests hastened southward into the Pasochoa Forest for cover. Suamox had seen its last day. They were on their way with their trophy to the new capital, the promised new temple of Balao.

When the woman with the red clay hair emerged from the forest, she saw Reventador in the middle of the burning river that Moche had set ablaze, but there was nothing she could do to rescue him.

The seeds she carried in her pouch could only grow things, but she couldn't grow water to douse the fire.

She could, however, call for rain. It would not be easy. Puyo Supai had always been fickle with her loyalties. She was Moche's mistress one day, then taking comfort in Mama Killa the next. Whose friend would she be today? Whose enemy?

The woman with the red clay hair could only hope to be lucky, and she called out to the monkeys in the forest to make the rain noise, and to make it loudly. They responded and Reventador heard them, catching on to the woman with the red clay hair's idea. He joined in by clapping his hands together. Each clap bounced off the sides of the canyon until it sounded like thunder.

Eventually, Puyo Supai heard them calling and came from the east where she had been sleeping over the rainforest. Clouds become agitated by noise and react by making a greater noise to silence it all. So, Puyo Supai came and released her torrents to quiet everything down.

The rain poured down on the flaming river and filled the stream that Tamaya and the people had started down the side of Antisana, turning it into a rushing river that crashed into the Tamboyaco and flooded the sandbar, lifting the hermit off and sending him downstream a ways until he washed up on the bank. There he crawled out and met the woman with the red clay hair, reaching her hand out to help him.

As they could see no sign of the fisherman, they assumed he had had come down closer to the mountain, or that he may be on the mountain itself. So they started climbing Antisana with the hope they would eventually catch up with him and help Queen Tamaya in her distress.

When they came to the fork where the Tamboyaco joined the new river, they followed the new one up the mountain, for a steep flowing watercourse like this would keep them safe and certainly lead them to Tamaya.

It was a salvific stream, the only path up the burning mountain, and a river that Reventador would eventually come to name the Condor Road.

28 TUNGURAHUA'S TOWER

Balao had fallen.

What once were streets full of stalls selling crabs, shrimp, bananas, and gold, were now all burning with crucibles of lava supplied by Tungurahua himself. They created an awful black and oily smoke that coated the town and all the mangroves around it with a thick sludge.

Out of their primitive soup bubbling red and blue, Heatheridge was overseeing the production of various shapes of quartz block. These were then carried off to the clearing, the same one where Unawqi had his fateful and ultimate battle, for there Tungurahua was using the quartz to build a massive tower, stacking the blocks high into the sky. They gleamed like blue beacons all the way to the top of the tower.

The intent of Tungurahua's spire would be to conduct an energy current that would be sufficient to burn open a hole in space through which Unawqi could be contacted, and if Unawqi, then all those in the qanaq'wa makuyhana.

Through the portal would Aakti then return, but only if Unawqi laid the path, for only he had the unique ability to do so. This is why Tungurahua needed the fisherman, to call Unawqi and draw him to act.

What Tungurahua did not know was that he did not need to build the monstrous tower at all. He could do the same thing with the phototeledar if he even knew it existed!

The closest he had come to it was in Kukanibo where it was concealed in Bachué's pouch and was now resting at her bedside in the house of Qayqa huk'ucha.

So the work went on: firing, scorching, forging, and stacking up the spire so high it seemed like it was a needle pricking the side of the Moon.

Inside her house, Naira could hear her guest waking, coughing, and yawning as she tried to raise herself from her long rest. Naira leaned over her with a cup of water and some fried plantain to nourish her.

"Where am I?" Bachué asked.

"You are here, back in Balao," Naira replied, looking deeply into the old woman's eyes to see if she could recognize the young Tamaya behind them.

"Back?" Bachué said, startled. "I have never been to such a place. And who are ---"

"But the metal spider in your pouch. Don't you remember? It was me who gave it to you when you were last here in Balao, the night your son was taken."

Bachué took another sip of water and started to put the story together.

"Tamaya. You gave it to Tamaya, I believe. Here. Wherever here is."

Naira now was taciturn, realizing this old woman was not Tamaya, but not knowing how an old woman came to possess what Naira had given to a much younger woman.

Naira then explained to Bachué how she had been laid at their doorstep by the flying beasts of Tungurahua, and that Tungurahua had taken control of the town and charged her husband, Ernest, to oversee production of the material to build the great spire that would bring the return of the Sun. Tungurahua, she explained, had promised that Ernest's reward would be consecrating Balao as the new temple of Aakti, replacing some place called 'Suamox'.

Bachué grew troubled at hearing this but became even more so as Naira continued to explain. Bachué's incomplete mission was still to destroy the bridge, for Titu was most certainly near to crossing it, and that would mean a horrible reversal of astral power.

But upon hearing that Naira's husband had sent some men of the town to find and capture a fisherman that they had previously let leave Balao the same day as Tamaya, Bachué felt she must somehow split herself in two directions.

Naira shared they wanted to bring the fisherman back to Balao now, but for Bachué, Naira didn't need to explain why. Bachué saw it clearly; it was to lure Unawqi into a trap.

"Stop!" Bachué ordered, not able to listen anymore. "You must help me leave at once, while there is still time."

"Time for what?" Naira asked innocently.

"Time to save who you think I am, and her entire world from a most certain death. She may have left here as a stranger, but she is now your queen."

"I cannot leave my hus---"

"You must! If you love him, you must, and now. There can be no farewell, or Balao will perish before tomorrow."

Bachué took Naira's hand, the same way Naira had held Tamaya's hand in the same bed. It felt warm and kind, clean of the impurities that were smothering Balao, a hand that felt like it had caressed many crying children to sleep. Bachué's eyes were pleading for help, better than any words could say.

"Come with me," she said, "I need you so terribly much!"

Naira's motherly instinct put her arms around Bachué's head and pulled her towards her neck. She did not know that the old woman she was holding like a baby was the greatest living power on Earth, the very mother of Aakti, the emperor, the Sun. All Naira knew was that this old woman was frail and sincere, and deeply connected to Tamaya.

Naira had never been outside of Balao. She had also never felt the urgency for leaving it as she did now. Her decision was impulsive, she knew, but she also knew there was something of a divine quality in Bachué's call that she couldn't ignore.

She picked up the pouch, gave it to Bachué, then put on her shawl and grabbed some walking sticks. The two left the house through the back door and went into the small trails through the mangrove forest Naira had used to gather frogs. She did not even tarry to snuff the candles out.

They simply left, and let the black mangrove be their last witness.

29 THE WESTERN DEEP

Perhaps no one will ever understand, not even in a million years, why Tamaya chose to do what she did on that most bitter of days at Antisana. No one, of course, except Tamaya herself.

She was encircled on all sides. Her young reign called for a heroic act, and her people were ready to fight at the sound of her call. The river they had fashioned from their own hands, given a little more time, was going to change the course of the battle in her favor. The knights were fighting their enemy valiantly and keeping him at bay.

All she had to do was shout back a call to arms. When she saw the new river was tumbling down the mountainside, she felt hope that the fires at the basin would subside.

As she looked up at the source of the stream above the Antisana Gate, where it all started, she caught sight of a simple spider web, moistened by the dew of the stream, which made the web sparkle.

Entranced by the small distraction, she approached it closer, and was admiring the perfection of nature that it was when the spider's leg pierced one of the dew drops, which in turn cast a tiny spindle of light out into the dark entrance of Antisana.

The spindle of light traveled even further, deep into the cavernous interior. There, the light hit a small pool, casting the reflection of another light above it, like a window deep inside the mountain opening to the other side.

Tamaya had never seen such an opening before, and she took the spider's act as a sign. She followed the dew beam back into the caverns, leaving her butterflies to continue on their own. Was it a piece of glass? A diamond? Another door?

Through the byzantine paths carved on the side of the cavern walls she made her way into a series of chambers she had never been to before. They smelled so much older, perhaps unvisited even before Moche's time.

But then she lost track of the light and she stumbled around in the complete darkness.

She was lost in her own mountain.

When she stopped to rest, the sound of stumbling continued, and she realized she was not alone.

"I'll get you, you wench! Ha! You won't even realize I've already taken my mountain back."

It was the voice of Moche. He had accessed entry to the mountain through the western side, a rear portal, which must have been the same light she was pursuing.

But instead of lunging out at him, Tamaya decided to use the darkness to her advantage. She followed the contour of the wall in the direction she had arguably been going, whispering as she went.

"Moche, it is I, the mountain. It has been a long time since you left."

Moche stopped cold in his steps, trying to detect the location from where the whisper was coming, but since it was a large chamber, the voice bounced from one wall to the other.

"Antisana?"

There was a pause, as Tamaya smiled upon her cunning trick.

"Yessss. Welcome home, Moche."

"My lady, indeed a victory to be your servant again, but it's been so long I can't find my way. Guide me as you have done before."

Tamaya treaded some more along the wall, looking to see if she could regain sight of the rear portal.

"Yes, Moche, you are not far. But first, tell me what became of you? I had heard you had left this world?"

Moche squinted intensely. He too did not know the western deep, and he could see no glimmer of light, no matter which way he looked.

"My lady, I thought you would know, but perhaps even your greatness is growing old. I came back across the forbidden bridge, there in Kukanibo."

Tamaya did not know of it.

"Koo-ka-neee-bo. Ahhhh yes! Oh, but Moche, why did you do what is forbidden?"

"I will tell you, my lady, for you are mine, and I am yours, but you must swear to me my answer will never leave the hollow of this black pit."

"This black pit," Tamaya replied, "is my heart. I swear upon it."

"Very well. The bridge is in danger, and may soon fall. Bachué already tried to destroy it—"

"Bachué? Our emperor's mother?"

"Yes," Moche continued, "and she would have succeeded if Tungurahua hadn't gotten to her first. I had to cross, for if she returns…"

Moche paused and swallowed the thought.

"Continue, my true one."

"She knows where Kukanibo is, and if she should succeed in returning to it, she will not fail a second time, and then Aakti will never be able to return."

Tamaya felt her way now to a smooth boulder, and went around it, and looked up. There she saw the open portal.

Moche called out, "My lady, time is fleeting. Tamaya will soon discover I am missing. I beg you, tell me the way out!"

There was no reply. Tamaya was scrambling up to the portal, and upon reaching it, heard Moche's desperate cry for help, imprisoned in his own mountain.

She crawled out of the hole, not much larger than the width of her own body, and found herself surrounded by a small band of her yellow knights, weakened and sullied, but still an encouraging sight.

On the western side, it was smoky and desolate. She felt no longer a queen there. She felt free from the burden, more like the goat herdess she used to be, and with nothing between her and the Pasochoa forest down below.

No one knew where she was, and that emboldened her. She looked up at the butterflies and questioned their strength to carry her, for no doubt the battle had sapped them dry.

Until, at least, one landed on her forearm, shaking the dust from his wings, happy to see her.

She smiled back at him and asked, "Do you know how to get to…Kukanibo?"

30 THE MUD RUT

They pushed south through the coastal lowlands under the pale Moon.

For the fisherman, the pain was maddening laying captive beneath the pile of wool blankets on the flat wooden bed of a wagon. Every stone the wagon went over felt like running into a tree. He would much prefer to walk if his captors, the priests, would let him, but they were traveling with haste and spared no time to listen. The only thing beneficial about his being buried under the pile was that he was protected from the splashes of mud and swarms of starving mosquitoes.

After several hours travel, he felt a steep dip of the wagon's wheel beneath him, along with a loud crack, followed by raised voices exclaiming insults at each other. The wagon stopped, and much of the cargo shifted or fell off the side.

One of the Suamox priests pulled the blankets from on top of the fisherman and urged him to get out. The wagon had gotten stuck in a mud rut and they needed to get all of the weight out of the back in order to lift themselves on to a drier patch.

The fisherman got out slowly and fell to the ground, his joints stiff from the grueling journey.

The priests cursed him and spat on his head, calling him a worthless ingrate, and he curled up into a ball to protect himself.

But then a smaller figure broke through the ring, a young girl who carried herself with some authority. Admonishing the priests, she held out her hand, lifted the fisherman to his feet, sat him against a small tree, and charged one of the priests to stand over the prisoner while she directed the rest of them to free the wagon.

The fisherman looked at her and found her to be an odd member in the mix. She wore no priest's clothing, and her accent was not from Suamox but something closer to his own, seasoned with tones from people working near the sea.

He did not recognize her, but before she left him, she looked into his eyes as if she knew him.

It was Qina, daughter of Ernest and Naira, the first betrothed of Unawqi, who had slipped her own wedding ring on to the fisherman's hand as he slept his last night in Balao.

Qina had been assigned by her father to lead the band and find the fisherman. She had gone all the way to Suamox, and not having found him there, enlisted the help of the priests.

As she withdrew from the fisherman at the tree, she slid her hand over his ring most tenderly, as if wanting to send him a message.

The priests heaved and pushed the wagon back and forth until they were finally able to wrest it out of the mud.

Naira and Bachué were on their journey north and saw the broken wagon in the mud rut from a distance.

Bachué stopped Naira from going further, sensing some danger in the situation. She reached down into her pouch, put her hand on the phototeledar and closed her eyes. The object pulsed energy through her arm and helped her feel there was a great power in and amongst the crowd ahead. She was certain it was the fisherman, and knew this was her opportunity to save him.

Feeling it was a dangerous scene for them to risk being seen together, Bachué turned to Naira and handed her the pouch, instructing her to keep it safe and to go into the bush and around to the opposite side of the gang where they would meet again to resume their journey.

If they did not meet there, Bachué told Naira she should hurry on forward to Antisana and deliver the pouch to Tamaya, staying out of sight until she got there.

Naira found Bachué's words distressing, for she was younger than Bachué and she worried for the old woman. So instead of stealing into the bush, Naira stayed on the road and watched from behind.

Bachué walked toward the priests intrepidly, for these were her own people – indeed, she was their goddess. She walked into their melee and they stopped immediately and fell to the ground, astonished at her appearance there among them.

She saw the fisherman being held up against the tree at their perimeter. He smiled at her, but at this moment Bachué needed to be at her most serious, and she did not smile back.

"Bachué," one of the young priests said, "how good it is to see you coming from Balao, for that is where we are headed."

"Silence!" the head priest interrupted, chiding his novice, and giving Bachué a patronizing grin. "The great Bachué has not asked you to speak."

"Balao, you said?" Bachué asked. "And what business does Suamox bring to Balao?"

The priests were silent, afraid to speak, looking to the head priest to reply for them. But he was guarded, looking for words.

"Very well," Bachué continued, "seeing you have no business in Balao, I will tell you that you will find nothing holy there, and therefore I order you to turn back and go home at once."

The head priest spoke reluctantly. "We cannot."

"Why not?"

"We have been summoned."

"Who gives you summons but me?"

"Your son, the emperor, our great Bachué."

Bachué heaved a deep sigh of disappointment.

"I thought for all of your years of training you should know better. The emperor was cast out, and by me!"

"Yes, our great mother. What you say is true, but his return is imminent if we but deliver---"

"His return?! Nothing of the kind is imminent unless I say so. Who has been feeding you these orders? Enough of this insolence. Turn around and go back at once!"

"He has a viceroy," the high priest said, closing his eyes to shield himself from Bachué's certain anger.

But Bachué already knew of whom the high priest was speaking. She looked at them with heavy eyes, saddened that their lives had come to this: veritable treason, and an abandonment of loyalty to her will. Inside she felt powerless to change their minds, but she did not want to appear to them that way on her outside.

"What changed you?" Bachué asked the high priest. "You joined in the wedding blessing of this fisherman, and now you hold him as your prisoner?"

The chief priest could not look Bachué in the eyes, but she knew he succumbed to greed and ambition, and Tungurahua was the one that spooned him the poison.

Naira, watching from where she stood a way off, heard movement coming from the road behind her. She looked and saw it was the towering Tungurahua, galloping toward them on his smoking gray horse. He had obviously found out that she and Bachué had fled, and was now in hot pursuit, trying to get to them before Bachué could run into the very group she was confronting at that moment.

Knowing she had disobeyed what Bachué had told her to do, Naira timidly tread along the side of the road toward the gang, with one foot in the bush. She was hoping to warn Bachué who it was that was coming. She was half of the way there when she spotted her daughter, Qina, standing to the side of the priests. It stopped Naira cold in her tracks, at which point pure motherly instinct took over, and she ran out into the road and cried, "Qina!"

Qina looked up and saw her mother in front of her, and with a most harsh look, gave her the same stern command Bachué had given:

"Run!"

Naira got the message loud and clear this time, and dashed into the bush, leaving Bachué to face the priests on her own.

"Very well," Bachué said to the priests, "if you must continue to Balao, you will surrender the fisherman to me, for I am need of him now."

The high priest protested. "But that is--"

"That was not a request, servant! Think for a moment who it is speaking to you before you dare say another word."

It was Tungurahua who would have the next word as he rode into the midst of them and dismounted from his gray horse.

"He needs to say nothing more, Bachué." Tungurahua shouted. "He doesn't answer to you anymore."

Bachué turned to face Tungurahua.

"Stand back, Tungurahua, you have no authority here. These are the priests of my temple."

"A temple," Tungurahua countered, "that, like you, is no more."

Tungurahua then pulled some smoke out of his horse's nose and hurled it at Bachué, knocking her to the ground. He then proceeded to place his boot firmly over her neck, pressing into her throat until she could breathe no more.

The fisherman tried to bolt from the tree to come to her aid, but two priests pinned him to the ground. Bachué fought back, clapping her hands together around Tungurahua's leg, but her energy was not enough. She looked to her side for Naira's help, but Naira was gone, vanished into the bush.

Bachué writhed on the ground, throwing her hands at Tungurahua, while the priests who once loved and protected her from harm, now stood over her, watching as she was smothered in the dust.

When she could fight no more, her arms fell to the ground and her body went limp. Tungurahua finished her off with the force of his foot as it snapped her neck.

He removed his foot and looked over at Qina with some contempt.

"Daughter of Qayqa huk'ucha, you have done well. I congratulate you. Your father will be smartly rewarded for my prize."

He then ordered the priests to put the fisherman on the smoking gray horse so he could personally take him back to Balao, leaving the rest of them to bury the old woman according to their own custom.

But for all of Tungurahua's ruthlessness, his cunning intellect was lost in his triumph. He had forgotten there was another who had escaped; someone who Tungurahua had never laid his eyes on.

Naira reached the other side and emerged from the bush, with nothing blocking her path now to the north. She looked back down the road and saw the Suamox priests kneeling and weeping over Bachué's body, mourning their mother and their part in this wicked affair.

But two were not so preoccupied. Qina and the fisherman looked directly back at Naira, as if they knew exactly where she would be. They stood still, doing nothing to encourage her to come back. They gave no gesture for her to rejoin them, for this was not her stand. They just stared at her, and then nodded for her to go on.

Whatever reason she had to be with Bachué, it was for the wiser. Wiser than the hell that was about to befall the place she had once called home.

31 SAVING REVENTADOR

There's a question that even Unawqi could not answer for me: Is Antisana the mountain of evil, or the mountain of good?

He said that it very well may be both, for it begs the question are we made good or evil by what we fight for? Mountain hermits are susceptible to the same influences as humans, even though they like to think they are transcendent. However, Antisana was exceptional because the hermit sister was sequestered for so long, leaving it to be tossed between the hands of human contest for hundreds of generations.

To explain more, he continued with the story.

Reventador and the woman with the red clay hair followed the Condor Road, the river forged by human hands to save Antisana from burning. As they climbed, they witnessed more bodies lying by the wayside, those that had made the very river and tried to use it to escape but then succumbed to Moche's poison gas and ash.

No one, nothing, had survived. It was a stark wasteland, but being who they were, Reventador and the woman with the red clay hair were not afraid of Moche and hoped they would find Tamaya and rescue her from his hands.

They reached the main gate, and Reventador announced their presence with his commanding voice, but it was Moche who had managed to find his way out of being lost in the deepest recess and emerged at the gate instead of the queen.

Moche shouted them to get off his mountain and go away. The queen was no longer there, he said in a mocking tone, and Antisana was once more his keep, and his alone.

In truth, Moche did not know where Tamaya was, and he had no force, not even a scout, to pursue her. Neither did he want to fuel the idea of her as an exiled queen, for that would seed hope for her return, or worse, an insurrection.

So, he told Reventador that Tamaya was dead; that she was the weaker side in a duel they had fought over the throne, and she had fallen into a boiling lake of lava, never to be seen again.

It was of course, a lie. The woman with the red clay hair remembered her similar duel with Moche a thousand years earlier inside the same mountain, and Moche was probably manufacturing Tamaya's death as a deferred victory over his original contest with the woman he would only call "Atama".

Hearing this made Reventador supremely angry and is the reason the two mountains have feuded to this day.

Moche, you see, did not have the pedigree of the other hermits. He was not one of the mountain gods. He was not part of the family. He was a usurper, a leech with magic of his own that fed off Antisana.

Reventador, therefore, cursed Moche, and threw at him a bolt of rock and flame, which Moche rather easily deflected.

Not wanting to see a new fight break out, the woman with the red clay hair, took ahold of Reventador's arm and asked him to reserve his energy, as this was not his land, nor was it his day.

She did not believe Moche, for she had known him longer, and he had a fumbling deception in his voice. So, she turned Reventador around and told him they should leave and devise a better plan.

They descended back down the mountain, and as they went, the woman with the red clay hair cast seeds from her pouch everywhere around her, reaching down into the bottom of her pouch to scrape up every last seed she could find in order to resurrect life back to the mountain.

Behind her, the seeds glowed green and bright, plants sprouted. People lifted themselves from the ground and dusted themselves off. The reign of Tamaya was something neither she nor Reventador could reawaken, at least not now, but the woman with the red clay hair knew that the very growth of life is insubordinate to the finality of death, and creates a greater balance of good over time.

Reventador could not see it--the sprouts in his footprints, the people behind him rising to their feet. They were now his people to reign, for he was the surrogate guardian of the Quijos. Nonetheless, he was too saddened to take note of his responsibility to lead, and just hung his head down and cried as he walked.

He had failed Tamaya. He set her up for something she could not sustain, and put her, an innocent, in the middle of powers that had led to her demise. He thought himself a fool for believing humanity could handle this fragile world.

The woman with the red clay hair sensed his trouble and stopped him, allowing the life she was planting to catch up to them, and surround them on all sides.

She took out the last few of her seeds from her pouch, placed them on his tear-soaked face, and brought him to the side of the path, more directly in the moonlight.

The once fiercely powerful mountain god who had inspired nothing but fear, Reventador was now completely collapsed inside of himself and could not get out.

It was something the woman with the red clay hair would not tolerate. She despised pity, and self-pity even worse, and wanted to save him before others took notice.

She knelt down and wrapped herself around his knees, and the seeds on his wet face caught the moonlight, making it glow and soften. Vines came around his shoulders and bolstered his back, giving him armor.

And then a single, yellow butterfly, one of the remaining knights of Antisana, landed on his wrist. Reventador lifted the butterfly to his face and looked into its eyes, this weary and battle-beaten insect who needed a place to rest.

For the butterfly, all was not lost--it still had gold on its wings, and it could fly. It just needed company.

It gave Reventador a breath of confidence, for while he knew they could not save Antisana, the butterflies were ready to move on, so why shouldn't he.

Indeed, the butterflies had saved him.

He lifted the woman with the red clay hair to her feet and embraced her for staying with him. "Thank you!" he said. "We are not finished."

They followed the Condor Road back down the rest of the mountain and crossed the Tamboyaco to the other side. From where they stood, one could hardly tell Antisana had been so recently ravaged.

It was beautiful. Lavender swayed in the breeze. Eucalyptus leaves danced in the moonlight. Burning fire had been replaced by the sound of mountain streams.

They had lost the dream of Antisana, but the first steps of getting it back were already behind them.

32 SANGAY

Her army decimated, Tamaya flew on the backs of a small detachment of Pasochoa butterflies, for the rest had taken refuge with Reventador, believing the queen to be dead.

They flew her south, staying on the warmer side of the cordillera where the occasional rainfall bathed their broken spirits.

They rested at the house of Sangay, another eccentric cousin in the family of mountains who lives in relative isolation, disconnected from the drama of the rest of her family and enjoying her remote perch above the Amazon.

Sangay was not adept as a host, and would often get distracted with her own mundane affairs while in the middle of conversations with Tamaya. Still, she did what she could to provide Tamaya and her regiment safe harbor. She particularly was enchanted with the yellow butterflies, and asked Tamaya to leave half of them behind as a parting gift for Sangay's hospitality.

Tamaya, however, asserted this was regrettably not possible, for the half that would remain her own were not strong enough to carry her to Kukanibo.

Sangay reacted sharply, exploding pumice and steam into the air to express her being insulted by the rejection.

"After everything I've done for you, and you want to just leave me alone? You are as bad as the rest, J....Ba...Wil... what was your name again? Oh, never mind!

"Be off, then, in the mor--wait a moment...did you say Kukanibo?"

"Yes, do you know it? Could you point the way?"

Sangay got anxious again, this time visibly shaking with fear at the sound of the name.

"Oh, no, no, no, child, that is a terribly foolish idea. That is a place we prefer to remain forgotten. Go there and you will never return."

"I have heard there is a bridge."

"Yes, but what is that to you?!"

"I have lost my husband and my son to qanaq'wa makuyhana, and I want to retrieve them, whatever it takes."

"Well, that is where you are misled, and better off to forget it."

"What do you mean?"

"Oh, you humans and your putting your nose into things too complicated for you to understand!"

Tamaya remained stone silent, not letting her curiosity abate. Sangay relented to explain:

"This 'palace' of which you speak is not a place fixed in a spatial frame. It is a way of referring to where you are **not** right now. That is why we call it the place of an eternal struggle, and why if you go to Kukanibo you will all the more be seduced in the riddle. That's what the bridge does to you."

Tamaya looked confused already, for this was a different interpretation of qanaq'wa makuyhana than she had heard before.

So, Sangay took Tamaya's hand and led her to a ridge at which they could see both her great mountain and the beauty of the rainforest teeming with life. She continued:

"From the mountain, you look at the rainforest and want to go there; it beckons. But once you satisfy your zeal getting to the rainforest, you look back at the mountain and find it so beautiful, that you want to go back. You go to the mountain and the temptation of the forest starts again. You see, we are always struggling to live where we are **not**. It seems like it's "there," but when we get there, it is no longer a "there" but a "here," and we want a new "there," a new horizon. We feel we are always displaced, always left behind, never at a destination."

"Yes, great Sangay, but I cannot live without confronting the one who caused death to my loved ones. I won't know what I can do unless I make the effort to get to the palace of qanaq'wa makuyhana."

"Mmm…very true, but I'm afraid you won't find what you're looking for. Even in our old age, the mountains have seen many people racing on journeys from their birth to their death, trying to resolve matters that all along were ready to be solved right at home.

"Take my advice, young one, and go home. You won't be retreating or running away. Believe me, you will accomplish just as much by letting the answers find you instead of chasing them into that nasty jungle."

Tamaya nodded her head in agreement, but chose to persist anyway.

"So you do know it. Can you help us or not?"

"I have already helped you and this is what I get for it? I've done more than my fair share, I think."

It was then that one of the butterflies came to Tamaya's ear and whispered to her that they would take her only as far as Kukanibo, but would not enter it, for they feared its magic was too powerful for them. They would instead hand her over to another guide who knew the secret paths.

Tamaya smiled at Sangay to try and enter a little charm to the otherwise tense conversation. She told the mountain that she would relinquish not half, but all of her butterflies to Sangay's dominion on the condition they first take her to the border of Kukanibo, and then she pledged they would be returned to Sangay.

The mountain was delighted with the idea, and her angry rants immediately turned into jumps and dancing, pleased with the thought that she would have her own knights.

Sangay drew out a map on a papaya leaf, although it had been so long since she had been to Kukanibo that she struggled to remember the details. She drew a bizarre and twisted line going south, then north, then east, then west--having forgotten one minor detail: that butterflies fly!

Tamaya humored Sangay, not wanting her to lose her concentration and momentary pleasure. Soon Sangay rolled up the map and placed it in Tamaya's hand.

Fearing Sangay might change her mind again, Tamaya announced she would leave at once, and made an oath to Sangay that the Antisana knights would be the Sangay knights in but a few days' time.

Using the map as a rough guide, they continued their flight south and then east where the air grew warmer but smelled of rotting carnage.

This made the butterflies nervous and the flight stalled and started again many times, for they were unsure as to whether the border was in front of them or behind, and if it was behind whether they would ever be able to return.

At last, they saw below them the shape of the river bend they had been looking for and they brought Tamaya down to its western bank. There they waited with her for an hour until her guide showed up.

When the guide appeared from the tall black grass of the riverbank, Tamaya dropped her jaw in astonishment. It was the chinchay, the same one from her own cloud forest that had been companion to both the woman with the red clay hair and the fisherman of Jaqunqay on their journeys, and here she was, so very far from home.

How the chinchay could know so much and travel so widely, Tamaya was at a loss to understand, but at the same time she was so relieved to see a familiar friend.

She turned to thank her butterflies and bid them their farewell. Indeed, it was a sad occasion. They appeared reluctant to leave her, and their wings folded back and forth in a melancholy way. They had sworn to be her guardians, they were proud of having been her adornment, and they had never been so honored until she had named them her knights.

She remembered the peach kernel, Tapaipi, between her breasts, and she pulled it out and opened it in the palm of her hand. It gave off the most beautiful rose-colored glow. She beckoned the butterflies to jump into her palm one by one, and feel the beauty of its warmth. They did so, and she took the time with each one to caress it, kiss it, and then send it off into the sky.

When the last one had left, the chinchay stood up from its haunches, came over to Tamaya, nudged her with her nose, and then pointed her head across the river to the dark and thick forest of Kukanibo.

The chinchay was very calm, as if she was prepared for whatever might come, and this made Tamaya feel confident too. The cat led Tamaya across the river on a crooked trail of steps, lily pads, and the backs of friendly caimans.

When they reached the other side, Tamaya looked back, but she couldn't see the bank she had left behind, for the view was pitch black as far as she could see. She was entirely at the mercy of her cloud forest friend, swallowed into the jungle and with no way back out.

But fear? No. Tamaya did not have it. She knew this was where there were answers. This was where she was needed. The chinchay seemed to know exactly where she was going, and the kernel over Tamaya's breast had never felt so firmly planted.

It was a paradox more than a paradise. In such an impenetrable wilderness, Tamaya had never felt more like she belonged, and she looked at the chinchay and said, "Yes, I am queen here, too!"

33 IN THE RING OF FIRE

It took Unawqi several attempts at telling what happened next. We would meet at St. Rita's, or even for an early morning coffee down by the pier, but what he wanted to say was still too close to the bone for him to separate himself from the pain.

He would just retread the previous parts of the story instead, to try and get a better run on it, but then freeze up with a ball in his throat or remember something particular that made his head hurt so bad that he had to get up and leave the table.

Having heard this much, I still didn't know enough to help him advance, but I, too, was also so deep in to just let the story go unfinished.

I reminded myself that I was listening to a dead man, at least as far as his story had said so. And yet it was the absence of the rest of his story and the unquenchable hope in his eyes that made me a believer that he was still very much alive.

I told him the story would come, for it was surely worth the wait.

He asked me if, in my world, it was good for a man to love another man, like he loved the fisherman. I told him it wasn't acceptable to everyone, but what I wouldn't accept was for him to speak of his love in the past tense. For me, it was inspiring and still is, and just like in his world, one must trust in Tapaipi wherever it is beating.

At last, he was able to break through.

We had gotten a late start cleaning fish one Saturday evening. The July weather was warm and allowed us to linger after dusk when the chores were through. We hung our feet into the cool bay off the jetty in Thea's Park. The moon was full that night, and Unawqi closed his eyes and bathed his face in the light.

Perhaps it was Mama Killa that finally helped him draw up the words, where the sun only seemed to discourage them.

He described how sore it was for the fisherman to travel in the back of the priest's wagon but being slung over the rear of Tungurahua's horse was much worse. The fisherman felt completely mangled as Tungurahua drove the horse like a burning comet to Balao. The Black Giant wanted to waste no time and take no chances with further interruptions.

They barreled through abandoned farms and fields, scaled down and up ravines, and forged muddy streams poisoned with the runoff of Balao's industrial waste. It was all so rotten that the fisherman couldn't recognize any landmarks to suggest where he was or where he was going.

While they were still a way off, the fisherman saw the great blue spire towering on the horizon and could only think it was something from another world, for it looked as if it was literally scraping the bottom of the Moon.

When they entered the town, the stench was unbearable. On top of decomposing fish, the sulfuric clouds of the forges made the fisherman choke and the lids of his eyes blister.

Tungurahua made straight for the clearing, where he expected to find Ernest Heatheridge overseeing the finishing touches of the tower's construction, for it was functionally complete.

But Ernest was at home, distraught over the disappearance of his wife, along with the woman that had been laid at their doorstep. Had the woman kidnapped his wife? He wondered if Tungurahua put them both to work somewhere. No one knew, as no one had seen them either coming or going.

For so many years, Naira was the mainstay of Ernest's life and household. She was the helm, the sail, and the rudder of their ship, and without her he was lost at sea, and he didn't know where to swim.

The howls of Tungurahua in the clearing broke Ernest out of his spell, at least for the moment, for they were especially shrill this time. He left the house and ran toward the clearing, hoping Tungurahua would know Naira's whereabouts.

As he came into the clearing, it was lit up by the illumination of the Moon casting through the prisms of quartz stacked one on top of the other above him. It was a spectacular feat of engineering he couldn't ever remember seeing the likes of anywhere in his travels.

There, in the center of the clearing was the fisherman, bound and scarred, looking like the chewed-up bait of a crab trap.

The fisherman's and Ernest's eyes met, and Ernest's face turned to a tortured anguish. This was the first time he had seen the fisherman's face so clearly; for their encounter when Unawqi died was one in which the light of the night was too dim.

The face that Ernest saw was a surprise. The two stared at each other, unable to say the thing they each wanted to. They knew each other well, but had too much to say, and didn't know where to begin. Ernest certainly didn't want to see the fisherman battered like this.

Tungurahua's shadow passed between them as he prepared the space around the fisherman with incantations and a thick ring of black oil.

It became clear to Ernest that he had been fed a ruse. Tungurahua's reasoning that the fisherman would be bait to attract Unawqi was true, but not to protect the fisherman from assassins. It was now evident that any presumed assassins were actually in Tungurahua's employ. Tungurahua was the assassin, planning to burn the fisherman alive if Unawqi could not deliver the required ransom.

Ernest called out to Tungurahua in a feeble voice, asking where Naira had gone. Perturbed by the interruption, Tungurahua hissed back at Heatheridge,

"Why do you bother me with petty questions, you immaterial man, at the hour of my deliverance!"

"Immaterial" was such an insulting term, it broiled Ernest's insides. He saw that Tungurahua had been using him all along and the Black Giant had planned to leave the wasted landscape around them as it was. The promise to reward him with a great endowment of knowledge and wealth was a cheap trick from the start.

Naira was also not a "petty" request. She was more than the Sun to Ernest, and so was the fisherman, and both were in great danger.

Ernest looked at everything around him, burning, boiling, rotting, vanishing, and choking; and saw how disgraceful he had allowed it to become; and how it was unworthy of his name. Perhaps Naira's normal routines over the years had masked the devastation he had allowed in his home, and then his town, which reflected upon his name.

Now, Naira was not there; an ironic gift that permitted the illusion to at last disappear from his view. Life was anything but normal. Balao was not safe. It was not the lavish new temple of the emperor. It was a living hell.

What would Qayqa huk'ucha do? Ernest thought of himself for a moment in the eyes of his townspeople.

Tungurahua could not be dissuaded or stopped by a man, but what about by a 'crazy mouse'?

The sorcerer finished his incantations and approached the fisherman, whispering into his ear. He explained to the fisherman in frank and simple terms that the fisherman was about to be tortured.

The fisherman would be given a chance to stop it by taking a unique opportunity to speak to his lost lover, Unawqi. All Unawqi needed to do was reach out and touch the top of the spire, opening the path between qanaq'wa makuyhana and Earth, allowing Aakti, the emperor, to return. And if Unawqi should refuse, then it would prove he never cared for the fisherman at all, and the fisherman would be consumed by the ring of fire.

The Black Giant walked away to commence the ceremony. Ernest heard the whole plan in his ear, but his mind was racing with other things.

"Call him," Tungurahua demanded to the fisherman. "You've waited long for him. He's listening now."

Tungurahua then rubbed the fingers of his right hand together until a dribble of lava formed between them, which then rolled out and dripped onto the black oil, igniting it. He made a trail of the oil from the fisherman's feet out to where it connected to the circle, and there the entire ring soon burst into flame. Tungurahua stepped to the side and into the back of the clearing, leaving the fisherman alone to watch the flames advance toward him.

The fisherman looked up at the Moon. Was Mama Killa betraying him once again? he wondered. Why could she not intervene? Had she returned to do the same as she had done the day she swept Unawqi out to sea?

Where was the condor?

Dead, he reminded himself.

Where was Reventador?

Where was the woman with the red clay hair?

Far from here, obviously.

Where was the chinchay?

Disappeared as well.

There was nothing and no one left to come to the aid of the fisherman of Jaqunqay. All he had was the open sky above him and piercing into the middle of it a crude, glowing, blue tower. The fire and smoke burned around him on all sides, blocking out any sight of the world he was about to leave.

How foolish an idea to talk to the sky, thinking Unawqi could hear him! The fisherman knew these would be his final moments, and that Tungurahua had nothing to lose in a dead fisherman.

Nonetheless, the fisherman raised his head to the sky, if to do nothing but let his last words be spoken to Mama Killa.

"Where did I go wrong?" he said. "I did everything my father asked of me. I learned how to fish with no one's help but that of the sea. But even the sea left me, and took with it the love I plucked from its grasp.

"Unawqi, if you can hear me out there, I want you to know I never meant to leave you on the beach like my father left me on the beach. I would never allow it. I came to find you and bring you home, to keep you safe, and I have been looking for you ever since.

If you can do this thing the sorcerer said, please, cast out a line for me. Let me hear you again. Let me see you, but once. I've never known how to do anything but save myself, but now, if you can, please save me. You're all I have left to ask."

The sky was as black as Tungurahua's cloak; and as cold, motionless, and unresponsive as a corpse. Nothing answered him, save the flames which crept closer, the heat starting to chap the fisherman's legs and arms. For all he knew, Tungurahua had already left, resigned that the fisherman would fail and therefore let the fire burn him to ash.

The thought of burning did not scare the fisherman. It was the sound of being so alone. It brought back memories of being alone on the beach, but now even the sea he loved had abandoned him, as he was no longer able to hear their calming waves in his brain.

His only choice, therefore, was to writhe; to let his limbs squirm, letting him pass his last lonely moments listening to the pathetic form of company that was his own body snapping and burning away.

He didn't want to see the flames come any closer, so he closed his eyes and listened to his own breathing, wondering how many breaths he would have to endure before his last.

And there, in his breaths, he heard something else breathing. It was two breaths, coming in and out in unison, like two lovers sleeping next to each other, making their lungs move together in concert.

Was the other breath Unawqi? The fisherman didn't want to wake it up for fear of losing the togetherness, so he spoke, but only with his mind,

"Unawqi…I am here. Breathe with me."

As he breathed, he listened to the motion coming in and out. He recalled doing the same thing as a boy when he first learned to breathe with the sea, sitting in the surf, and letting the waves move him as they directed, the fish and seaweed taking a hold of his hand and guiding him. His tension lessened, and he let his breathing take control.

It was then he heard the other breath say, "Do you remember the lights?"

"What lights, Unawqi?"

"The trail of illuminated jelly fish you left for me on the beach at Jaqunqay."

"Yes, my love, I remember."

The recollection made the fisherman smile, a little embarrassed at his overprotective nature.

"Unawqi, I made them so that if night should fall, you could find your way back."

"It worked," the other breath said. "I found my way back."

Tungurahua scanned the sky, and there, at the very farthest point of the constellations, he saw the blackness begin to pale as it bled into the stars around it.

It was a light spreading itself out like a spring crocus. It formed a path from one star to the next, making its way toward them in larger and brighter strokes.

Tungurahua used his smoldering hand to raise Ernest's chin up so he would notice the phenomenon moving toward them.

It was working. Unawqi was coming, and with a mighty sword in his hand.

34 CONVENING THE CONGRESS

Now that she was dead, Bachué was in qanaq'wa makuyhana like all the others who have met their fate in this story. However, having both the emperor and his mother share the same house was the recipe for a titanic war. Quarreling with her son was raised to a new level, demoting the rotating struggle between Unawqi, Titu, and Aakti to that of small skirmishes.

The truth of the matter was that on Earth, Bachué was a goddess who received the highest worship, but in the sky, she was seven times more than that. The constellations worshipped her, and saw her reemergence among them as somewhat of a miracle. They instantly yielded more authority to her than to her own son, the emperor.

For many days on end, the throne room of Aakti was a veritable burning furnace. Bachué had transformed herself into a blazing white star, and cast her lashing tongue upon the emperor and everything around him, braiding him up and down for his history of abusing his power; for violating every law of the universe; and for failing to live up to the family name.

Try as he might, the emperor could only mount doleful ramparts against his mother's fury, and increasingly shrunk into a weak shadow of himself on his throne.

It was only the beginning. The worst was still yet to come when Bachué stopped her tirade. When her heat subsided, every material thing the emperor had possessed to remind himself of his stature was charred to a crisp, and he sat in a bleak landscape of ash.

Bachué announced: "I shall call a congress!"

"No!" Aakti protested with a look of terror. "That is a right the law affords me, and me alone."

"The law which you have made a folly," Bachué said. "Try and stop me!"

Aakti could not. Whenever he thought he might, he quickly convinced himself he would be wasting his breath. He no longer desired his throne as long as his mother was there. He could not undo what had been done. In fact, even though it was Tungurahua's hands that had done the deed, the murder of Bachué on Earth was a part of the emperor's larger plan, a step he now regretted in his scheme to reclaim his dominion. He had thought that matricide would have a harmless consequence, for it would only remove her from Earth and place her securely by his side where he could control her.

Bachué was anything but "by his side" as he now came to see. He could not control her in the least.

The congress came; the giants of the sky: Centauri, Sirius, Rigel, Canopus, Vega, Altair, and Capella.

The emperor could not have been more humiliated, for they arrived to see him sitting in a pile of ash, with nothing left to parade in front of them to prove his superior status. He looked burned out, like the charred wood of a fire after a morning rain.

Instead, they looked to Bachué to speak, and for her to tell them what she desired, dismissing the capacity of the emperor to do the same.

As the congress encircled the emperor, so his trial began, as he had to answer for his many counts of crimes. They would require many more days before a verdict could be decided.

Always the opportunist, Titu took advantage of the emperor feuding with his mother and the deliberations of the congress. He had found the missing elements and completed his formula for activating the bridge at Kukanibo. The struggle had given him ample access to knowledge that humanity would have never gained on its own, not even in a million years. He now had all he could ever want in his head.

All he needed next was to escape back to Earth when the others weren't looking and implement his science to harness the Sun's power.

The timing of it all was grave. Little did the congress know that while they engaged with their debates over the fate of the emperor,

Unawqi was at the same moment burning his way through their treasury to rescue the fisherman, and Titu was ducking out behind their backs with the keys to Kukanibo and a device to enslave them all.

35 TOUCHING MIBA

As the Stars were meeting in their own tribunal, working toward a judgment on the emperor, it just so happened that at the same time, a similar meeting was being called on Earth.

Humble Naira, the cause of the meeting on Earth, came out of the Pasochoa forest and saw the blackened western face of Antisana. Not a single tree was spared and it had not been the recipient yet of the regrowth the woman with the red clay hair had started on the other side.

Worried for Tamaya, she hurried on her journey to the northern side where she hoped to find a sign of something better. There, at the bottom of the Condor Road, is where she ran into a couple coming down from the mountain.

It was, of course, Reventador and the woman with the red clay hair, neither of whom Naira had ever met. They cautioned her not to go up the mountain, for it was still not fully healed and full of poisonous traps. But Naira insisted, saying she had something very important to deliver to Tamaya.

"Tamaya…" Reventador shaking his head in sorrow said, "Tamaya is no more. It is the foul wizard Moche who once again rules this mountain."

"What is it that you have brought her?" the woman with the red clay hair asked.

This made Naira afraid, for she did not know if she could trust these strangers, but the woman with the red clay hair felt the energy around Naira's punchu, and instantly recognized it as the same energy as the demon on the wall she had last encountered in Suamox.

"Are you by chance carrying a demon?"

Now Naira was doubly frightened, and she made a break to run past the strangers, but the woman with the red clay hair caught her and sat her on a rock.

"Calm yourself, girl. Whatever it is you have, we don't mean to take it, but you certainly don't want to give it to Moche. He is a malcontent and the opposite of who you seek."

Through her blindness, the woman with the red clay hair saw one of the legs of the phototeledar poking out of the pouch.

"Ahh, yes, there it is! Tamaya brought it to the house of my grandmother, and then both it and she disappeared together. I have been looking for her ever since."

"Your grandmother? What is her name?" Naira asked.

"My apologies. I haven't introduced myself. I am the one they call Atama, and my grandmother is the great Bachué. Is she coming behind you?"

Naira's face turned a pallid gray, and the woman with the red clay hair stood back, not liking the feeling of it. Naira did not want to be in the position of having to be the first to share the sad news, but if not she, then who else would?

"I am very sorry, but as you have told me that Tamaya is no more, I must tell you that the same is true of Bachué."

"What? No! This cannot be! Surely, you are mistaken!"

Reventador grabbed ahold of the woman with the red clay hair to keep her from losing control, and took over Naira's questioning.

"Where did you get this impossible news? Who told you?"

"No one had to tell me. I saw it with my own eyes. It was the terrible Tungurahua who came on his smoking gray horse. He killed her amidst the company of his inferiors, but not before Bachué helped me to escape, and she told me to bring this to Tamaya. Now you are telling me I am too late."

Naira started to cry out of futility and her own failure, and Reventador reached out and comforted her.

"Don't weep, young woman. It would have been even worse if you had not found us. We are loyal to Bachué. Did you see a fisherman with them, too?"

"Yes, in fact. He was taken prisoner by Tungurahua and they rode away, I think back to my village of Balao. It has become a terrible place, not any longer of this world."

Reventador shook his head, understanding now for the first time that the gravity of the situation went far beyond his duel with Moche.

"Come with us to a safer place, where we can help you do what Bachué has asked."

Reventador led Naira and the woman with the red clay hair off the mountain and across the river, followed by a growing chorus of yellow butterflies.

When they reached the base of his own mountain, they came to place called tunqur amaru, "the snake's throat," a cove of dark caves hidden behind the drapes of the forest. Reventador insisted the woman with the red clay hair take Naira to the summit where they would be safe, and where he could join them after he took care of some important concerns.

When they were securely out of sight, Reventador descended into the tunqur amaru, slick with dew and guano. It was a filthy hole, making even Reventador skittish, but it was the only place from which he could simultaneously communicate with the rest of the family of mountains.

He dropped down into one recess in the shale after another, crawling deep into the bowel of the Earth until, at last, he caught sight of what he was looking for. It was an exceedingly difficult place to find, not even a place but more an anomaly of nature where the rock had peeled away to reveal a scaly flesh underneath, pliable when touched, and throbbing like a heart.

It was what the family of mountains called their "miba". The part that Reventador found was just a fragment of miba, a greater mass that is connected to everything. Miba is the glue and tissue that lay at the foundation of all the mountains, and something only they know of at their feet. If one of them touch the miba, all the other mountains feel it too.

Reventador took advantage of the fact that Tungurahua was not tending to his own mountain and was therefore disconnected from miba. Reventador wanted the rest of the family to hear what he had to say without Tungurahua present, so he touched miba, and at first it shrank back, for it is quite a sensitive thing. Then it stopped resisting and let Reventador rest his hand on it and hold it there.

Eventually, the other mountains felt it as one might feel a bug resting on one's foot, and they came to investigate. Cumbal came, as did the sisters Pichincha, Kayambi, and Imbabura. The brother, Cotopaxi, usually too caught up in his own vanity, arrived as well. Sangay, however, did not respond, as she had become numb to miba in her ever-growing dementia. Unsurprisingly, Antisana was silent, for she had long been presumed dead from Moche's poisonous spells.

Still, Reventador had a quorum, and he put his mouth close to miba, and spoke to them in a whisper. He asked them to do something he hoped he would never have to ask: expel Tungurahua from the family, never again to give him aid.

Naturally, the mountains were astonished at such a petition, and Cotopaxi, who had always been closest to Tungurahua and most tolerant of Tungurahua's rebelliousness, protested the loudest and threatened to leave the reunion.

Reventador begged them to listen and explained that Tungurahua had risen to a much higher level of treason. Reventador made the case that Tungurahua was flaunting the laws of nature and co-opting humanity to stage the return of Aakti, the banished emperor.

"But Bachué herself has banished Aakti," Cotopaxi argued, "so what business is it ours to meddle even more?"

"And Tungurahua, our own kind, has murdered Bachué," Reventador said in all sobriety.

"What! That's impossible," Cumbal said. "Our brother does not have the strength against a goddess."

"I am afraid this is where we have not been paying close attention. He has gathered power for himself from Kukanibo, a place so old you may have forgotten it is the place of passage to stars, indeed, to qanaq'wa makuyhana.

"Apparently, Tungurahua has harnessed the magic of Kukanibo to form a mutinous alliance with the emperor, and because of this, he is more powerful than any of us have given him credit for. It is upon us now to stop him, if we can."

"What are you suggesting we do, brother?" Imbabura asked.

"He will soon use miba to enlist your allegiance to his cause. You must resist with your silence. You must not give him assistance when he comes to you together or individually. If all he has is himself and no one else to join him, he will eventually exhaust himself and resign from his subversion."

Pichincha, always the most philosophical of the family, interjected,

"There is something that keeps bothering me, Reventador. The murder of the emperor's mother is certainly villainous, and we have always been cognizant of his contempt for the laws of nature. But aside from these things, what can be so bad about the return of Aakti? We were much better off with his light in the sky, and Tungurahua is orchestrating just such a return? Doesn't the good balance out the bad?"

"Ah!" Reventador replied. "This is where my intermingling with the world has brought me knowledge to which you have so far been excluded.

"Let me remind you that I am the confidant to none other than Atama, who we should remind ourselves is none other than Aakti's daughter, and she is with me at this moment. She has always known more than anyone else about her father's true intentions.

"If that is not enough, I also must remind you that I presided over the wedding of our queen, Tamaya, who is mother of the emperor's heir, the prince, Unawqi. Unawqi is also in qanaq'wa makuyhana, as is the groom of the queen. I don't think anyone needs to question the unique and deep knowledge I have into the affairs of the other world and that so much of Earth's dynasty is suffering destruction.

Aakti, my brothers and sisters, does not wish to return to Earth; he wishes to destroy it!"

The mountains gasped and exclaimed denial at such a preposterous claim, but Reventador spoke over them, saying,

"Yes, that has always been his intention. It is why he races around the world every day, trying to capture his rebellious daughter, to stop her from spreading his life. The emperor gives his warmth and light, but reluctantly so. It is his daughter we should be thanking that we are alive, and she is just as unwilling to let us die."

Pichincha, still unsettled, continued her questioning. "What of this prince, Unawqi? What does he want?"

"Unawqi..." Reventador struggled to explain, for the hermit had never met him, and understanding Unawqi's desire was an elusive exercise. What Unawqi was trained to do as a hunter was the pedagogy of Moche, and not necessarily representative of Unawqi's sense of purpose. Plus, Unawqi was rather young when he was removed from the world. He hadn't very long to think on his own identity. He was pulled between the missions of Moche and that of Titu Ilumán, not to mention the new life he had fallen in love with on Jaqunqay. It remains a mystery as to which one of these missions Unawqi truly was dedicated. Was he an amalgam of them, or was he a rejection of all three?

"Unawqi is indeed the question. He was raised to hunt the Sun by Moche, a thief of our sister Antisana's dominion. This thief is not one of us, and so we do not know his ways or who he is seeking to please by his presence among us. And yet I am the one who also wed Unawqi to a fisherman–that's right, a man to a man, something I thought I never could or would do–but I did. Why? Because the strength of their love made me see Unawqi was not a product of Moche, or even of Aakti. Despite everything he had been through, he showed himself to be resilient, and to cherish and fight for a fisherman instead of a god. It made me unconvinced that Unawqi hunts to kill. I believe he hunts to conquer, to overcome all our monsters, whatever they are."

Kayambi was the first one to be settled. "I am with you, Reventador," she said.

"Tungurahua will hear from me no more," Imbabura concurred, then Cumbal.

Pichincha and Cotopaxi, however, stewed on it longer. They, too, were mostly ashamed of their brother Reventador and his repugnant acts, but Reventador was asking them to abandon one of their own in a preemptive way, without Tungurahua being able to mount a defense of his own.

That is when Reventador took an ember of carbon smoldering nearby and drew onto miba the glyph of the condor.

"My brother and sister, remember it was my son, your nephew, whose blood was spilled to burn Antisana to a desecrated crisp, right in front of your eyes. Do you need any further proof of the evil befalling us as each day passes?

"Soon, Moche will gladly lend Antisana to Tungurahua's war, for that would bring Moche the powers he has sought for near a thousand years. For the sake of my son, do not allow Moche any such victory. Stop Tungurahua before he can reach the gates."

This was enough to make Cotopaxi and Pichincha fall in, and the union was unanimous. Reventador gave them a blessing in appreciation, and began to scramble up the crevasses between the shale, up through the caves underneath his mountain.

When he emerged, the birds of the cloud forest greeted him differently. He was not the same raging hermit he used to be, and they felt it. Reventador was more purposeful, more worldly, less of a hermit at all.

The path up the mountain was quiet and peaceful. Mountain jasmine was blooming, having adapted to the Moon for its light. The tranquility of Reventador represented a new chapter of resilience of Earth, a place that set aside its ferocity to make its restoration a higher call.

Reventador didn't look up to notice Unawqi's comet, now a bright ginger-colored streak racing toward the Earth. Instead, he was focused on the trail at his feet, on *this* place, on being grounded.

36 REUNION

With relative ease, Tamaya passed her way through the fortress Tungurahua had made of Kukanibo. The peach kernel given to her by Bachué protected her from being molested by his spies, as they saw her as being just part of the fabric of the jungle.

She had nothing else with her, and no plan in mind like Bachué's to destroy the bridge. Tamaya was not a schemer of great plans. What drove her was curiosity, and she was fine to confront whatever she found at the end of her wandering with the wits of the moment.

In addition, the chinchay was an excellent pathfinder, which made finding their way to the bridge more efficient, at least compared to the effort Bachué had suffered.

Tamaya, too, passed through the creek of water that was not wet, and climbed the bank on the other side to see the enormity of the Kukanibo Bridge towering above her and disappearing into the infinity of space. It was far more astonishing than anything she had imagined.

Thinking on what Moche had said in the western deep of Antisana that soon Bachué would return to destroy the bridge, Tamaya thought she should camp there and wait for her, for she was curious to understand why the Sun's mother was intent on such drastic measures. Part of her wanted to help Bachué, for she knew Titu was up to no good, and the bridge's downfall would stop him for good. Then again, her heart was also caught up in the same conflict between love and vengeance, a struggle that had welled up there so many times before.

The temptation was strong. She could cross the bridge right now and be united with Titu forever. What was there to stop her? She could be useful by intervening, persuading him to change his mind, and then return with him before Bachué arrived so there would be no need to bring the bridge down.

She laughed a bit as the whole notion was rather naïve, but she would, if she could, allow her curiosity to prove it either true or false.

Alas, the bridge was massive and seemed to go in so many different directions she didn't know where to start. What if she chose the wrong way? What if she got lost in the heavens, alone, and with no one to help her find the way back? What if she didn't make it to the other side before Bachué crossed over and destroyed the bridge while Tamaya was still on it? Then all would be for naught.

She would have to think about crossing the bridge later, for along the span she saw what looked like a group of people coming toward her, which meant the bridge was, indeed, traversable. But who were they, she wondered? Soldiers? Pioneers? Fugitives?

She had to know, and had no fear in setting out to greet them.

When they came into closer view, she could not believe her eyes. It was Titu, Bachué, the fisherman, and leading them all, her son, Unawqi, who had never looked a stronger man!

They all came across the bridge like an odd parade that was still looking for its intended route, and they were just as surprised to see Tamaya standing there in such a forbidding place.

They wasted no time and rushed into each other's arms, all of them, that is, except for Unawqi, who did not clearly recognize Tamaya at first.

Bachué noticed this, and asked Tamaya to show Unawqi the peach kernel so that he could hold it. Tamaya could not take her eyes off of him as she withdrew the peach kernel from her breast, held it in the palm of her hand, and brought his hand over it as well.

Unawqi was truly the prince he was destined to be. He stood straight with a strong spine, his shoulders and chest built like forged armor. There was also a light in his eyes and an aura around his head that was grown up and revealed an inner tranquility, one past the age of cavalier, contempt. He was, in every way, the great man she dreamed he would become, and that many women would fall at his feet to be his bride. This was the man she had given birth to, and not the man Moche had raised.

He took hold of the peach kernel Tamaya had put in his hand and let it roll between his fingers.

"Hold it tighter," Bachué urged.

Unawqi did, squeezing it now in his palm, and that is when the memories returned. He saw a crying young woman outside of her hut, handing over her newborn infant to a small and ugly wizard. He saw a goat being left in the forest for him to eat, and a woman disappearing behind a tree not far away. He saw the last breaths of his own life when the same woman had taken justice into her own hands, punishing the one who had both raised him and killed him.

Unawqi opened his eyes, gasped for air, and then looked directly into Tamaya's eyes for the truth.

"You…are…my…?"

Tamaya couldn't wait and finished his sentence for him.

"Mother!"

It was still too much for Unawqi to take in, but he was nonetheless happy and held her to his chest as she cried.

Unawqi looked behind him and called for the fisherman to join him.

"Mother, I want to introduce you to Tomás."

She already knew him as the fisherman of Jaqunqay, but not until now by his name. In her being so enamored with her son, how quickly she had forgotten that he was already spoken for and married to the fisherman at her own wedding to Titu.

Quite embarrassed, she laughed at herself, and held her arms out wide for the fisherman.

"My gentleman! How long has it been?"

Tamaya embraced them both.

"My gentlemen!" she said again, and they laughed even harder with joy.

Standing behind them was Titu, whose face was brighter than the Moon. She gave him a coy look and he smiled and blushed a little as he looked down at his feet.

It was a sign of something good that Bachué was in his company, considering the danger she said he posed. Something must have changed, but Tamaya was in too high of spirits not to suspend her suspicions for a moment and offer him welcome.

"Come to me, Titu."

As they wrapped their arms around each other, she felt the same warmth and energy as when they were young and rolling in the corn fields in the Quijos canyon. It was as if Titu had brought them both back in time.

"My Tamaya," he said, "please do not worry, for from now on, I am just Titu, your Titu."

But for all the conviviality of this unthinkable reunion, Tamaya knew nothing of how it had come to be.

Bachué knew this would soon be asked, and reassured Tamaya.

"I know you have a lot of questions, young girl, and we have a large story to tell, so let's light a fire on the edge of the bank there where we can get some rest."

Tamaya took Bachué's arm to help hold her up, for the Sun's mother was weary and tired.

"It all began," Bachué started, "when your son-in-law called for help. That's all it took to turn heaven and earth upside down."

37 LIGHT COMBAT

If a happy reunion could be the end to all our lives and all our stories, it would be a beautiful expectation, but no doubt you have remaining questions on your mind. How is it that the party came across the bridge together? Whatever became of the others back in Balao, and in the Quijos? How did the fisherman join their company?

It is all very simple, really—they helped each other, without any one of them expecting to. There are rare moments in our lives when someone pulls us up from the roots, diverting us from our lesser need to their greater need, and without any regret, without a bitter flinch, we just go their way and abandon ours.

By the time the Congress of Stars was beginning its hearing of the arguments against the emperor, Titu was already well into his journey across the bridge. Truthfully, he would never survive a day at the other end of the bridge in the jungle of Kukanibo, as it would swallow him up with its deadly traps if it didn't first starve him to death. But he wasn't much concerned with getting all the way over.

He was headed for the core pin, the ballast in the middle of the bridge that was its hinge. He wanted to turn the bridge around! That is how he would change the balance of power, and instead of the bridge being a path to qanaq'wa makuyhana, the palace would now be on Earth's side, and Titu Ilumán would be holding the leash around the yellow ball on the other side.

He had the formula he needed to rotate the pin. He had worked on it from the first day of his captivity in the palace, drawn from gases and minerals he had scraped from the Sun when the emperor was sleeping.

Titu arrived to the core of the bridge, a noticeably wide section with a massive column coming up through the center. He was laying out his materials for the event, when he heard a sound he had almost forgotten—the vibrations of the phototeledar, ringing in his ear. Could it be Tamaya? He scratched his head in confusion.

It was Naira, dusting off the phototeledar with her hands.

"Tamaya?" he asked. "I hear you. I am here."

What was this? Naira wondered. The metal spider was speaking, and using Tamaya's name?

"No, I am not Tamaya, little spider, but I am seeking her, too." Naira said. "I did not know you could speak."

"What do you mean, is she missing?" Titu inquired. "She is queen of Earth. How can you not find her?"

"Oh, no, spider, you must have been sleeping. Tamaya is not in Antisana, for Moche has reclaimed it for himself."

The answer shocked Titu. In all his scheming, he had never accounted for the whereabouts of Moche, nor his motives or plans. That Moche had gone back over the bridge ahead of Titu posited a very dangerous situation. It contaminated Titu's own scheme, for Moche would once again be a competitor in pursuit of the Aakti Amurugana.

Magic and science would be rivals once more, and Titu had depended on all the magic being rooted out.

What pained Titu even more was that his one true love had an unknown fate. He could not bear the thought of her being Moche's prisoner, and if Moche had done worse and killed her, that would call for the utmost of Titu's powers to avenge her death.

Naira's voice surfaced again:

"Spider, do you have anything more to tell me?"

"I am not a spider. I am Titu Ilumán, Tamaya's husband, given to her in marriage by Reventador."

"Reventador? He is on his way to join us. He married Tamaya to a metal spider?"

"No, no, I am merely talking through the spider. It is too difficult to explain. Where did you last see Tamaya?"

Naira was indeed baffled, but she humored him.

"Oh, I have not seen her for a long, long time, but I was told by Bachué to bring you to Tamaya at Antisana before she died. When I arrived at the foot of Antisana, I was greeted by Reventador and a woman with red clay hair, who told me not to go further, for Tamaya was not there and Moche had returned."

Turning the bridge was now but a minor thought in Titu's mind. He was completely preoccupied with Tamaya, for if she was gone, what would be the purpose of returning to Earth at all? There was nothing there for him if there was no Tamaya.

"Listen to me," Titu said. "Whatever you do, don't lose the spider!"

Titu now needed to use all of his devices and knowledge in order to locate his wife. He had always failed to put her first in his life, putting his experiments and his lust for discovery higher. Now beyond life, he had the first clear chance to do something right, for what is fame if fame doesn't need you, and the only one who ever did need you may just need you still.

Relying on Naira or her companions to locate Tamaya would take entirely too long, and his tether to them was too fragile. He needed the help of the skies as well, but who was there to call when all in the palace in the sky did not know he had even left?

The Moon! He could ask Mama Killa for help. He called out to her and offered her all the science he had accumulated to brighten her light, and for as long as he could possibly hold out. In exchange she could illuminate the world as bright as the Sun so his dear Tamaya could be found.

Mama Killa accepted. She was almost empty of the light that she was giving to the world on her own and desperately needed to rest. She had also been party to the wedding of Tamaya and Titu, and sincerely wanted to see them together.

So, Mama Killa came closer to Titu, and he in turn diverted upon the Moon all his harnesses of the Sun's power that were to be used for the turning of the bridge.

The entire world lit up like a fire in a dark cave. The beasts and people of Earth stood up and cheered, praising their gods that the severance from Aakti was over, and that the emperor had returned to guarantee them life again.

Titu had never yet been the focus of Earth's adulation like this, although that had always been his dream, though under quite different circumstances. After all his years of trying another way, this was his moment. He couldn't stop now, nor could he bear to tell them the truth. The world was happy, and stuck there on the bridge, he was their savior.

For the duration of the trial, the Congress of Stars imposed a rule that required Aakti to temporarily abdicate his power as emperor and cede it to the next in line of succession, who was Unawqi. But Unawqi had no desire to pass the time sitting on a throne. He unlocked the treasury and nearly burned up all the Sun's energy racing toward Earth to save his own love, the fisherman, from harm.

Titu was unaware of Unawqi's covert mission, and so in his effort to illuminate the Moon so he could find Tamaya, Titu unknowingly diverted Unawqi's surge for his own purposes. The resulting brightness of the Moon reflecting from Earth blinded Unawqi, so now he could not see his way clearly toward the Balao tower that was his target.

The three--Titu, Mama Killa, and Unawqi--all had the best of intentions, but they struggled against each other to direct themselves to different goals. Unawqi pushed, but Mama Killa pulled. Titu illuminated, and Unawqi diminished. The result was that the light pulsed in and out from the sky, changing hues from yellow to orange to white, without anyone knowing the source of the challenge.

Tungurahua was greatly troubled by this, for he much to lose if things failed to according to his plan.

As Unawqi made his final descent, he had lost sight of the tower that was guiding his way, and the tower was what Unawqi had sensed was threatening and torturing the fisherman. He then saw his lover in the clearing not too far away, the same clearing that was the scene of the end of Unawqi's own life, and this made Unawqi doubly angry.

However, visibility was continuously blurred by the brightness of the Moon, so he called for Mama Killa to lower her light and let him continue with his mission.

Mama Killa, however, could not abandon Titu so easily. She had no warning that Unawqi was coming, or why. How could she even be sure it was him?

Unawqi had to act. He had no more time, for if he simply continued his course, he would crash into Earth and annihilate it altogether, fulfilling his father's will that he wanted to thwart instead. Unawqi had to direct his energy somewhere else and rescue his lover, and do it now.

Then it came to him, a solution that would not solve everything, and one that had only a small chance of success:

Unawqi would take the life of his lover!

He would prefer to protect him and let him live a useful life on Earth, but he could not see Tungurahua's tower. He could, however, see the clearing. Directing his energy at the fisherman, still a mortal human being, would of course incinerate him, and the fisherman would die in one life and join Unawqi in qanaq'wa makuyhana to be likewise immersed with the eternal struggle.

Unawqi thought back, and now wondered if perhaps his father, Aakti, had also looked at death as an act of reunion, and not as punishment. What if the emperor's intention in removing Unawqi, or Titu for that matter, was to unite them together? Was qanaq'wa makuyhana all along not a place of struggle, but of working out our conflicts? Was struggle itself another word for love?

These questions spinning through his mind, Unawqi had no time left to determine right or wrong but had to choose to do something. He resigned himself to his plan.

It came first to the fisherman as a rapid flow of sweltering heat, which he thought was the approaching circle of fire set by Tungurahua, but soon he saw the blue gamma rays that were the Sun's radiation. He felt a high-pitched vibration through his body, his bones began to crack, his internal organs burst open, and the hair fell from his head. The rest of his demise was instantaneous, when an explosion turned his body to ash.

Unawqi then hurled himself, hard and to the left, and barely missed the planet, sailing past it into space.

With Mama Killa and Titu consuming his energy, Unawqi did not have enough to return to qanaq'wa makuyhana to join the fisherman. It was only in the course of his final moments that he realized this would happen, leaving the one he saved from torture to be removed to the imprisoning palace, but also unable to join him. Instead, Unawqi was doomed to flying through space alone on the back of a flying comet.

Leave it to a great fisherman to know how to catch a runaway fish!

Transported to qanaq'wa makuyhana but seeing the trouble Unawqi was in, the fisherman's swift instincts took over. He took the ring from around his finger and threaded it over a long ray of the Sun from Titu's machination with the Moon. He then positioned himself directly over Unawqi's spiral downward into space, and when Unawqi circled around again, the fisherman cast the line and ring at his lover, singing:

"I will not let you go; I will not let you go until you take me in your arms."

Unawqi looked up and burst open with a smile at hearing his song being sung by the fisherman, a song he had first heard the fisherman sing after saving him from the sea.

The song meant even more to Unawqi. It seemed to define him ever since he had ridden on the back of the condor as a boy, raising his arm as in victory. He loved the hunt, and hearing his lover sing made him feel invincible again.

He jumped off the back of the comet into the irrevocable void of space, reaching out as far as his hands would stretch and closing his eyes in faith the fisherman would catch him.

"Catch me, my fisherman!" Unawqi exulted. "Do not let the white vipers bring us down!"

Unawqi beamed widely as if gratified those words would be his last, but the next feeling in Unawqi's hands was the surface of a warm golden ring, and he grabbed hold of it with all his might, like the back of the condor that never let him go.

The fisherman pulled him up securely on board, and they laughed until the breath was out of them, rolling around and over each other, sometimes wrestling, other times kissing and wiping away the tears from each other's faces.

"Unawqi, I plucked you from the sea, and now I plucked you from space. I will never let heaven or earth take you from me again!"

Unawqi looked back into the fisherman's eyes like they were the prized pearls in an oyster, so precious to behold and too costly to lose.

They had never needed to know each other's name on Jaqunqay; they were all each other had. In fact, the fisherman only came to know Unawqi's name through others, but now Unawqi was feeling a little embarrassed by the fact, for there were others nearby in the palace who would need to be introduced.

"I am Unawqi, hunter of the Sun," he stated, quite proudly. "By what name shall we call the great fisherman of Unawqi?"

The fisherman laughed, for it had been so long since he had been washed away to Jaqunqay, he nearly had forgotten his own name. But when he thought of his mother calling out to him from the shore of Balao, his name came back.

"Tomás!" He beat his chest with pride and smiled again. "My name is Tomás!"

38 QINA'S ARMY

The tower still stood, and now that Unawqi's comet had passed, the battle of lights in the sky was fading. It was enough for Tungurahua to glean that his plan had failed, and his promise to Balao would also be broken.

The town would not be so forgiving. They had sacrificed everything for the fulfillment of Tungurahua's pledge. They had made their home a noxious and irreparable wasteland believing Tungurahua would deliver them the Sun. Without his mountain for refuge, they would soon unite to destroy him.

Ernest Heatheridge had stood by and did nothing to help when Tungurahua put the fisherman into bondage and proceed to incinerate him.

He knew Naira would be no less forgiving of Ernest than the town would be of Tungurahua. Indeed, the fisherman was their son, Tomás, who Ernest had long ago lost to the far away Jaqunqay, and tried hard ever since to forget him, simply because Tomás had loved another man.

Ernest had permitted a colossal construction of lies to be said and accepted about his son, and then about the promise of New Balao, as the town would be called in its new manifestation as the temple of the Sun. He recognized that as brilliant as he was, nothing he had done so far had qualified him to be a man.

It was not as if he could hide it. Qina had arrived some hours earlier and had watched the events in the clearing unfold. She had put her faith in her father to always come through, to bring about the best results for all concerned. She loved him so much that she made excuses for him to advance to others his better and hidden nature. That is why she forfeited her own wedding ring, and put it on her brother's finger instead, giving up her own promise to be married to Unawqi. She wanted to project a generosity and righteousness for her father if he could not muster it himself.

Ernest looked at Qina's greatly disappointed face and realized that his last hope of grace was quickly vanishing.

As Tungurahua quietly mounted his gray horse and snuck away into the rotten and dense mangroves, so Ernest called for Qina to come with him in pursuit of the Warlord of Fire. They mounted two horses belonging to the Suamox priests, and went after the terrible mountain hermit.

Tungurahua was still too powerful and could burn the entire town instantly in defense, so his pursuers needed to be discreet and follow him without his being aware. On their way out of town, Qina picked up every able man and woman she could recruit, and in no time, Ernest had Qina's army behind him.

They caught up with Tungurahua at the mountain pass where lies the high Lake Iuzpa. It was there that Tungurahua noticed Qina's forces on his heels and became mightily afraid of their numbers, so he tried to cut south to Kukanibo where he could head them into his traps.

Tungurahua would terribly overestimate his friends and underestimate his foes, and as he came over a ridge he was ambushed head on by a surge of the Sangay knights, Tamaya's former brigade, who flew in front of him in such great numbers they completely blocked his path.

He blasted a furnace at them from his mouth, but there were far too many of them to fight, and so to help him escape he retreated north by a small and narrow trail.

With the help of the yellow butterflies, the forces of Balao were the ones with morale on their side, and Tungurahua's only choice was to run as fast as his horse would carry him.

He arrived to his own mountain ready to mount a strong and violent response. He could have gone up to his lair and rain down fire and smoke on Qina's army, now made up of soldiers from many towns along the way, such as the Déleg, the Chunchi, and the Yanayacu.

Qina's army surrounded Tungurahua's mountain, and Ernest dismounted and climbed the mountain on foot so he could kill Tungurahua with his bare hands.

Tungurahua, however, was so afraid, he decided not to climb to the top of his mountain at all, but to instead call for the reinforcement of his family, sure that they would come to his aid.

So, he went to a cave on his mountain named the same as the one on Reventador's mountain, "tunqur amaru", and slid and squeezed himself down inside until he could find miba.

It was a perilous task for the shale was brittle and could collapse right on top of him. He wedged his way down into every crack and crevice, stuffing himself as far as he could go between the debris of the erosive interior, constantly being showered by falling shale. He then broke through a final flooring of shale with his foot, which opened into a small hole, and he dropped himself into it. It was so tight, he could barely move his arms and legs about, but it was there to his eager delight, he found miba.

Miba was at the edge of the hole, around the side of a tough wall, but it was almost unreachable and he could not turn himself to fully see it or get closer to it. So, Tungurahua stretched hard in back of his own shoulders, using his fingers to claw up and alongside the underside of the rock, until at last, he felt the scaly skin he sought.

To his terror, the skin felt cold and unmoving. Tungurahua's plan was to call his estranged family of mountains and ask for them to rescue him. If he touched miba, they would hear him, but miba was suddenly not miba. It was stony and lifeless, no different than the rock face around it.

Try as he might, no one responded to Tungurahua. No one came to his aid.

Ernest had followed him all the way, and listened to Tungurahua's cursing of his own family, threatening them with his vengeance. Seeing some loose shale near his feet, Ernest pushed it into the hole on top of the hermit, and then climbed out the same way he came in, pushing more rock and mud down as he went, burying Tungurahua beneath the mountain alive until he was a prisoner in his own castle of hell.

When Ernest crawled out from the entrance, Qina's forces were there, and they filled the tunqur amaru with all the rocks and trees they could find. When that was done, they climbed further still to the crater, and toiled day and night to smother the volcano, condemning Tungurahua to silence for a long, long time.

39 THE CONGRESS DECIDES

In the ruins of the Great Hall of the Sun, the Congress of Stars was closing its deliberations. While some confessed they felt sympathy for his motive to bring his daughter back to his side, his means of wanton destruction were nothing short of bloodthirsty, and they could not find a way to pardon him for the lives he had taken.

Rigel was elected to speak on behalf of the Congress as a whole. He presented to the emperor their accord with Bachué, but Aakti had already acquiesced to this outcome and looked away despondently.

Bachué had made it clear she was not a kindly grandmother, but a seeker of the highest and best justice. She wanted to protect her son, but even more, she wanted to protect the trust afforded to his name (and her by extension), which was a trust he would need to earn again.

During this whole time, none were aware of the defeat of Tungurahua; none were aware that Titu had left to return over the bridge to Kukanibo; and none were aware that Unawqi had burned his way through space on an undertaking to save his human lover.

So, when Unawqi entered the hall with the fisherman, it was a complete surprise to everyone. Though Bachué was speechless, caught between delight and bewilderment, the emperor was bilious at seeing the pair and he hissed at them without hesitation.

Aakti was outraged with their being reunited and stood up screaming at the top of lungs, forcing the two strongest of the stars, Altair and Centauri, to hold him down. He felt the true drain on his imperial power was not Unawqi, but the unquenchable force of love the fisherman had planted. This human love was blasphemous to Aakti, as damnable as the Aakti Amurugana being indiscriminately spread around the earth by his daughter. All that love and amurugana served in common was to create beauty and inspire hope for a future that Aakti in no way wanted to sustain.

Seeing this reaction from Aakti, Bachué began to calculate what sentence would be advisable for the congress to ratify, and she turned to address her son and the assembled stars.

"All these years you have spent hating," she said to her son, "trying to get rid of everything that aspires to be bright and invigorated, even your own son–indeed, the entire world. You welcome nothing; you abhor everything except yourself.

"My error in casting you out was that you already had company with you to subject to your bitterness, giving you pawns to play with in your game–a game which you would always win.

"But that's it, isn't it, Aakti? You need others around you, even if it is only to assert that you are larger than they are."

Bachué walked up to face the emperor directly, and set her severe black eyes upon him.

"If you need to do that in the first place, my son, then truly you must be too small to be an emperor!"

She looked to her right and saw nearby the sunflowers the fisherman had thrown at the emperor in their battle in Suamox. They were nearly buried underneath the ashes she had made of the Great Hall, but she went over and picked them up, shook them off, and presented them to her son, saying:

"You can start again with these."

She decided that Aakti's sentence should be to give him what he had always wanted from the start: to be alone. He could retake his throne, and what was left of his palace, but he would be placed under the guardianship of the stars around him. They, in turn, would be authorized to ensure he could neither destroy nor leave Earth. He would do what he had been entrusted to do, and he would do it alone.

Rigel and the rest of the Congress were fond of the nature of the sentence and were in full agreement to act as overseers of--and restraints on--the emperor's rule. They informed Bachué they would call another Congress if and when they felt his sentence could be lifted.

Bachué, Unawqi, Tomás, and Titu would be allowed to cross the bridge, leaving qanaq'wa makuyhana forever. They would live new lives, find their new homes, and build a new world under the surety of the Sun.

This is when Bachué first wondered where, exactly, Titu was. Where had he disappeared to? After searching, they realized there was no place he could be, at least in the palace. There was only one way out, and the portal door to the bridge to Kukanibo had been left ajar.

40 CROSSING OVER

Long after the others had drifted off to sleep, Bachué continued to recount the events to Tamaya over the dwindling fire in Kukanibo. Bachué was tired, too, and even more eager to bring her story to a conclusion so that she would have enough energy the next day to leave the impenetrable jungle with the rest.

She told Tamaya how their group had left qanaq'wa makuyhana and found Titu along the way, and that it was Titu who had lit up the world for fear that Tamaya had been lost in the dark, and he wanted to find her. She told how Unawqi had sacrificed himself to save the fisherman, now known to them as Tomás, and how, in turn, Tomás had saved Unawqi from being cast out into space. She concluded by explaining that Aakti, the emperor, would never again be a problem for the world; his menacing and abuse was now put in check, and he was condemned to live alone in perpetuity while carrying out his obligations under the guardianship of the stars.

As the fire faded, Tamaya noticed something neither she nor the rest of her world had seen in a very long time: the first light of sunrise in the east. The emperor had truly returned after his long absence, although his light looked more tarnished than she had remembered.

One might think that Tamaya would be glad to see it, but she looked troubled instead. The emperor was returning, yes, but in chains? It did not sit well with her.

Yes, it was Aakti who had ruthlessly burned the Quijos without any regard for his infant son in his path, tried to kill him again in the skies over Jaqunqay, and then ultimately succeeded in the mangroves near Balao. It was this same emperor that had killed her husband and that devised the murder of his own mother through Tungurahua. If it weren't for the larger-than-life efforts of Bachué and the Congress of Stars, all of them would still be in qanaq'wa makuyhana instead of safely sleeping around her by the fire.

Aakti deserved the justice Bachué delivered…or so Tamaya thought until Tapaipi began weeping between her breasts. Tamaya leaned her head over Tapaipi to listen, for whatever the peach kernel said was the truth of the heart that is greater than truth of any other kind.

For Aakti to now be enslaved to Earth in involuntary servitude was indirectly handing Titu what he had wanted all along, even though powers far above and beyond Titu were the ones who had rendered that sentence. Nonetheless, Titu had gotten his slave, and on a leash that would last forever.

The notion violated something deeper beneath Tamaya's hunger for vengeance, and Tapaipi was digging and scraping, trying to pull that something up, hoping Tamaya would wait and listen.

She felt separate from Bachué's justice, and that maybe, if her privilege of being a queen meant she could have a vote of her own in the Congress of Stars, she would have perhaps cast the only vote of dissent, even though she did not readily know why.

Bachué was now finished recounting her stories and had moved on to talk of the fripperies of this life, her sore bones and back, her craving a papaya, and how she would like to make Kukanibo a more orderly garden.

But Tamaya's eyes were not paying attention to Bachué. They were fixed in wonder at the timid trim of the sunrise above the horizon. It looked lifeless, humiliated, as if it was apologizing for its appearance and limping into the sky.

This was what she would have to greet every day? She wasn't fond of that.

She looked at Unawqi and Tomás, and she loved seeing them happily sleeping in each other's arms. Titu, dozing with his arm crossed over both Tomás and Unawqi, had come back home, not as much to a terrestrial space, but to his better self.

For Tamaya, all of this contentedness was at the expense of retribution, of leaving the Sun to talk to his own misery for time without end. She could not find anything in her heart to agree that was fitting or right. To choose to be alone, she thought, is a rightful privilege, but to be condemned to be alone is the greatest of all wrongs.

Bachué laid down by the fire and fell fast asleep. Tamaya looked at all of them again and saw in them Earth restored. The tranquility in their faces—their togetherness—was her greatest achievement.

She called the chinchay over to her side and thanked the chinchay for being so faithful to both her and to the rest of them on their journeys. But then Tamaya asked the chinchay if she would do one last favor for Tamaya by guiding everyone there sleeping out of Kukanibo when the Sun had finished rising.

"May everyone be so blessed as this," she told the chinchay, "but the blessing will always be a lie if there is even one we leave behind."

Tamaya then stood up, turned herself toward the bridge, and walked across it, not once looking back.

When morning came, the chinchay led the company out of Kukanibo, but they walked like mourners in a funeral procession, for Tamaya was no longer with them. In time, they would understand where she went, and then it would make sense. She was every bit the monarch for all of us, and in all of us.

Every day since, this is why we look up and feel so lucky to be alive. It is not just our gratitude for the Sun returning instead of abandoning us to suffer the night, it is knowing he has good company.

41 OLD MAN

I had come back to St. Rita's several times to help with other events like that Thanksgiving breakfast where I first met Unawqi. I enjoyed meeting other people and hearing their stories, but none of them compared to Unawqi's.

So, I always looked for him in the crowd, hoping there was an empty chair across from him so I could sit with him and hear where his last adventure had taken him. Sadly, he stopped showing up as well, and I was left to wonder whether he had left Tacoma to go hunting in another place, or whether he had maybe succeeded and his hunt was over and he had gone back to the Quijos.

He said he wanted to take the whole world home with him, but I was still here, so I couldn't let myself believe it was truly over.

As I was walking back home past the edge of Ferry Park, there was an old man standing there with sunflowers in his arms. I realized I had seen the same man pacing back and forth down Ainsworth Avenue, stopping at the steps of St. Rita's to cross himself. He was never apart from his sunflowers, whose amber glow lit up his face, even in the winter.

The reason I noticed him as peculiar on this occasion was because sunflowers don't grow in Tacoma in the winter, and for that matter, neither do they blossom so easily in the summer. But the stubbornness of the sunflowers wasn't as unusual as the man himself.

He was without either family or friends to accompany him, and yet he had such a radiant kindness about him. It made me wonder what or who fueled his happiness. It was as if the perfume of the flowers was also the air in his lungs. He breathed such beauty that it was difficult to find as good a word to match the charm of his simple hellos and thank yous.

However, when it came to the flowers, he showed a more complicated nature. Since it was a Sunday, a woman on her way to church approached him, wanting to buy one of his sunflowers for her hat. His face took on a devastated look, as if he was being asked to give up one of his children, but he didn't know how to be impolite in a polite way. He swallowed and started to sweat, and after a few tormented moments, somehow produced a refusal in broken English: "Forgive, I can no do this."

From then on, people just learned to leave him and his sunflowers alone.

Since I was something of an avid gardener myself, I was curious to know where he grew those sunflowers, so I followed behind him when he left the park.

All he had to call home was a small, white shed, on a flat stretch behind the Alaska Street Reservoir. It had been converted from a standalone garage by his landlords, who lived just few steps away. Grass surrounded it on all four sides, with the exception of a little bird bath the landlord had made himself by setting an old sink on top of a stack of river stones. Clearly, there was no garden to speak of.

I was not alone in wondering about the old man. Some neighbors of mine suspected he had a sunflower "grow-op" percolating under his floorboards. Others claimed they had spotted him plucking the sunflowers from the clouds when they brushed down low enough to reach. It grew more absurd the more I indulged them, so I left the question open, and continued to watch.

One day in the heat of summer, the old man was sitting, as usual, at the edge of Ferry Park, admiring a family as they danced to the radio to work off their Sunday picnic.

The grandmother was swinging her hips better than the grandchildren, and the mother–much pregnant with yet another– was trying her best to boogie, but couldn't control her laughter. They danced, rolled, weaved, and laughed themselves silly for their lack of coordination, which is typically the symptom of good cooking and summer weather.

It was then that they noticed the old man peering through his sunflowers, laughing, too.

The grandmother called him over, saying,

"Well, now! If you think you're just going to sit there and watch the show, you're going to have to be in the show too!"

The old man was horrified that he had had been discovered and closed the sunflowers back over his face, but it was too late. The children rushed him and snagged his arm before he could get away. "No can dance!" he whimpered, but they would not take his excuse.

They pulled him over into their circle and danced around him as he clung to his sunflowers for dear life and giggled nervously. Eventually he relaxed into the rhythm, and his eyes became brighter, and his laughter mixed in a note of exultation to his usual, self-effacing kindness.

But all it would take was one turn of overconfidence for things to go awry. He lost track of where the ground was and landed on the side of his heel, and it was like a crashing building from there. He fell to the ground, knocking the radio off the table's edge, sending all of his sunflowers up into the air for a push of wind to scatter them across the park.

As soon as his face hit the ground and he tasted the humid soil against his teeth, he realized what for him was a mortal situation. He had been severed from his yellow stars, and he rose up to his knees, pale as a ghost.

He looked around half-dazed, like he was blind, and cried out, "My flowers! Where my flowers?" His arms thrashed about to feel where his flowers might be.

The grandmother commanded the children to help him quickly by picking up the sunflowers and giving them back to the old man. As soon as he felt them fill his arms again, the color came back into his eyes, and the lines of his brow softened.

When that bit of catastrophe settled down, so, too, did the flowers relax in his arms.

"These," he said, "are my responsibility."

The petals of the sunflowers rested on the pillow of the pregnant mother's belly next to him, and she could feel their cool tranquility soothing her, inside and out.

At first, the grandmother dished up a slice of chocolate cream pie for the old man, but then she thought that perhaps the other one, a peach pie, might be more medicinal. She put in front of him a generous helping of her peach pie, and then put her other hand on his shoulder.

"Now, you just set yourself there and eat some pie," she said. "You don't need to fear a thing or go anywhere. The day's young and you and your flowers belong right here with us."

The family talked on in their normal way. Even though he couldn't understand everything they said, he was well-attended. Occasionally, the pregnant mother would lean over him to pour some iced tea, or the children would sit next to him on the picnic bench and swing their feet underneath while singing to the radio. He was no longer an island of kindness. Quite by accident, he found he belonged to an archipelago of kind strangers like himself.

When the day was slinking to the west and he could feel the mosquitoes snapping at the back of his neck, he felt it was the right time to be on his way home and rose from the table.

The pregnant mother grabbed his hand and gave him a look full of gratitude, longing for him to stay. It was as if she were one of his sunflowers, not wanting to be severed from his belonging.

He withdrew one of his precious yellow stars, kissed it, and looked up to the stars for a blessing, then placed the sunflower in her hands.

As she held it against her breast and thanked him, the petals came alive and blazed like the rays of the sun, illuminating her countenance with a golden luster that chased the dusk away, and made the day last a little while longer.

That night, the grandmother died peacefully in her sleep, and the very next morning the pregnant mother, not having but a moment to grieve, gave birth to twins at St. Joseph's Hospital.

Before she was able to get her first look at the newborns, the doctors' faces gave her the signal of something inexplicable.

In the twins' tiny hands was a peach kernel, as if they had been given it to share or struggle over during their journey in the womb. Not knowing exactly what the nature of this omen was, the mother saved the kernel. When she was well enough, she planted it on the side of the family's house on Ainsworth Avenue as a memorial to the deceased grandmother, the one they lovingly called "Maya."

42 THE EMPEROR'S ROBE

When the twins were a few years older, they were playing by the side of the house near where the peach kernel was buried. They stopped playing when they heard exotic music coming from beneath the ground. They took their toy shovels and scraped away the dirt until a green sprout emerged, which when they stroked it this way or that it let out the sound of a wooden flute.

Fearing what their older siblings might do to it, the twins kept the singing sprout to themselves, nourishing it with water and sunlight whenever they went out to play.

The sprout grew so quickly, that by the time the mother noticed, it was a handsome peach sapling, and it sang just as hauntingly to her too. In fact, it wasn't bashful about singing or swaying with the breeze for any of the members of the family when they approached. Whenever any one of them needed to lean up against it in a moment they felt heated or diminished, they loved how it cradled them with the flute's lullaby. The music was other-worldly, taking their minds to faraway hillsides, dotted with sheep and sapphire lakes.

Even in Tacoma's mild summers, the tree not only yielded fruit, it generously gave the bounty of an entire orchard. The peaches were heavy with a mellow cordial that made their eyes water with memories of dancing in the park. When the mother bit into one, the flesh was so succulent it reminded her of her first, passionate kiss. Paradisiacal, rapturous, humbling, aphro-peach-iac, Hilltop Hooch— they used many words to try and capture the powerful experience of those peaches.

Word got around, and as you might imagine, something so unusually splendid like this would sooner or later become the object of greed. And so it was on one occasion that a Seattle businessman came down to Tacoma and proposed a partnership with the family. He would cordon off the tree to protect it from poachers, and demand a price for the fruit that would make them all rich.

At first, the family would hear none of it, for that would take advantage of the miracle in their midst that asked for nothing and gave everything. But the Seattleite was persistent, and eventually the family succumbed to his reasoning.

He went to great expense, not just to build a fence, but an upmarket storefront, and an amphitheater where the family would coax the tree to perform for audiences. He then launched a big advertising campaign across the country to draw all kinds of outsiders to what he billed as "The Phenomenal Peach Patch of Tacoma."

Sure enough, people from all corners of the earth swarmed to the so-called peach patch on Ainsworth Avenue, and as the money flowed in, the family started to count on the idea that this peach tree was going to send the children to college and buy them a much bigger house.

However, it wasn't long before the tree started to hold back. It produced less fruit each coming month, and the flute music whistling through its branches became scratchy and flat. In response, Peach Patch Enterprises, the corporation formed between the family and the Seattleite businessman, raised the price of the peaches.

When the tree produced even less, they raised the prices even more. Within a year, the tree's voice was so harsh it shrieked like a clarinet with a broken reed. The concerts had become an embarrassment and had to be cancelled. The peaches still tasted like heavenly candy, but the price had become so dear and the yield so insignificant, only the world's wealthiest few were treated to the rare occasions on which it gave fruit.

The day finally came when the fate of Peach Patch Enterprises had to be called. The cost of protecting the tree had outstripped even the highest price it could win for its fruit. The family had sacrificed all of their earnings to keep the business from going bankrupt with the hopes the tree would enjoy a better season, and they had nothing left to send the children to college.

The tree had all but shriveled up, and most of its limbs were diseased or suffering from dry rot. A security battalion had to be employed around the clock to defend the tree, and a single fence was no longer enough. Several concentric 12-foot walls were built, each topped with shards of broken glass from surrounding hot shops, to prevent vandals and poachers from damaging what was left.

The waiting list was long and its members restless for a taste of the phenomenon of Ainsworth Avenue. A cattle baron from San Antonio, a prince from Nepal, a consortium of Nobel-winning scientists–all just waiting for a single peach from the withered tree in Tacoma, but the tree refused to yield any more fruit.

One late autumn morning, when the mother was certain the tree would rather die than go through another winter, she decided to pay a visit to a local tailor to request a proper funeral pall be prepared for the tree.

The tailor's shop was a damp, 10x10 room in the basement of the Courtney Building, the air heavy with the aroma of mothballs and guayusa tea. He cleared a place from a table piled with clothes for them to sit and talk over a pot of tea.

As a rainstorm shook the basement windows, the two took their time talking about everything in their lives that had passed them by. Even though the tailor appeared to be a young man, his stories were much longer than hers, and contained more adventures than his age could possibly hold.

When the mother eventually got around to laying out the business at hand, she described the pall she had in mind as a big, cotton smock. The tailor interrupted her and said,

"I know this tree, and it is much too important of a tree to die in a cotton smock. It must be buried in a silk robe, made for an emperor."

The mother sat back, startled at how quick the tailor had been with his assessment. The mountain of silk that would need to be imported would be far more than what she could possibly afford. She swallowed the rest of her tea and countered the tailor:

"I beg your pardon, but I am not the emperor's bank, and the tree is nearly dead! Besides, how would you ever make such a thing with so little time?"

"Me?" The tailor laughed. "Oh, no. I would leave the making of the robe to my assistant." He pulled a basket of leaves off a nearby shelf and carefully lifted each leaf out, inspecting the bottom of every leaf before he put it down. Eventually a smile spread across his face as he pulled up one leaf from the basket and placed it on the table. On top of the leaf crawled a small little worm, spinning a thread of silk.

The mother peered down into the basket and realized they were peach leaves.

"Yes," the tailor explained, "I've been collecting the leaves of your tree, when the wind blows them across the walls and into the street. The leaves here are the perfect condition for this worm to make silk, up to one pound every day!"

The mother was still skeptical and inquired of the tailor how much such a robe would cost. The tailor shook his head and said,

"It would be our honor to give the emperor his burial robe, for he has nurtured the earth and paid his due. We only ask for the privilege. However," he continued, "for the silkworm to make such a magnificent robe, he needs more than the leaves in this basket. He needs to belong to the tree itself."

Partly out of admiring the brave eccentricity of the tailor and partly out of feeling a little sorry for him at the same time, the mother shrugged her shoulders, thinking no harm could come of it. So, she invited the tailor to bring over the silkworm that evening to let it loose in the tree, but she planned the next morning to go elsewhere to find someone willing to make her the cotton pall that she originally desired.

The tailor was punctual and greeted at the door by the two twins, who escorted him out to the tree. Even though it creaked and moaned in the cold moonlight, the tree still managed to make the tailor shiver with awe over its mysterious power.

When he was sure he was all alone, the tailor spoke to the tree: "At last I have found you, Aakti. You thought you could hide yourself inside this tree, but I am a clever hunter, and you could not fool me.

"Do not be afraid—I am not here to kill you. I am only here to do what I have always wanted, to embrace you in my arms and claim you as my own."

In a crude box in his hands, he carried the worm, and he opened it at the base of the tree.

"In but a short while this little friend will regale you again with your honor, and soon you will take my side in the skies as father and son. The sunflowers never left your arms, and because of it you have replenished Earth with their beauty these many long years. So now Earth will replenish you with its gratitude."

When he was done, the tailor retreated back into the house where the mother was preparing to thank him for his visit with some warm peach cider she had pulled from her special reserve, for while she believed he was deluded with a fantasy, she was nonetheless grateful for his sincerity.

When she got herself ready the next morning to go find someone else who would make her a cotton pall, she looked out the kitchen window and couldn't believe her eyes. The entire upper part of the tree's canopy was shrouded in a golden luster!

The worm was working!

The mother went out to the base of the tree and stretched her neck back to peer up into the golden canopy. It formed a blinding kaleidoscope of color as the sun reacted with the silk to paint hues of orange, pink, and silver she had never seen before.

Most certainly, not only did this create a whole new curiosity that caught the attention of neighbors, the Seattleite businessman noticed it too! He wanted to re-open the amphitheater and begin to immediately give tours of this dazzling sight.

But the mother disagreed, shaking her head in resignation to another sense of time and opportunity.

"No, the tree is dying," she said. "It deserves this one miracle for itself."

There wouldn't have been much time for shows, anyway. Daily, more pieces of the tree disappeared underneath the blanket of golden silk, and only the family was able to glimpse the increasingly intense cauldron of color trapped inside the canopy.

Within a week, the little worm had completely mummified the peach tree in a resplendent robe, burying itself alive, and thus becoming one with the tree forever.

The tailor couldn't have been more accurate in describing that it would be fit for an emperor. The elements of light and oxygen had given the exterior of the silk a patina that enriched the colors coming through from the inside.

The family sat in funeral silence, beholding this exquisite orchestration of art and nature unfold, studying every crease of the red and gold finery emerge over the body of their mysterious giant. It was a decomposition that lived as much as it died and grew more beautiful and supple with each passing hour.

Even as they slept through the night, from the base of the trunk to the highest branch, the robed tree sparkled sufficiently to rival the constellations overhead.

The truth of the matter is that the tree had not gone silent at all. Inside, it was teeming with energy no one could see from the outside.

Early in the morning before the rest of the family awoke, one of the twins shuffled into the kitchen to pour herself a bowl of cereal. She was the only one to witness what would happen next.

The robe started to fade, and ever so faintly that same, strange music the tree had played in the past whispered to life again.

Increasingly, she could see through the veil, not a tree, but what appeared to be an elderly couple, dancing. They were as tall and as big as the tree, but as the robe continued to break apart, the size of the couple shrank to a more human scale, leaving behind nothing but open sky over their heads where the tree once stood.

The girl was too mesmerized to cry out, and instead stepped outside to get a closer look before it completely vanished. As she got closer, she noticed that between the dancing couple was a rather homely bouquet of sunflowers, pressed between their bodies, and a little bit faded by time and circumstance.

The elderly man of the couple was the first to notice the girl standing there, and turned to her, his eyes brimming with pride and pleasure, as if having arrived home. He held the sunflowers out in his arms, and gave them all to the girl. Every. Single. One of them.

"Shake them up a bit ever so often," he said. "Let the seeds fall where they may, and life will happen."

The elderly woman smiled and waved from a distance, and in the palm of her waving hand was a peach kernel, a lucky charm, perhaps.

The couple rejoined and took each other's arms, walking quietly away around the high wall, and disappeared, leaving nothing in the place where they danced but a patch of green grass, happy to catch the fleeting autumn sun.

Having heard the kitchen door open, the rest of the family raised themselves from bed and made their way there. The morning light streamed in like it hadn't in years, and in the center of their new solitude, their new barrenness, a young girl with sunflowers in her arms.

43 THE END

I was the last to leave St. Rita's, this time on New Year's Eve. I had long stopped looking for Unawqi in the empty chair on the other side of the table, and sat myself down to dry silverware after the guests had gone out to watch the fireworks.

The door was left open and the moonlight streamed in with the crisp winter air. I thought of going over to close the door, but then thought about how good it was to relish Mama Killa's ebullient pride. She was so happy and bright these days, why not let her cast her shine as far as she could, and add some polish to my silverware?

It was then that two young men came through the door, and I was about to inform them the holiday dinner was over, when I recognized one of them as Unawqi.

I ran over to embrace him. He had not aged a bit. I assumed he had gone back to the Quijos, done with his gardening, done with tailoring, and done with hunting.

"What are you doing here?" I asked.

He turned to introduce me to the other man and said,

"This is Tomás, the man who never left me. It is true, we are going home, but he reminded me of my promise to take the whole world home with me. Would you like to come with us to go fishing for the stars?"

GLOSSARY

The non-English vocabulary used in this book consists mostly of original words loosely derived from Quechua in addition to actual Quechua words.

Aakti – the Sun, emperor of the universe

Aakti Amurugana – seeds of the Sun

Amaru – a serpent that travels between the underworld and the heavens

Antisana – see the Family of Mountains

Atama – an invasive weed, used derogatively to refer to the old woman with the red clay hair

Chinchay - a medium-sized yellow cat with black spots, similar to an ocelot.

Family of Mountains – hermits who are also gods and are personifications of the mountains they inhabit: Antisana (the vanished sister); Kayambi (sister); Chimborazo (brother); Cotopaxi (brother); Cumbal (the northern sister); Imbabura (sister); Pichincha (sister); Reventador (brother); Sangay (the southern sister); Tungurahua (brother).

Guadua – a thick and large variety of bamboo.

Huasquila – an endemic and massive tree to the Andean cloud forest known by its abundant vines.

Ilumán – the place of healers.

Jaqunqay – the island home of the fisherman.

Khirkinchu – armadillo

Kukanibo – the swampy land at the end of the world, home to the bridge spanning between the Earth and the cosmos.

Mama Killa – the Moon.

miba – an organ or tissue that lies at the base of all the mountains, connecting them together.

Moche – the sorcerer of Antisana.

Papallacta – the western range of the Quijos.

Puyo Supai – the goddess of the clouds, or cloud spirit.

Pasochoa – a forest to the south and west of Antisana.

Punchu – a poncho.

Qanaq'wa makuyhana – the palace where they are forever struggling.

"Qayqa huk'ucha" – crazy mouse, a nickname given to Ernest Heatheridge by the people of Balao.

Quijos – the valley lands between Antisana and Reventador; the birthplace of Unawqi.

Reventador – see Family of Mountains.

Tapaipi – the peach kernel that contains the essence of all that is beautiful and good.

Tamaya – in the center.

Tamboyaco – the river separating Antisana and the Quijos, which eventually flows itself into the Quijos River.

Tarapacana – a hardy and tall-growing shrub that grows in the heights of the Andes.

Titu – difficult.

Unawqi – anointed.

Yarumo – an Andean tree with broad leaves.

Yawar Wiki – a cloud forest tree that produces a medicinal red sap.

ABOUT THE AUTHOR

Kali Kucera is an American artist and author of 'new lore'. Since he was 9 years old, he has been composing plays, operas, short stories, and multi-disciplinary experiences. He has been both a teacher and performer as well as an arts mobilizer, founding the Tacoma Poet Laureate competition in 2008. After some time being a teller, Kali was concerned about the absence of both original and local lore, and no one seemed to be preserving the tradition of creating new narratives, tales, and myth about why the world around us is the way it is. He therefore devoted his energy to filling this void with several short tales of the South Puget Sound and continuing with new tales emerging from the inspiration of the high Andes of South America.

Visit his site and follow activities at https://kalikucera.com

OTHER BOOKS BY KALI KUCERA

South Sound Legends and Tales: A compendium of short stories
The Less Told Tale of Never Never Land
South America Borders
Lady Charlotte: The Witch of McKinley Hill
Strawberry Hill
Bay's Charm: Tacoma's mysterious island
Milo's Curse
The Legend of Golden Fern
The Amocats
The Meadow over Tacoma
Sticky's Sanctuary: The odyssey of Tacoma's most famous cat
Vic, the Anxious Waiter

All can be located on Amazon if not your nearest bookstore.